THIS IS PARADISE

WILL EAVES was born in Bath in 1967. He is
the author of two other novels, *The Oversight* (2001)
and *Nothing To Be Afraid Of* (2005), and a collection
of poems, *Sound Houses* (2011). For many years he
was the arts editor of the *Times Literary Supplement*.
He now teaches at the University of Warwick.

Also by Will Eaves

SOUND HOUSES

NOTHING TO BE AFRAID OF

THE OVERSIGHT

WILL EAVES

THIS IS PARADISE

PICADOR

First published 2012 by Picador
an imprint of Pan Macmillan, a division of Macmillan Publishers Limited
Pan Macmillan, 20 New Wharf Road, London N1 9RR
Basingstoke and Oxford
Associated companies throughout the world
www.panmacmillan.com

ISBN 978-1-4472-0236-3

1 3 5 7 9 8 6 4 2

A CIP catalogue record for this book is available from
the British Library.

Typeset by CPI Typesetting
Printed and bound in Great Britain by
CPI Group (UK) Ltd, Croydon, CR0 4YY

Visit **www.picador.com** to read more about all our books
and to buy them. You will also find features, author interviews and
news of any author events, and you can sign up for e-newsletters
so that you're always first to hear about our new releases.

'Need I say more? Need I say more than that?
No. Reach out and touch.'

Aretha Franklin, *Live at Fillmore West*

BELLEVUE

Great Big Baby

'It's not as bad as all that.' Irene offered her daughter the same glum reassurance with each visit to Bellevue Place. 'You won't remember the pain afterwards. *I didn't.*'

The goading emphasis made Irene's teeth rattle with pleasure. Emily feared the threat of weakness more than the pain, and wondered, staring past the elfin stoic at the foot of the bed, what she would find in the next six months to sustain her; what books and daydreams, letters, incidents and friends – what family – could possibly absorb the vacancy of her prospects. The doctor's orders were for complete bed rest, which Emily dreaded the way she dreaded long journeys.

Irene was seventy-four, tiny and spry, clad in a pink woollen coat that she never took off. She lived along the road in Malvern Terrace in a house like her daughter's with three rickety floors (one rented out), a sloping lawn, a Singer and treadle, the bed that sounded a minor chord when you lay on it, a few chairs and no heating. To the children, Liz, Lotte and Clive, she gave delicious teas; to their mother, a feast of stony looks. Or rather – stranger – like the coat, a sort of sympathy for all seasons done up to its neck in pride. *Oh, you poor thing. I expect you'll live. How ever did I manage, on my own?*

A threat to survival and nothing less roused Irene's pity. Sometimes, not even then. She came from Hanley Road in North London, where seven families topped and tailed in five-room houses. Her husband had died while she was pregnant with Emily. They were penniless after the birth, unable to pay the hospital bill. Men arrived to take Em and her brother into care, but Irene's doctor intervened, waiving his fee. She took in work, making dresses, sleekly beautiful coats and skirts, sewing hems by evening candlelight until her head nodded and hit the bridge of the machine. At four she rose to scrub floors until eight, then walked up to Drummonds in Dalston for more piece-work. Bombs fell. Irene could not afford to stop for them. Besides, Matilda Voy upstairs had read her leaves and said she'd live to go on a journey West, maybe as far as Basingstoke. The children meanwhile, clutching kitbags and labelled underwear, were sent to Dorset. Irene took them to Paddington and returned home to find Miss Voy shaking beneath a tin tray on the edge of a crater two streets long. *Didn't see that one coming, did she? Don't talk to me! You think you've got it bad.*

Emily thought nothing of the sort, although perhaps she should have done: another pregnancy, and in her late thirties, had placed her in great danger. No matter – in Irene Coker's world, the instinct for self-preservation cringed before the civilizing virtues of self-sacrifice. The right to be distressed, or ever to complain, did not exist. All cries for help went up in smoke.

The ashen residue was sarcasm, a diet of sly belittling designed to toughen Emily and make her grateful, which she was. From Irene Em got her wit, know-how and dexterity. She was both educated and practical, a minder and a maker: she stitched and patched and sang and laughed. Made quilts, sold them. Bore kids, raised them. Cooked meals from almost nothing, ate them – standing up.

Her talent to deride was a less certain inheritance. Once only she tried to cow her mother, to pay her back in kind, and the attempt blew up in her face.

When Irene moved to Bath, to Malvern Terrace, to be near the grandchildren, she brought with her the high bed, the Singer, a suitcase with all her clothes in it, and an album of photographs. Somewhere along the line she'd also acquired a brown Hoover that ate the carpet. The sac, fully inflated, bobbed gruesomely. Emily turned it on and nearly lost her toes. 'This thing's dangerous. You should get a new one,' she shouted above the noise. 'We'll help.' Her mother wrinkled her nose and made no reply. The monster stowed, they spent the rest of that morning shaking out sheets and stocking a chest of drawers left by the previous owner with Irene's things, light sweaters especially, many of which surprised Emily with their softness and scent of violets. She did not associate her mother with any kind of feminine sen- suousness or with the word that sprang to mind as she lifted, unfolded, folded and set down on tissue paper a shell-pink crêpe de chine slip, cut on the cross – 'luxurious'.

The French-seamed silk belonged to the pre-war era and a mother she could not remember. She was willing to bet the slip had been made, not worn, but the plain fact of its discovery was enough: the long-sought, frail and thrilling proof of Irene's vanity; of fallibility. Emily gave an eagle cry of victory – and then spotted the letters. There was a small bundle of them tucked into one of the suitcase's peach-coloured lid pockets. At this point, Irene was downstairs, investigating the fireplace, snapping kindling. It was January. From the upstairs bedroom window the tiled roofs of the crescent below Malvern Terrace bared themselves at the sun like hardy souls determined to enjoy the fresh air on deck.

The letters were neatly folded into handkerchief-squares, their envelopes tied together with a shoelace. They were from Emily's father, the father she had never met, and – a quick glance told her – spanned many years.

The top one was from 1924, quite late on in the marriage, and postmarked Baden-Baden. The hand was evenly spaced but shaky; some of the looped fs and ps did not connect to the next letter. Each sentence, in the manner of the time, heaved with a kind of formalized yearning. Emotions struggled and writhed beneath set phrases, pleasantries, so that the letters as a whole were never simply decorous. For all their awkwardness they communicated things the person writing them would not have been able to say out loud:

We are all well looked after here, my dear Renie, though it is perishing in the huts at night. There is enough food at least for us, and for which I am thankful. What a carry-on it is for the ordinary people hereabouts. They must push money around all day just to eat, and even then they come up short. Well, the machines are nearly done and then I will come home to you and little Arnold. It will not be long now, I think, but I am counting the days, as you may imagine.

Your loving husband, A

Looking up from her father's bottled longings, Emily felt the necessity of a response. So she laughed. And having laughed, immediately sat down on the bed, as if she had been pushed. The machines would have been aeroplanes, for Luft Hansa, she knew that much. Her brother remembered playing with the armfuls of worthless Marks that their father had brought home.

The next envelope in the pile contained a much earlier letter, sent from Montreal during the War, along with a certificate of demobilization granted by the Canadian Expeditionary Force in June, 1915. It exuded eagerness. He had been happy. By this point, he had an understanding with Irene and a heart defect. They intended to marry when he got back. Something – his happiness maybe, or her own eavesdropping – struck Emily as a dreadful betrayal. It was like confronting a person with their private habits and making a joke of them. There were things about people you might know, but were not supposed to know: the way they laughed without meaning it, their misshapen feet (Irene had a gnarled green toe), their peculiar sensitivities and coverings-up. Of course there was nothing misshapen about this letter, which was innocent and light-hearted, almost gaseous with hope. But her father had died of pneumonia. He'd been born with a hole in his heart. The adventurous, affectionate husband who'd written this, the letter she was holding, was not that man. A different man had existed. A different father, and a different mother.

'What are you up to?'

She had not known him, and she had not been told the truth about him, if such a thing could even be done; at any rate, no one had tried. It was a double blow.

'*Em*. What *are* you laughing at?'

The enquiry came from the top of the stairs.

As she held on to the letters, Emily wondered at her own nerve. She was powerfully angry and upset. Terrified, come to that, of who the woman now advancing down the short hallway might turn out to be. But the violent feelings were not enough in themselves. She required a declaration, as a murderer requires a victim, in order for her passion to enter the world of consequences.

Irene was in the room, smiling. She had glaucoma and needed to be close up to her daughter to understand the source of amusement. When finally she did understand, she gave a little shrug, making no attempt to wrest back the bundle of letters, admitting and denying nothing.

Emily read out a few choice endearments, astonished to find herself still laughing between the lines. Her mother listened unembarrassedly. Emily turned again to the letter sent from Baden-Baden. 'Dearest, sweet,' she recited, almost crying with frustration. 'I am counting the days. Your ever loving husband. Dear. *Sweet*.' It wasn't the sentiment in the letters that beggared belief. It was Irene's toleration of them – her weakness for them, one might say. Between what Em knew for certain of her mother's disdain for romance and the wizened coquette now tutting and giggling at her side, a gulf of implausibility opened up.

'I don't know why I kept them,' Irene said at last.

'Oh, you *liar*, Mum!' Emily exclaimed with real delight. 'You big fibber.'

But as she crowed, she glanced about her – at the bed, the green eiderdown, the half-full chest of drawers, the nets – and saw the room of a woman, a widow, the silent correspondent, whose circumstances had always been reduced. Seen like that, the myth of sacrifice – that comforts had been refused, that there had been the option of refusing them – was one way to a kind of self-respect.

'Well, aren't you clever, being inside my head.'

Now Emily felt weak. They went downstairs and boiled the kettle in a dark kitchen at the back of the house, below street level. Cars drumrolled overhead. Nothing in the kitchen was flush. The yellow Formica tallboy did not fit against the wall – it wobbled if you pushed it – because the floor was uneven. The sink came away from the tiles. The paint bubbled with damp. They took their cups into the front room, which was warmer. It had a number of items picked up from Old Jack's, the junk shop on Walcot Road: a pair of wing-back arm-chairs, a glass cabinet on splay legs, a drop-leaf dining table. And a coal fire.

Irene sat back with her tea and asked for the letters.

'I just want to see.'

Emily handed them over and her mother re-read the first two or three, carefully, considering. After that she seemed to grow bored. The two women talked about Don going to America for a term and what that would mean, about Clive's splints, Summerfield. Em said there was no question of her joining Don; he hadn't asked her, and anyway she didn't want to go. Irene grunted, listening, and reached for the tongs to open the fire door. She fed the flames one letter at a time, as if to eke out the waste with an equally consuming and purposeful thrift.

The memory of those exploding intimacies made Emily's face warm, so that on his arrival Dr Pattison took her temperature.

'Normal enough,' he said, tilting his head back to read the thermometer. 'Though God knows it shouldn't be. It's absolutely freezing in here, Mrs Allden. Have you not got a heater? Of some description?'

She explained that the electric heater needed a new element, without adding that she did not know what an element might be (she was simply repeating her husband's diagnosis) and that in any case it cost too much to run.

'And I'm only up here for a couple of hours in the afternoon. It'll be warm soon. It hardly seems worth it.'

Dr Pattison, who was younger than he looked, smiled and sat on the bed. In the doorway Irene opened the clasp on her handbag and started fingering dryly through its meagre contents – stamps, small change, her pension book.

'I won't stay, Doctor. I just popped in to give my daughter this.'

She took out a postal order for five shillings.

'This is for Clive, Em. He wanted to get a book, he said, and I've an idea he wanted to choose it for himself. He told me the title.'

'Five shillings! Oh, Mum, you are good.'

Irene was quiet a moment, looking a little enviously at Dr Pattison and his patient. The vow of silence she observed with most visitors, anyone who was not family, could be relaxed in the doctor's favour, but the opposing discretion with which he listened made her nervous.

'He's a one, isn't he, Em,' she broke out. 'Little monkey. But he does read beautifully. I quite look forward to it.'

'He must enjoy it or he wouldn't run along so eagerly.'

Dr Pattison smiled. He was looking down at his lap, hands folded, entranced by awkwardness – a short, rather solid man, in whom a combination of shyness, soft-spoken professional competence and a surprising delicacy of movement and touch suggested sadness. His eyes were forget-me-not blue – too eerie against the dark stain of his cheeks. Others said that he drank.

As if in response to some unvoiced dissent, Irene added abruptly: 'They'll all be after him, you mark my words.'

'He's only eight,' Emily objected. 'Give him a chance. I *am* sorry, Doctor. Anyway, what about the girls? Liz's going to have a nice figure.'

'Liz?' Irene sounded irritated. She had been put to work at twelve, and Liz was eleven or fast approaching, a little woman. 'Liz is like you. Lotte's pretty. Was there anything else, Em? If not, I'll be off.'

When she had gone, Dr Pattison asked how Emily was, and how Clive was getting on with the splints and the spectacles, and Emily was relieved to report that she was feeling quite all right and Clive was being brave and Liz was already such a help in the house—

'Have you and your husband discussed the letter, Mrs Allden? Have you looked at the forms? You do know that you'll have to decide very soon.' Dr Pattison shut his eyes as he marked the words with pauses.

'Yes I do. We have, Don and I have read the – papers.'

The doctor nodded.

'And I'm so grateful to you for everything. I understand everything you've told me – and I just can't bring
myself to sign them.'

'You're aware of the risks?'

'Don has said it's my decision. He backs me up.'

Downstairs, the front door opened and the noise of
traffic flowed into the passage along with the children
back from school, arguing.

'It's *will*,' Clive was saying furiously, his phlegmy
treble charged with adult exasperation, 'not "shall".
Shall is weaker than will. It's feminine and the last line is
masculine. It's *will* never be slaves, Liz, you *moron*.'

'I know what you must think, Doctor. But I can't do
it.'

' "Britons never, never, ne-ver *will* be slaves".'

'Have it your own way,' a girl sighed. 'But it's still
"shall". Mr Meyler said.' And with that Liz took Lotte,
who was crying, downstairs to peel potatoes while Clive
began his painful, expostulatory ascent to the bedroom.

'He'll be all right,' Emily assured the doctor. 'He likes
to do it on his own. It takes him a while.' She raised
herself onto her elbows. 'Are you managing, Clive? Dr
Pattison is here. Do you want him—'

'Mr Meyler said. Mr *Meyler* said. Who *cares* what
that fat oaf thinks? He's not a proper Briton. He's from
Swansea.'

'Clive?'

A gulp halted the invective at the bottom of the stairs.
'How would *he* know?'

Clive was really her favourite child. The idea of having a favourite horrified her, but there it was. Many years later, when he returned to visit her and she could barely mumble his name – when names no longer meant anything – a part of Emily still knew this, and though by middle age Clive himself fumed with neglect, nevertheless she clung to him. In the chill passageway beneath the framed butterflies, she turned to her other grown-up children, saying, 'I love this one. I can't help it. It's true.'

The same part of her tried to concentrate, now, as Neil Pattison told her all about placental insufficiency, but it was no use. Emily heard only the short-breathed stagger of her son in the background. Clive had been born blue, with the umbilical cord round his neck. Every day when he clambered up the stairs, her heart leapt at his restoration, the joy of knowing that he had survived and she had not been left on her own. Because that was the worst thing by far about a still-birth. Worse than the fact of it was the stillness and isolation of the room they put you in, the un-marked afterthought with a lone bulb in which you were abandoned to get on with things. And the dead two – one before Liz, another between her and Clive – had been hard deliveries, and she had screamed for hours, probably. When it was over, the nurses were never kind enough. They took the baby away, shut the door and let you have a good cry. Two days later, you were dressed and sent home with antibiotics. And you always felt you'd failed, no matter what people said, which wasn't much. Clive had nearly died on the way out, but not quite, so he had to be lucky.

'I'm lucky, I know.'

Dr Pattison, nodding, was saying, 'You have three lovely children,' and seemed prepared to leave it at that, then changed his mind. Some gear of impartiality slipped as the boy stumped nearer.

'You will be in this bed for the next twenty weeks, all day and night except for one hour or two at the most, and you could still lose the child, or it will be born with defects, or it will die shortly after birth. Or you will. Having this baby could kill you, Mrs Allden – Emily. I mean it, and I wouldn't be much of a doctor if I left here feeling I hadn't got this across to you. Do you understand?'

Emily looked at her hands.

'You could die from any number of complications that we mightn't be able to detect until—'

Clive came in, elated.

'Beast!'

He saw Dr Pattison and stopped.

'Oh, *Clive*. You did it all on your own again, didn't you?'

The little boy, thin as a seed, held himself against the edge of the door, his head angled away from the doctor and his mother. He moved his jaw around, stuck for words in front of the man sitting where he, the hero, would normally sit at this time of day. The doctor smiled and checked Clive's legs, tapping the shinbone and the clamps, asking if anything he did hurt any more than usual. Clive looked at his mother out of the corner of his eyes.

Dr Pattison left and Liz, the capable one, cooked dinner. At eight she put Lotte to bed, checked on Emily, and ran Clive's bath. Don had gone back to work at the Technical College. Between tasks, Liz walked about the house on her hands.

The next morning, after his father had left for the day, Clive returned to his parents' bedroom and gave Emily his glasses to clean.

'Beastie not getting up no more? Beastie staying flat for ever and *ever*?'

A posture went with the nasal voice – shoulders hunched and arms locked straight down by his sides.

'Maybe not for ever.' Emily spat and polished. 'Here.'

'Beastie continue to pretend she's alive by being brought tea and toast in morning which Beastie can't eat because Beastie stiff as a post?'

Don had brought her some breakfast on a tray.

'Is that what you'd like?' she said.

Clive chewed the insides of his cheeks and gave her his sideways stare. He went to the toilet next door and steadied himself. It was a fine day and from the top of the house you could see small birds speedboating across the open sky. He was full of exciting title music and fast getaways.

The possibility of a defective birth had not occurred to Emily until Dr Pattison mentioned it. Whatever the risks involved with this pregnancy, for some reason Emily took them to be of the all-or-nothing variety. She could not imagine an alternative or compromised outcome, a state between absolute loss and complete gain – which was strange, considering her job at Summerfield and considerable experience in such matters. Summerfield was the school behind the cypresses behind the approach golf course – a joke and a threat to dim kids elsewhere in the city. The children in her care were all ESN, with a range of incapacities, from the merely slow to the bawlingly disturbed. Emily minded them with great compassion: there were pictures to cut out, collages to be made, chaotic trips – occasionally – to parks and gardens to be survived. She thought it a shame that they suffered their imperfections as they did, but her sympathy couldn't extend to real empathy because she did not for a moment question the necessity of their segregation from the rest of infant society. Assessments had been made and that was that. Only now in the empty house, after Liz had led Clive away, did she consider that assessments were indeed *made* – by someone, somewhere – and that, as a result, of all the children born equal, or not obviously deformed, there were a minority who passed from the Eden of normality into a world of certified inadequacy, for ever. They were a separate concern.

But her brother was blind in one eye. Her grandfather had had a cleft palate. Cousin Phyllis, in Edgware, could not be trusted to go to the shops and still depended on her mum for everything. And Julie Naish, Emily's best friend over the road, who played the saxophone with one lung, smoked as though she had three to spare. Was anyone the full shilling?

She heard Irene's words, repeated with a prophetic insistence: *you won't remember the pain afterwards.* The pain that was fear and threat and dire uncertainty, a sum of conditions only secondarily, historically, physical. Her mother had carried her despite the shock of bereavement, and they had both lived. Perhaps she was right. Perhaps it was all or nothing in the end.

The thought reoccurred to Emily on several future occasions, each time with a rush of adrenaline and woozy relief. The first was when the Gas Board finally installed a heater – downstairs – on Benjamin's sixth birthday.

The gas fire had three upright bars, each the size of a large Cadbury's, and a dial at the side with two settings, Super Heat (all three bars) and Miser Rate (one bar). There was a turning-on tea-ceremony-cum-birthday party at No. 2 – this in the middle of the Energy Crisis – and as the weak flame leapt Irene had an inspiration. 'Take off your clothes, Benjamin,' she quavered, from deep within her pink fastness, 'or you won't feel the benefit.'

Benjamin did as he was told, and stripped. He'd seen, besides, something in his grandmother's comical, indulgent eye that his mother might have missed. It was fun, nudity, and the idea stayed with him. Spring and summer of that year were both hot, so one blistering day Benjamin decided to walk home from school naked. It started as a dare with his schoolfriend Daniel and turned into a demonstration. Daniel needed a lot of persuading just to unbutton his shirt and then refused outright to take off his trousers. Benjamin sighed pityingly. If he had to take the lead, he would.

He arrived at the front door with his clothes tucked under one arm.

'D'you see your Benjum, then?' gasped a neighbour.

'You won't be able to do this when you're grown up,' his mother said, and sent him back to look for the sock he'd dropped along the main road.

Don and Emily eventually got a new element for the heater in their bedroom, but it smelled funny, and on balance, and because they were the children of their generation, they preferred to do without. Nothing was safer, too. A while after the gas fire had been fitted in the front room, someone left it on unlit. The hiss was scarcely detectable beneath Clive's own hum of concentration as he settled down to watch TV, shivered a bit, got up and struck a match.

Em heard the *whoomph!* from the kitchen and was by her son's side before he had recovered himself enough to cry out. His forehead was the colour of Empire; the air smelled of burned hair. Clive brushed away his scorched specs. Little black filings – eyebrows – tickled his cheeks.

'See?' Emily cried, shaking the teenager, who had a notorious temper. 'You're still in one piece, aren't you? See? *There* you are. Oh, Clive!'

Her emotion caught up with her. She fought it back.

Clive's eyes had started to leak meanwhile and Emily, noticing, reacted as though robbed of her own fear. She almost snapped: 'Would you believe it? Clive Allden, you great big baby. It's never as bad as all that.'

Treatment

One of the things Clive lacked was an appetite for excuse-making: he had missed his appointment, and whether or not he could have caught the faster 113 instead of the 103 was a side issue. *Patients arriving more than 15 minutes late for their appointment will not be seen.* Unreasonable no doubt, and wonkily handwritten, but understandable. The point of any order, as Napoleon might have said, was that it kept its tactical justifications a secret. Or, as Uncle Arnold, who worked for the *Standard*, once put it: Never Apologize, Never Explain.

How disappointing, then, to hear Mr Naish say, in front of the whole room – receptionists, guilty-looking adults and sheepish children, everyone – 'I'm *sorry*, Clive, but you're late. I can't treat you. It wouldn't be fair.'

He wasn't sorry, and Clive wasn't fooled. There'd be time enough if Mr Naish spent less of it chatting; if he cut down on the flirtation with Sharon or Patricia, swivelling about in their cave of files listening to Radio One. If he didn't wash his hands every half-minute. Why not admit the truth – that he didn't *want* to treat him, and that, like most people, he enjoyed the exercise of power? That would be honest. That, Clive, in turn, could have forgiven.

As Clive backed towards the door Mr Naish raised his hand, bouncing Clive's notes in the air as though he were about to throw them on a table. Somewhere inside the receptionists' radio, the DJ reached a point of critical jocularity and exploded into static. The tension in the waiting room eased; Sharon – smiley, hair-do, little gold cross – wheezed while retuning.

Mr Naish shook his head. 'I don't know,' he said. 'Clive Allden. You're a funny lad, aren't you?' He smiled, and to Clive the smile indicated a person at once less menacing and more fatherly – a confusing transformation. 'We hear these amazing things about you. Read about them, too, in the paper – your drawings, your own exhibition at the grand old age of, what is it, fourteen?'

'Amazing,' Sharon echoed.

'And yet you can't keep a simple appointment.' Mr Naish paused to flick open Clive's file. 'You've got a birthday coming up, haven't you? That's nice.' He coughed. 'Well, nice while you're still the right side of the fence.'

The room rippled, and a lady with twin daughters opened her mouth to reveal a complementary pair of teeth.

'Have you asked for anything special?'

Clive, momentarily wrong-footed, said he had not and apologized for getting the slow bus. For his fifteenth he had, in fact, asked his mother for a good copy of *On War* by Clausewitz, which his uncle would probably track down. The red slab of Bourneville from Nellie next door he didn't have to ask for: it would arrive on the nearest Sunday, along with the weekly bag of Milky Ways for the others.

'That's all right. Just try to catch an earlier one next time – and perhaps you'll get an alarm clock on the big day, you never know.'

Clive smirked, not wanting to show his teeth. At the counter he waited for Sharon to finish shushing over the pages of the appointments diary, and stared instead at the pictures of dental caries and gum disease on the walls. The giant choppers spoke to him, in some dreadful way, of age and moral decay. Like Ayesha, withering and shrivelling in the eternal flame, they belonged to the realm of the once beautiful, now corrupt.

'I'm putting you down for a week today, Saturday 26th, Clive. Clive? Is that all right? Will you be able to make that, dear? You need to say now if not.'

Clive was fascinated by the images of self-neglect. You could always shut your mouth, he reflected, or grow a moustache to hide it. The trouble was that people, especially women, liked to have an image of themselves as lovely and young – and the image stayed young while they aged. As they got really old, the gap between the image and the reality broadened into black comedy. The first time his grandmother had taken out her teeth, Clive had been scared; in a tight voice he begged her to put them back in. And she had tittered at his dismay, perhaps a little scared herself.

'I'm going to write you out a card, so's you don't forget.'

The receptionist's lips parted while she filled out the appointment slip in a round hand, the word 'Clive', which should have been tall and proud, lost in a coil of curves. 'There you are, young man. Now you've no excuse.'

Mr Naish lingered behind Clive, on the threshold to his clinical rooms, in no hurry to see the next delayed patient. They were all waiting for the appropriate blush, a mark of faltering respect from the boy before he left.

'We'll see you next week, then,' said Mr Naish finally. Clive nodded and pushed his glasses up his nose, where the skin was still pink from the gas fire. With a shiver, he conceded his accusers' victory – because it was in his power to make the concession – and took the card.

'I'll do my best,' he said, to which Mr Naish replied, 'Super.'

The practice was on the other side of Bath, not far from Clive's school, but Mr Naish actually lived nearby, in one of the 'villas' with the long, steep gardens his wife could no longer climb. It was a shame that she, Julie Naish, had not married Clive's doctor, Neil Pattison, in whose quiet expertise the whole Allden family had such faith. The piped music in Dr Pattison's Pulteney Street surgery came from a compilation of Russian Marches with the stirring if not quite appropriate addition of the *1812 Overture*. People tutted during the cannonade. Dr Pattison had heard of Clausewitz and, years ago, spotted a logical error in the deployment of one of Clive's minutely detailed armies. He was the right sort of man to appreciate Julie's humour and strength, her curt cultivation. Instead she had married the dentist with bristles – a pseud whose deep voice drew attention to itself; who wore a blazer at Christmas Drinks, and put his hand in the small of Clive's mother's back when the time came to say goodbye.

But Mr Naish moved with grace and was, as Clive had heard it said, 'well put together'. Beneath that absurd tunic, with the womanly buttons, one sensed heft and muscle, the appeal of strength. However great Dr Pattison's appreciation of tactics might be, however distinguished his surname, it was impossible to imagine him as a credible opponent in the ring. Mr Naish, on the other hand, had the comfortable solidity of a Sullivan (perhaps it was the whiskers) or a Corbett – someone whose experience commanded your respect, even if it failed to excite fear the way a killing machine like Marciano could. All of this was, again, by way of concession. To the high aggression and luminous reflexes of the great black boxers (by which, inevitably, one ended up meaning Ali), the best white contenders were as cap-tipping subalterns. Naish would go down in three. Five at the very most.

Clive got off the bus and strode confidently across the asphalt to the station's PhotoMe booth, tucked behind the 317 stop, next to the drivers' office with the smoked glass. Noise came from within the office, the sound of fleshy laughter and disdain for the poor sods waiting outside.

This part of the station, in the no-man's-land between the National Express coach stands and the shopping centre, never got much use: the 317 went to Peasedown and Radstock once an hour, and its few passengers bowed their heads, as if on their way back to prison, or the stone age. Clive took a last look around to make sure the coast was clear, and hoiked off his sweater.

It was a nice paradox, he felt – the publicity shot created with the minimum fuss, an almost complete absence of publicity. So different to the tumult of open training, with fans and followers paying a dollar apiece to see the dental practice taken apart and a succession of receptionists called Sharon or Patricia bapped about like speedbags. Sessions like that took their toll. Afterwards, Clive needed the consolation of solitude, though of course sparring and withdrawal went together in the end. That was the purpose of training: to feed the ego; to monumentalize a fighter's indifference to criticism, to the merest possibility of attack; to create a routine of truly volcanic boredom out of which a brilliant anger might emerge, dancing, needling, jabbing. From the better part of himself, from family and friends, indeed from the whole of society, he, Clive, the Pretender, would retreat into a smoky chrysalis, a little like the driver's office or this modest cell – a slave cabin, unfurnished but for a stool and some thin curtains – to await the final unveiling. Against the harsh light of this self-realization, and to obtain the photograph necessary for his passport application (the Alldens were going to France in August), Clive slipped into the booth and raised his fists.

'Excuse me,' said a friendly voice. 'I think you'll find this one doesn't work. That's why there's the sign.'

A man's hand had pulled wide the drape. The day's dusty light searched and found Clive, bare-chested, sat sideways on. He was trying to look down into the maddeningly hidden camera – looking down over his fists, because that was the angle at which the best pictures (Clay, before Clay vs Liston) were taken.

'Heavens above. You look like you've been in a fight. Are you all right?'

'Oh God,' said Clive, fishing for the glasses that had been in his lap. 'No, I'm fine. Thank you. I was just practising. Silly really. Completely stupid.' He couldn't see to find his specs. The man was standing in his light. 'Thanks anyway, I'm fine now . . . Thanks a lot.'

'There they are! By your right foot.'

The man was a fool.

'Has it taken your money?'

'I'm sorry?'

Clive had got his specs back on by now and was struggling into his V-neck. The wool pulled over his glasses and dislodged them again.

'If it's taken your money, and it probably *has*, you should ask in the office. They've got a key, you see, to the machine.' He paused. 'Is it Clive *Allden*, by the way? To whom I find myself speaking?'

Through greasy lenses, Clive faintly recognized a teacher from Lyncombe. No one who taught him, thankfully, but a familiar presence nonetheless. His name was Pascoe – the boy scout. The stunted one who wore shorts to show off his hairy pins and went about jangling keys in his pocket. The head was blurred, but the sweet smell of brilliantine was unmistakable.

'That's me, I'm afraid.'

'I thought so.' When Pascoe laughed, his shoulders jacked up and down in the manner of a cartoon. 'Well, be sure to get your money back. Or it's a swizz, isn't it? Ha ha ha.'

'I will, yes. That's great advice.' Clive could feel the pressure building inside him. 'Thanks for stopping by, Ted.' He reached down for his bag. 'Terrific.'

But the teacher failed to register any embarrassment and stayed where he was in front of the booth, blocking Clive's escape.

'We're all looking forward to your exhibition, Clive,' he said. 'Or should I say, exhibition *match*? Is that what all of this is? Yes, I think I see. Have you swapped fine art for the sweet science? Pencils down, gloves on! Are you happy to *draw*,' and here Pascoe nodded, 'a crowd instead?'

Clive's forehead twitched.

'No, of course not. I *was* being comical.'

On his way over from the Peasedown bus that had just pulled in, disgorging a larger than usual number of housewives, quarry men, miners and rural youth, a driver stopped to remark on the uselessness of the PhotoMe franchise. He spoke colourfully, indicating the Out of Order sign taped across the face of one of the blow-dried models on the instruction window. Clive counter-indicated its faintness and small size.

'It *is* very small,' said Mr Pascoe with feeling.

'Surprised you can read anythin',' the driver said to Clive, pointing. 'What d'you clean them glasses with, then? Margarine?'

Adults were never more disappointing than when they thought they were being funny at someone's expense, Clive considered. And it was one of the trials of youth that you had to tolerate such sallies. You couldn't answer back, without risking a cuff, a grab of the neck, or a throwing out. A waste of aggression all round. Violence should be stored.

The machine gave a chemical grunt as four images arranged two by two dropped unexpectedly into the delivery tray. Clive took them quickly, deaf to the expostulations of Ted Pascoe and the walrus in uniform.

He had no quarrel with the photos' snowy brightness, no interest in their presentability at Customs. It was the element of make-believe he could not stand to see in them. The fists – anyone would notice – were raised too high, making it hard for the fighter to see his opponent, while inside the matchwood cage of his forearms an un-protected chest edged down into ribs as sharp and thin as the tines of a dinner fork. The hair lay upon the neck and wept.

Apart from that, things were shaping up nicely.

Most of us keep our heads level when we walk. Clive didn't, because he loped – in long strides pushing off the balls of his feet into space, into a thrilling contest with gravity. Down he came, often to find himself lost on the corner of a street he didn't recognize: he'd approached it from an unfamiliar angle, perhaps, or a shop had suc-cumbed to inflation, its windows blanked by whitewash. The stride was fast; alas, it came up hard against the sluggishness of reality – people with bags waiting for the lights to change, cars failing to indicate, the whole com-plicated flow of misdirected persons and traffic going the wrong way. Clive bubbled with frustration, on the brink of what his father delightedly called a 'tizzy'. Where was he? How had he got here?

At home, Don got a kick out of goading his son. Clive could not believe what he knew to be the case: that his father, salivating before sucking the glee back in, wanted Clive to throw a tantrum so that he might vent his own envy and displeasure. Why? The torment of disbelief possessed Clive, and in its throes the original disagree-ment, whatever it was, disappeared from view. When the fit had passed, Clive would feel, as he did now, bereft;

bewildered by the way people pretended nothing had happened. 'Oh, don't go *on*, Clive,' his father would say, triumphantly. 'I've already forgotten about it.'

The world shrank from consequences. It moved in grim suspension around the street corner now, and in the curved plate glass of Milsom's, the big music shop on the far side of the road, Clive could see a dark figure, waiting, his head cocked, tilted upwards, looking back at him.

He turned and bounded up the steps of the City Library and Victoria Art Gallery. There, inside the stone foyer with its lattice-pools of light, he stared at the alcove where his drawings would be displayed. They wouldn't make much of an exhibition, he thought. The alcove was a darkened recess beside a broad staircase that led to the main gallery on the first floor. Passers-by would have to look closely and carefully to spot the drawings, and then closer still to appreciate their detail. They were panoramas of epic battle, viewed from a grand height, with hundreds of quarter-inch horsemen and infantry engaged in vicious combat. On each soldier warrior, the tunics, swords, shields and *ricti* of exertion were depicted by soft-lead pencils sharpened to vanishing point. They were scenes of diminutive but horrifically realistic engagement. Men fell, clutching their bellies, trying to fend off incoming blows. Horses reared and grappled the air. Bleeding captains led reinforcements into the arms of death. And perhaps to the north-west of the field, behind a ragged outcrop or a bony tree, a handful of blue capes might gather about a nervous little traitor, clad in red.

The Alldens lived on Camden Road, beneath the beechy fringe of Beacon Hill. An approach to the house from the garden, especially in summer, gave a good view of its open windows, the sunny two-tiered lawn, and an even better one of its occupants' animated self-involvement. Clive's mother would often be found between the kitchen and back door, calling to one of the children, getting the names in the wrong order; or in the garden itself, with Benjamin who pretended to plant things; whose whole life, it seemed to Clive, was a pretence. Benjamin did nothing with the ideas and enthusiasms he stole: his taste was for the fancies of the Narnia books, for words and jokes he did not understand. If you told him they were not original; that Lewis's Jadis was a dilution of H. Rider Haggard's Ayesha, he got amusingly, then tiresomely, upset. The little boy might also be accompanied by Lotte, practising her pliés on the top lawn, and overseen from the window-ledge of the first-floor studio by Liz, writing cavalierly about set books she had no intention of reading, or else drawing pictures of herself and chewing her hair. Finally, behind Liz's long-limbed sedation there scuttled Don Allden, darting to and fro in his jazz-flavoured lair, a big white room of frames, lengths of wood, box racks, glass, tool-kits, knife-scored work table, auction catalogues, and flat-plan drawers filled with prints, papers, card and gold leaf – materials that lined the family nest.

Such a close inspection of each family member always revealed to Clive a source of irritation: his mother's anxiety, a solitary aspect like the tiny hairy mole on her cheek; his father's practicality, which concealed a short man's doubts; Elisabeth's attractiveness, a given (but by whom?); and Charlotte's blonde, thumb-sucking not-quite innocence. Lotte was angelic, and yet her skin simmered with psoriasis. Her handwriting flowed faultlessly on in 'what I did' stories of trance-like banality. *Me and my friend Shuna. Me and friend Fiona.* Benjamin's attempts to ape his elder brother did not count. And he was at least willing to put up his hands and be thumped before mealtimes.

Each of them had failings. Not one saw these failings as Clive did – rationally, dispassionately, fairly. Whether as parents or sibling rivals, they were individually flawed; but together – like a scene of tribal earnestness, a fête or a fayre, glimpsed romantically from the deep cover of the hawthorn that straggled over the garage – they were good, an ideal almost; necessary, and at the same time vulnerable to change. Clive did not like to think of what would happen if they disappeared or moved. If a bomb dropped, or anyone left home.

He climbed the garden steps. The window to the sitting room was open, and through it floated the earnest chatter of *Grandstand*. Clive's father, like a monitor lizard, occupied the whole of the brown sofa into which his farts plunged so resonantly one seemed to hear a distant crash of plates.

'Yeah,' Don said, as Clive ran in. 'Just started. Spurs are good.'

'Spurs?'

'Looking good. Could be their day. Arsenal haven't got anyone. No imagination. There they go, passing it back. Can't understand it.'

'But what about Ball – and Brady?' Clive objected. ' "The sorcerer and his apprentice" – and *Kennedy*. Kennedy's the best player in the league.'

'Again,' Don said. 'Passing it back *again*. Who was that – Brady? There you go. I tell you, they're finished. It's all over for them. Useless, useless.'

'You don't know what you're talking about.'

'I know, don't worry.'

'Name the rest of the team, then, go on. Name *any* of them.'

Don chortled to himself, but a fleck of spit had appeared on his lower lip and a light had entered his green eyes. He hugged himself on the sofa.

'Clive,' said his mother, in the doorway; then, softly, 'Don.'

'What?' complained Don, who was enjoying himself now that Emily had embarked on one of her elaborate facial mimes. 'Let him have – what? I don't know what she's on about. We're just discussing the game. It isn't a question of winning, Em. I'm not trying to win anything.' He waited. '*Hopeless*.'

Clive stood up, his hand in his hair, cursing an absent referee.

'He just lies there!' Clive protested.

Don stared on, smiling open-mouthed at the screen.

'He doesn't have an argument. He isn't even interested in football.'

'I'm not *arguing*, Clive, about anything.'

'He hasn't the first idea. Look!'

'Hey. Hang about. I'm allowed to watch, aren't I?'

But Don sensed the ground shifting. Like any torturer, he soon grew tired of pain and sought distraction from it.

'Now you mention it, Clive,' he said, letting out a yawn, 'I'm *not* interested. Not any more. Too boring. Do what you like with it, it's all yours. Over to you. De da, de da, de da . . .'

He got up, shaking off pleasure, avoiding his wife's gaze.

'Oh, Don,' she said. 'You know it upsets him.'

Clive leapt about as if on hot coals. 'I don't need your pity, you harpy. No, ugh! Get your claws off me. He's an ignoramus. He doesn't care about *anything*. Get off. Get away from me, both of you. You make me ill.'

'Here we go,' said Liz from the stairs. 'I'm making some tea.'

'Now that,' Don said, approvingly, 'is a good idea. I don't know about anyone else, but I'm going to have some of that cake.'

All Clive could do was stare as his father dived for the door. Don and Liz were soon laughing like old friends while on the telly Liam Brady, who ran as if he were cold and wet through, picked his way past the Spurs defence and hit the bar. Clive sat down again, got up again. Fled to his room.

At 4.30, he slunk back into the sitting room for the results. The *Grandstand* teleprinter, bobbing away at the bottom of the screen, reminded Clive a little of his dad – always on the go, except for the occasional panting lull. Merrily it spat out the scores from every division, and Clive found himself as ever consoled by the appearance of letters and figures, teams and tallies, from the snuffling nib. Then it was over to the commentators in the field, shouting above the noise of the departing crowds from Highbury, Anfield, Upton Park, somewhere in Scotland. A ditch in the Wirral. Arsenal had won – 1–0.

The greater victory, Clive felt, was his. Arsenal had triumphed and his father's desire to influence the outcome, to thwart, had been exposed as vanity. A similar vanity, expressed as superstitious fear, afflicted his mother during Wimbledon fortnight – 'If I leave the room, perhaps she'll win.' The interesting quality, in both cases, was self-awareness. Clive felt that his mother knew she was being irrational. Don, on the other hand, had no sense of his own ignorance; and so it followed – this began to take the edge off Clive's delight – that he did not, after all, feel particularly exposed.

An hour later, Don Allden made dinner. This was done, as always on Saturdays, in a spirit of friendly self-congratulation not even Clive could despise. There was little art to poached eggs and baked beans on toast, but his father dished them out with fervour nonetheless. 'Lovely. Corrr!' he kept saying, and Emily, catching the children's eyes in turn, smiled her encouragement. Liz was the first to splutter into laughter.

'Here it comes,' she said. 'Watch out, Egon.'

Liz worked part-time at a restaurant in the Upper Borough Walls, where she'd already cooked for parties of twenty or more. She was seventeen. Emily had still not recovered from seeing her eldest fillet a whole salmon in front of her, or from realizing that she was having as much sex as the notorious Osborne daughters on the other side of the city. Alan Rowe, a curly-haired student from the university, and rock singer, was the latest.

'These eggs are really great. Get a load of this.'

'A load,' Liz repeated.

'Superb, Dad,' agreed Clive, inspecting his portion. 'Just a quick word about the ratio of bean to egg. Any chance we could make it 2:1?'

'Loads here. Loads.' Don went round the plates in turn, dabbing tiny quarter-spoonfuls of beans onto half-slices of toast. 'Lovely.'

It was a peculiarity of his, on which Emily had often remarked, that Don could be first at the bar with other buyers, artists and musician friends, but was unable to judge portions when it came to his own family. And yet he loved food, and ate it with his mouth open, chomping and sucking in breaths between gulps. He was a sort of glutton of niggardliness. Somehow, too, he always contrived to end up with just a little more of the little there was than anyone else.

He thinks I don't see, thought Clive. Although there was another explanation: he knew that Clive saw and didn't care. Round the table he went again, spooning largesse. Clive had set the room off by now, and Lotte, in particular, whose laugh quickly spiralled upwards into skylarky hysteria, was having difficulties keeping the food in her mouth. The chef scraped the pan and sat down to eat.

'I don't know about you lot, but I'm getting stuck in.'

Liz, blinking, looked at Clive. Benjamin laughed: she was like a different kind of parent – a more exciting one, who did as she pleased; someone you always wanted to be caught up with. She could do anything.

'Dad, we've finished. No, look – they were good. Really.' She waited, wondering if it would be worth the effort. 'The whites, Dad – were a bit rubbery. And not that – not quite *with* the rest of the egg.'

'They go like that. That's what happens.'

'Did you put vinegar in the water?'

Don stared straight ahead, nodding, not listening.

'You put some vinegar in the water. Dad? And when you crack the egg in, you stir gently around the outside to keep the white flowing inwards. So that it stays in one piece? Anyway, it doesn't matter. I'm just saying.'

'Sure, sure.'

'It's just a thing you do.'

Liz considered her father again, and stuck some hair in her mouth.

Emily didn't like to see one of the children managing their father so blatantly, so she flew to the subject that put her at a disadvantage instead.

'Are you seeing Alan tonight, Liz?'

'We might go to Moles. If we do, I'll probably stay at his afterwards.'

Alan lived with two other language students, the Periss brothers, in a flat at the bottom of Margaret's Hill. Soon after meeting Alan at a gig in the Pavilion, Liz had stayed over, and there had been no dispute because Emily hadn't the nerve to confront her daughter. Liz's confidence made her wholly responsible, she told herself, suppressing as she did so the thought of her own up-bringing, with its peculiar restrictions and silences. She didn't think it wrong that Liz was taking her life into her own hands at such a young age, but it made her sheep-ish. It was so unfamiliar and alarming – as if a separate person, or spirit of discord, were standing between them, whispering into Liz's ear, taking her over.

'You know he's always welcome, here.'

'I know, I know.'

'Or he can come to lunch tomorrow, if you like,' Emily added, feeling that the offer was really too boring to be acceptable.

'Maybe.'

'Or to France,' Don said. 'If he can get there.'

Emily thought this was a good idea. She liked Alan a

lot. If only the spirit at Liz's side would relent. Under its gaze, she turned into a spoilsport, and found herself creating obstacles – the (borrowed) car would be too small, what with the luggage; Alan couldn't, surely, ride his bike all the way to Aix; Liz certainly wasn't going with him, not on the back, not on French roads.

Liz closed her eyes and spoke in the voice she'd used to explain the mysteries of poached eggs: 'Mum. It's all right, we'll *hitch*. Of course he won't be riding all that way – it's hundreds of miles, for God's sake. We'd be lucky if we got as far as Ramsgate on that crappy Honda.'

'Don, back me up.'

'You can zap down the autoroute in a day or two.'

'A day,' Clive scoffed. 'I'd like to see that.'

'Five pounds,' Liz said, mildly.

'*Don.*'

Clive was impressed. 'Five pounds? Where are you going to get five pounds from? More to the point, where am I?'

'Yeah. I'll bet you five pounds,' Don said, to a yelp from Clive and a cackle from Benjamin. Lotte was complaining about things being unfair: she'd been thirteen for ages; she wanted to hitch with Liz and Alan; and Emily could hear her own mother as she said, 'He's doing it on purpose. Would you believe it?'

'I could walk it faster than you,' Clive boasted, not quite emptily. He'd nearly completed the school's Centurion walk last year – a hundred miles along the Kennet and Avon towpath in forty-eight hours – and was determined to finish it this year, blisters or no blisters.

Liz scoffed. 'You'll have to if you don't get your passport done,' she laughed. 'That'll be you, trailing down the hard shoulder.'

'See you in September,' put in Don.

Benjamin frowned. 'Why September? Mum?' He knew his question didn't really matter, but the list of things he felt like asking was so long, and the way they always got brushed aside just because, like now, someone wanted to see some stupid photographs, was very unfair.

On production of the PhotoMe snaps, Emily sat back in her chair. Clive was immediately on his feet, dancing and shadow-boxing.

'Ain't she ugly?' he yelled, while his mother shook her head. 'Ain't she the ugliest thing you ever seen?'

'He's mad.'

'Can she dance? Beast, can you – like *this*? Can you shuffle?'

Between the low cupboard and the dresser, just in front of the door, Clive stood sawing his feet back and forth, socking the air.

'You'll have to get them done again. Time's running out.'

'A left, another left – and a right. Oh, *what* a combination. *What* an incredible man! He's off the ropes. Oh my goodness me! The Beast is down, she's down – and she's not getting up. It's all over! She doesn't know where she is, she's being helped to her chair. Ali was too much for her. She threw everything she could at him, and he soaked it up, and then in the eighth – with seconds to go – Ali, Ali awakes. *Ali boma yé*. You can hear the crowd. *Ali boma yé*. We're not quite sure what it means. It means . . . "Kill her, Ali", apparently. Well, let's hope that's not literally true, but, oh what a night. There's the measure of the man! That's why they call him "The Greatest". One-two-three!'

'He's mad.'

Lotte had begun to cough, so Benjamin hit her rather hard on the back. She let out a piercing shriek and was soon incoherent.

'You've learnt that from your brother. It's a *nasty* thing to do and I won't have it,' Emily said. Benjamin was seldom in trouble but this time, without warning, he found himself hauled up by the arm and shaken. 'Do you hear me?'

It wasn't easy, impressing on Clive the importance of practical tasks. He was the sort of boy who longed to get things right, yet found himself as often as not in the wrong, or mistaken, or just perplexed, all of which he had come to see as being one and the same. The gap between his abilities and his deficiencies made people suspicious. How could he write and draw so beautifully, with such unfussy skill (so different to the shrill striving of precocious children), and not be able to add up?

How could he read Milton and stumble over four times four? Clive received no praise that wasn't accompanied by mild exasperation, as if to imply that he was faking his bad maths, could see perfectly well, and had never had problems walking. It pained Emily to read in his bewilderment and sideways-glancing surprise a deepening sensitivity. He knew that he was suspected of being lazy, of hiding a normal personality beneath a mask of perversity. And in the register of others' annoyance he was learning to rank his talents alongside his vulnerabilities as flaws. Don was no help, Emily felt, being rather on the side of Clive's teachers, most of whom shared in the snobbery that sees cleverness as an inverse proof of impracticality. So Clive was trapped: he inspired unease, and in response had developed his own weapons of cynicism. What people said to him was hardly ever what they thought. The gentlest 'suggestions' betrayed the deepest mistrust and disappointment.

Emily had to be so careful. Every remark unbalanced him. And the more cautious her approach, the more terrible – and likely – the prospect of his distress became. She circled him after dinner, while cutting his hair, snipping away at his lines of defence, until he could see her point – the simple necessity of cleaning his teeth, of going back to the dentist (or Julie Naish would get to hear about it, and he wouldn't like that, would he?), of getting his passport photos done without squaring up to the lens. He bore the nibbling lecture in silence.

Finally, in his haste to get away, Clive flinched from

the blades' last few passes, rebounded into them, and with a cry sprang from the chair. He was out of the room before his mother could see if she'd drawn blood: there was nothing on the end of the scissors. Slowly she climbed the stairs to the bathroom and the one mirror in the house.

'For Christ's sake, keep that lunatic away from me,' Clive was shouting at the glass. 'Look what you've done, you hideous crone.'

Should she go in or not? Emily didn't know; she half-hoped that Clive's fury was part of a frantic bluff. She laughed, on the safe side of the door.

'Why is she *following* me? It's like something out of *Jane Eyre*. I'm bleeding to death and she's pawing at the paintwork. Leave me alone, woman. Go and burn down another wing.'

In her bedroom, Liz turned up the radio.

'Is this what you call being sensible?' Clive opened the door and pointed at two tiny dots of red just below his ear. 'Is it?'

Downstairs, the jangling of the doorbell brought their bout to an end. Emily wondered aloud who it could be, while her husband hummed his way to the door. The humming stopped to admit silence, the absolute peace of the street at night – and an awkward gasp. It sounded, from above, as though someone were losing their balance on a ledge, or being caught mid-fall.

'What's that?' Clive whispered.

Emily frowned at him before slipping down quietly to

the half-landing. Another scuffle and a vexed sigh. '*Oh.* Look, you don't have to—'

As she descended the last few steps to the hallway, two men passed her on their way to the studio. One of them was Don, the other a very ordinary-looking customer, someone she'd never seen before, about the same age, with a white shirt, a sports jacket, and the pink ears of the fair-skinned; neat rusty-brown hair, parted, clean-shaven, a little padding at the waist. His contours were soft, girlish even – but he was big. He glanced at Emily as he passed, eyes wide and furious, the flesh of his cheeks reddened and lifted. A ring bit hard and deep into his finger. He had a handkerchief in his pocket and her husband in a necklock. The door to the studio was ajar, but Don's head soon butted it open. When they were fully inside, Emily turned to Clive, dithering behind her, and told him to go back upstairs. He went as far as the half-landing, with its shelves full of books about African art, birdlife, and R. D. Laing. There he waited with Liz, who had emerged from her room, alerted not so much by the bell and the exclamations from below as by the unnatural cessation of hostilities between her brother and the Beast.

'Understand me?' the man was saying as Emily entered.

'Yes. God, yes.'

The city's wooded hills raised a cape of shadow above its lights in the window. Don was sitting on the floor by the plan chest, one arm poised to ward off blows, as though his legs had given way. A goatee of blood dripped from his face. He looked amazed – hungrily contrite.

'I absolutely guarantee,' he stuttered. And still the man's arm, cocked, threatened to strike again.

Absolutely, thought Emily. Of all the words.

The dumpy man sounded gentle, almost caring. 'Do you *understand*? Mr Allden, if you so much as clap eyes on me or mine ever again, so help . . . .' And then the threat was choked off by competing emotions. Don sneezed his way through spittle and sobs to an apology, and the man's already high colour deepened a shade. Bending over, he punched Emily's husband three times in the face, very precisely, three little jabs of disgust.

He stood up, holding his own hand, the hand that had done the damage, walked back along the passage to the front door, and shut it behind him.

Emily looked on top of the chest for a paint rag that wasn't saturated with turps or wash. She found one and handed it to Don.

'I am sorry,' she said, and went to meet the family's enquiries.

'It's all all right now, Lotte. Liz, can you take Lotte – no, Lotte, can you, please, go back to bed. Dear, it's all right. The man has gone and he won't be coming back. I'll tell you about it in the morning.'

Liz's face betrayed no emotion. She looked weary. Her chin sank into a tiny bulge of determined opposition: she was still going out later.

With the girls packed away, Emily pushed Clive into his room, where Benjamin was fast asleep. Clive touched her arm, his breath the usual draught of soiled milk and sausagemeat. When he asked what had happened, she found that she could tell him, though it seemed to her unfair, as she did so, that Clive of all the children should be the one to hear the depth of anger in her heavy hinting.

'Sometimes, grown-ups make silly mistakes and . . . start interfering.'

'Why, what happened?'

'And then they get found out and other people, the ones they've upset by interfering, are angry and want them to pay for their mistakes.'

'What mistakes?'

'And that's what's happening now,' she whispered. 'I'm afraid your daddy's paying for his mistakes.'

It was one thing for Don not to know who played for which teams in the league, or to claim Ali had been lucky against Chuck Wepner ('Yeah, Wepner won it. Fixed, man.'), and quite another for Clive to see him literally beaten. It was an awful sort of devastation, too. Clive stared, now, while Don appeared at Emily's side in the ticking dark of the room where Benjamin slept on undisturbed, and muttered his apologies. 'In time, I hope . . .' his father was saying, with a tooth hanging over his lower lip. What could it mean?

The bell rang again and Emily raised her head. She left Don and Clive and went to the door, where the letterbox fluttered inwards. Leaning down, she met the keen white smile of Jeremy Naish.

'Wrecking your Saturday evening no doubt, but – wondered if I could have a very quick word?'

Unable to refuse, she found herself moments later in the kitchen making tea and listening to her neighbour's concerns.

From Clive's silence on the matter, Emily had already gathered that he'd missed his appointment. That wasn't why Naish had called, though he said it was. Julie, his wife, was wasting away. Jeremy, pseud that he might be, worked five days and Saturday mornings to keep himself sane, then came home to look after a woman who didn't want to be looked after. They were going through a tough patch and the truth was he needed company.

But Jeremy nettled Emily, for reasons not obviously to do with his dull material ambition, the way he mentioned the pedigree of his son's teachers rather than his son, the way he told you where he'd got that little painting (London), the blazer he wore at Christmas, the buttons on his T-shirts, or the necessary reminders which were really playground pinches of condescension ('Give me a call next week. Oh, you can't – just drop round then.') The way he just dropped round. And here he was again, at the worst possible time, rubbing her nose in it. Tragedy lay behind his boasts, his advice, his crafty handsliding. They were part of a pretence that life was normal for him, too – which it was not. Jeremy had lost his first son, and marriage, in a climbing accident when

Benjamin was born. On a trip up the back with two other boys to look for fossils in the overhanging rocks, Peter Naish had freed a boulder and got in its way. Now trivial things were serious, banalities utterly captivating. 'Yes, Emily, two, please. I know it's bad for me, but I just can't resist.'

He had a habit, too, of laughing whenever Don was mentioned, or introduced socially. 'And this is Emily's *Don*. He framed most of these, beautifully – and so reasonably! Including this super little Townsend, here . . .'

Emily knew what would happen. As soon as she saw Jeremy's teeth in the darkness she knew. And sure enough, while he was talking about *The Stepford Wives* and complimenting her on her own excellently even dentition; even as he used the word 'special', that awful word, to describe Clive, she saw his pupils contract. Don blundered in, panicky with a bad liar's inspiration. He came forward with a piece of bloodied tissue in his mouth.

'Goodness,' said Emily.

'Damn bit of wood jumped up. I was holding it down and the vice slipped. Think it knocked out one of my teeth. Just happened, Christ.'

Behind his father, Clive lurked by the banisters, the glow of the kitchen reflected in his spectacles. Emily went to him.

'It's never happened before,' Don was saying. And Jeremy, replying, said that it certainly put a cap on the evening. Though how he would know, Emily, busily distracting her son, could not begin to speculate.

'What are you dying of, again?' Clive asked Julie Naish the next day, when he went round for his remedial maths lesson. They never did much in these lessons, because Clive was innumerate. Julie had told Don and Emily, who didn't seem to mind. They saw that Clive got on with her, and that was enough. She played the cello and the saxophone and was, in a small way, a boxing fan, having lived in New York for a time. Clive appreciated people with skilful passion. They talked about books, sport, or listened to Sinatra. 'Is it leukaemia?'

'Leukaemia? God no,' laughed Julie, reaching for her Rothmans. 'Can you pass me that lighter, Clive darling? That's just what I tell my dreadful husband. He'll believe anything.'

'What is it, then?'

Jeremy was waving at them from the garden side of the front window.

'Galloping boredom,' she said cheerfully, and waved back.

Clive pondered this. Though he enjoyed any opportunity given him to feel superior – and Julie's laughing dismissal of Jeremy was surely that kind of invitation – he was also afraid of being laughed at himself, and therefore discreet.

The following Saturday Clive caught the more reliable 113 to Mr Naish's practice and presented himself at reception. One of the spinning assistants asked him to go through: Jeremy wouldn't keep him waiting. After about half an hour, the dentist appeared, apologizing. Clive listened in respectful silence, his head to one side. Then he rose up from the green chair and said brightly, 'I'm sorry, Mr Naish, but you're late. You can't treat me.' And walked out.

France

It was the end of a hot July, the day before the Alldens set off for France, and everybody seemed restless to the point of enervation. Clive and Alan Rowe were outside trying to inflate a blow-up tent, while Lotte and Liz sheltered in the kitchen, where their mother had just taken delivery of a spin-dryer. It was a labour-saving device, the shop said, and Emily was already terrified of it; annoyed, too, that she might be seen as giving in to soft living. The delivery men had cautioned her against putting her fingers anywhere near the drum while it was still spinning, which only confirmed her prejudice against technology in general. Things that screamed and span.

'I shan't like to touch it,' she said to Liz, who scoffed crossly.

'Don't be so ridiculous, Mum. You can't spend your whole life at the sink. It's perfectly safe. All you do is chuck the clothes in—'

'He said to squeeze them first—'

'Give them a quick squeeze then. But you don't *have* to, that's the whole point. It does it for you. Oh, never mind.'

'I'm confused already,' Emily laughed, while on the other side of the round kitchen table Irene muttered disloyally, 'Go on. Shush, Em. Let Liz do it.'

'Never mind,' Liz repeated, picking up an armful of sopping washing from the sink. 'In they go, like so. And you put the webby thing on top, like that. Put the pipe into the sink, or you can run it outside into the drain, it's up to you . . .'

Emily objected with a sort of weary cough.

'Mum, listen – lid down, and press start.'

The machine wobbled to life and began edging its way across the kitchen floor. Lotte giggled. 'It's walking!' she squealed. 'It's going for a walk.'

At Liz's command, Emily pushed the throbbing dryer back towards the sink. She watched nervously as sudsy water leaked from the pipe, in a mean trickle at first and then in a satisfyingly thick, steady flow. After a bare minute, the flow diminished, dwindling to a series of grey blurts. Emily clung on to the dryer's sides, fearful lest her new purchase should lose patience with her altogether and make a dash for the garden. There was no more water now but the dryer still shook and whined. If anything, it seemed to be speeding up, getting louder and louder, becoming hysterical.

'I don't know how it stops!' Emily cried out. 'How do I stop it?'

Liz lifted the lid, and the machine cut out with a groan of disappointment. As the drum slowed, the white strands of the plastic web inside unblurred. The clothing became visible, pinned back against the cylinder wall, and Emily reached for it. Liz yanked her back with a shout. 'Wait!'

'Tsk,' Irene muttered. 'You'll catch it.'

'Wait, or it'll have your arm off.'

'I wish I'd never bought the wretched thing.'

Technical matters were her husband's department. A boy of the war, Don liked to be absorbed by making and mending: he knew how to tinker with engines, lag boilers, lay pipework. Of course he did – he was a proper carpenter, among other things. And when Emily had decided she didn't much care for driving, he had let her give it up. But she could hardly delegate the washing.

She saw the funny side and laughed, relieved.

'You don't want to lose your fingers,' Irene was saying. 'I chopped the end off my forefinger once when I was doing the sausages. And I was so scared, I picked it up, and I—'

'Not this story again, Mum.'

'You don't know. You weren't there,' Irene cried while Lotte scratched herself. 'Don't listen to her, Lotte. I was so scared I picked it up and put it back on and I held it there. The doctor said I'd saved my finger.'

'Right,' said Emily, in a different voice. 'I see how it works. You unwind the pipe and put it in the sink. In goes the washing. Down with the lid, and on.'

'Very good, Mum,' said Liz.

'It was the pipe, you see. I couldn't – I was worrying

about the pipe and the water going everywhere. I could just see it happening.'

As the machine juddered and shrieked, Emily grew tall with her daughter's approval. She felt calm. The others looked on contentedly, deafened into acceptance. The noise had a human quality, this time, coming in bursts as if with breath, as if it originated at some distance, outside.

When the cycle ended, the scream continued: it was Benjamin, his voice sailing high above the traffic. Emily ran up the stairs and out into the street, where he stood on the far side, eyes saucered with alarm, putting first one foot into the road and then the other, threatening to cross by himself and stepping back because he knew he mustn't. She forded the stream and his tears came, the passion dissolving into sobs of relief and then a kind of stunned silence, gulps of air mixed with the strange, solitary elation of being safe and knowing it. For a moment the smell of laundry and the sight of familiar faces (and Irene's pink coat) held him in a trance, before the horror returned.

'The men,' he bellowed. 'It was the men – in the van with the cage.'

'What men?'

'The *men*. They had dogs and they were coming after me. Robert Naish said so, but I saw them too. They were in a three-wheeler and they had gloves on at the top of the hill. And Robert said they took people away and they saw me and I ran all the way home.'

'Well, you're all right now.'

'You're not listening.'

'I expect they were delivering the papers,' said Irene.

'I *am* listening, Benjamin. What am I supposed to say?' Emily sighed and immediately regretted it. 'You *are* all right, aren't you? You're in one—'

'But I'm trying to *tell* you something,' the little boy interrupted, caught between anger and dismay. Why did she not know what to do or say? Where was the kind voice? What had he done wrong?

Liz came forward, put her arm around Benjamin's shoulders and tried to interest him in the spin-dryer. The machine was new, and his pride was torn between the reflected prestige of the white object, which he'd heard his parents talking about – its expense, its size – and a natural sense of outrage.

'Or they were from the Gas Board,' Irene continued. 'Or the Electric.'

'I'm not saying you're making it up, Benjamin,' his mother remarked, 'but didn't you think it was funny the men weren't coming after Robert?

Reluctantly, Benjamin had to admit this was significant. Though Robert was older, and therefore safer. If only they'd been *there*, at the top of the beech-clad path that wound down the hill from his school, they'd have understood. If they could have seen the car crawling around the corner of the road in that creepy way three-wheelers had, making less noise than a milk-float, splitting gravel, stalking prey. He was hotly aware of having thought he might die at any moment, and then discovering in the comfort of his own home, with Gran and Lotte smiling at him, that life went on as before – Gran tutting and saying that Em should have a word with Robert's parents, Mum saying (of course) she didn't like to make a fuss. And now the whole nasty experience was wearing off. The shame of being wrong evaporated in the presence of others' excitement and the way Liz treated him as a grown-up. She gave him a cup of tea with two sugars, saying, 'I know what you mean about those grilles, in cars. They do look like cages, it's true, especially with dogs behind them. You did the right thing.'

There was a word for all this, Benjamin thought. It was a word he'd heard his brother use the first time the family had gone to France, three years ago. Benjamin had been very young then – not yet five – and his parents had decided to leave him with his other grandmother, Agatha. But before they set off, Don had taken Benjamin down to the canal in that part of the city behind the station called Widcombe. And Benjamin came home delightedly to tell everyone that he'd been to Widcombe France: a land that looked ordinary and yet was not.

It was called being *something*, Clive said. Something to do with seagulls.

Now, in the passage, Clive announced that the tent was up, and it seemed to Benjamin that just by thinking about his brother he had made him appear.

'Vraiment, vraiment,' Clive was saying. 'Nous avons dressé la – la grande maison de vacances—'

'*Tente*. It's the same word.'

'You blow it up next time, you're so clever. La grande tente, then. Viens. Viens, yes, Gran, come on, you too. Dans le manteau pink . . .'

So they all trooped out into the garden, the top half of which had disappeared beneath the puffy panels and ribs of a blue plastic igloo. Its door was a zip, and sticking out of the slit above the zip was the curly head of Alan Rowe, who wanted to know what the fuss inside had been about.

'I was being gullible,' Benjamin remembered.

Alan grunted. 'Nah, you're just a victim of circumstance, like me – ' with a look at Liz – 'like all men.'

Liz rolled her eyes, but looked happy.

Squinting sceptically, Irene wondered how they'd ever get it to stay up and Alan agreed that it was quite hard. You just had to keep pumping away. Lotte grabbed the tyre-pump Alan had produced as evidence and ran off with it to the bottom of the garden.

'It's mine now,' she gabbled. 'It's mine and I'm keeping it.'

'She does that if we're playing a game,' Liz explained to her boyfriend. 'I don't know why. Lotte takes the ball and runs away. It's her thing.'

While Lotte was distracting the others, Alan motioned to Liz to join him in the tent. In she crept, and Emily was glad of her mother's innocent reminder of the time, 'I ought to be getting back, Em.'

'You're welcome to stay, Mum.'

'No thanks. I've got a piece of cod.'

'I'd like to go to Iceland,' Benjamin said, following his own train of thought, which skimmed over fish and seagulls and the battles his brother drew. There was a war in the news, although Benjamin knew it wasn't a real one. All the same, he wanted it to end so that he could go back to being interested in Iceland for its volcanoes. Hadn't Bath once been a volcano, or was he making that up? And hadn't there been a Mexican farmer who'd noticed a hole in the ground that became a volcano and buried a whole town?

'Actually, Mum, did you know there aren't any volcanoes in *France*, but there are three in Italy including Mount Vesuvius, and that's the next one along so we'll be quite close really, won't we?'

'Yes, dear,' said Emily, simply. 'I'll pop in tomorrow, Mum.'

The heat produced in everyone a sensation of relaxed hysteria. Benjamin was full of questions right up until bedtime, but when he finally crawled in between his sheets he was asleep before he'd found his usual position on his side. He lay instead, like a baby, in a sort of dropped sprawl, his face distorted by the pillow's edge, breathing.

Instead of seeing Irene, Emily called on Julie Naish the next morning and the two friends had an affectionate row. Julie was cross with Emily for having kept quiet about France and Emily accused Julie, whom she hadn't seen for weeks now, of lying about her condition. She looked dreadful, wrapped in her stepson's dressing gown and adrift in the shiny blackness of an armchair steered close to the window. Julie coughed and grumbled, one tremulous hand scattering ash from her cigarette over her lap. A string quartet sighed on the stereo and Emily bridled defensively at her friend's plight.

'You should have let me know you were this bad.'

'That's good. Perhaps if you got a phone, the rest of the world wouldn't have to send carrier pigeons to the front line of working-class pride that is the Allden household, and you could let me know if you're on safari this week or not.'

Emily made her usual open-mouthed appeal to a non-existent third party and went on to explain that the house they were taking in France had been lent to them by the Pattisons; and that, while it was technically true they could afford one, neither she nor Don wanted a wretched phone: 'The noise.'

The tip of Julie's cigarette glowed unsympathetically. 'Dear me,' Julie commiserated, 'friends who can give you villas rent-free *and* a jealous regard for privacy. You have come up in the world.'

'Besides, I don't want to go. I'm dreading it.'

'Three weeks by the pool! No opportunity to suffer! How will you cope?'

Emily found herself shyly moved by a piece of sarcasm that, even to her disbelieving ears, failed to disguise its actual affection. Her friendship with Julie had always struck her as a minor miracle. By rights the second Mrs Naish ought to have been a figure of terrible authority, someone to fear: an open grate of fags, former lovers, licence and disease, where Emily was a nest of duty and sacrifice. Julie courted no good opinion and faked no responsibility. She felt sorry neither for her husband nor for herself. Above all, Julie refused to pity *her*, and of course Emily liked that a great deal because it set her free. It meant she could complain as much as she liked with no fear of being taken seriously, no polite resentment of her manipulations.

'Holidays are nice for men,' Emily was claiming. 'For us it's a different story, isn't it? There's so much more you have to do, so many more meals to cook. The food . . . Everyone is with you all the time and you don't know where the shops are or how to work the cooker. And people expect you to adapt instantaneously! "Mum, where's the milk! Mum, we've run out!" '

Julie grunted. 'Give them cheese on toast. That's what I do.'

'If you – if I – relax for a second, something happens. You go to bed even more exhausted than when you're at home.' Emily paused and shuddered. 'It gives me a turn just thinking about it.'

The surf in Julie's throat took a while to clear.

'Don't go, then,' she advised at last. And Emily told her not to be ridiculous.

'I mean it, don't go. Stay here and keep me company.'

'But I—' Emily began, in confusion. If the suggestion was so absurd, why did she feel the pain of having to make a decision? Julie carried on smoking. 'It's the family holiday,' she continued weakly. 'They need me.'

Julie sent Emily into the kitchen to fetch another ashtray so that she could think. Having decided to abandon the subject of holidays, she was about to ask after Clive when the sight of Emily returning with an injured expression – and a saucer – made her change her mind for the second time.

'You're always telling me how independent they are, your lot. Elisabeth practically runs a restaurant, Clive's off redecorating the Sistine Chapel, Don's in the auction room day and night when he's not framing the whole of bloody Cork Street. It doesn't sound as if they need you so very much, or not all of them and not every minute of the day. OK,' Julie sighed, 'Lotte and Ben still do, probably. Even then I don't know, children are so resilient. Look at Robert. He's had to do without a mother before, and he'll have to do it again.'

It came out harder than she'd intended. Emily wilted.

'It's only three weeks for Christ's sake, but, Em dear, if you didn't like the idea in the first place, you should have said. How can you be so indispensable and so helpless at the same time?'

Sitting there, weak-limbed but inwardly aflame, Julie looked like a dragon after a soaking. Smoke dripped from her nostrils as she raised her eyebrows.

'It's all very well for you,' her friend snapped back,

suddenly bold again. 'Not everyone has your confidence. I'm not like you. I'm not a *strong woman.*'

Julie's laugh leapt an octave with delight. She stared at Emily, took a long drag on her cigarette, and squealed again, more purely than ever, like a small child caught up in the silliness of other people on a bus.

With her back to the window's brightness, Julie's face was cast mostly in shadow. Two strings of smoke connected her to the clouds outside. When she spoke again her voice was the most real and present thing about her. You could see the lips moving, a hand bringing the fag down to her lap – but these were the actions of a mime; the voice belonged elsewhere. 'I'll miss you.'

It was Emily's turn to laugh. 'It's only three weeks,' she echoed. 'I'll be back before you know it.'

A train crossed the far side of the valley in a referred whisper. For some reason it called to mind not the journey she was about to make, to another hot country, but the shorter daily to-ing and fro-ing of people in rooms, on staircases, down aisles in supermarkets, which was where she and Julie had first met. The swirl of trolleys Benjamin so enjoyed. It made her feel enormously happy, and then enormously sad, and then both at once.

She'd left the house not more than half an hour ago with everyone in a state of chaotic elation, children carrying single items, Don enjoying the jigsaw-puzzle challenge of loading the car, Clive loudly pitying others' efforts to help. On her return, Emily found the packing done, the family ready and waiting, but – what? There'd been a change. In her absence, someone had said something. The two girls were leaning against the borrowed car (another loan from the Pattisons), looking as though they'd been told to keep a secret. Benjamin was already in the back seat, fretting about missing the hovercraft.

'All done?' Emily said brightly, silently going through the list of things no one would have remembered to bring, tin-openers, matches in case, Savlon and plasters, toothpaste, sunglasses. 'Where's Clive?'

'Saying goodbye to Gran.' Lotte looked at Liz as she spoke to make sure she was doing the right thing.

Liz closed her eyes. 'Dad and Clive had a row,' she explained. 'Clive decided he wanted to take his drawing things and the big pad after all and Dad said no.'

Emily said she was sure they could sort it out and went into the house.

'He said it was no good just having talent,' Lotte called after her.

'Where's Clive?'

'He's along at your Mum's. Should be back any minute.'

Don, unusually, was sitting down in the junk-shop studio armchair, with a notebook in his lap. He was fiddling with a drawing, shading methodically then scribbling an outline, and smoking a thin panatella. The room felt emptier. The big trestle in the middle was bare, all the knives and vices, rulers, mount-books, brushes and pots of glue stowed. Finished frames leant against the wall in their brown-paper wrapping. Empty ones, for display only, stared blindly.

'Has he got his things ready – his sketchpad?'

Don turned his head on one side – like Clive, Emily thought – and finished what he was doing with a flourish. It was the draughtsman's equivalent of his tactic when involved in an argument he had no hope of winning, which was to declare himself uninterested.

'Jesus, I don't know. You'd better ask him. I guess so – I hope he gets back soon. We've got to be at Ramsgate by four. How was Julie?'

Don looked up guiltily, his eyes hazed. Behind him, the panorama of the whole city waited for an answer and Emily felt sick again, weakened by conflict. It was an act of hostility to dampen a young boy's unconfident enthusiasms, bad enough in a teacher, but unforgivable – unfathomable – in a father. And yet she couldn't call her husband to account: she feared the power of an accusation, that it might crush him. It was mysteriously safer to indulge his envy. The bad part was, the children did it, too.

Emily gave a so-so account of Julie, not concentrating on what she was saying because her thoughts raced elsewhere. They invoked Clive, white with vexation, in tears that leapt into his specs – but when their son actually appeared, he seemed relatively calm. Impatient, and rather smelly, but calm.

'Don't you want to take your drawing stuff?' Emily asked, going next door into the boys' room and producing Clive's A2 pad from under the bed.

Clive gave her a sharp look. 'Never mind about that,' he said, loftily. 'I've stopped doodling. Come on you two. We've been ready for hours.'

It was as though Clive had fired a starting-pistol.

'Yeah,' said Don, springing up from his chair. 'Let's hit the road, Jacques.'

He was at the car door when Clive's voice stopped him again.

'Have you got everything, Dad?' his son enquired helpfully. 'Are you sure? What about your things? What about *these*?'

From behind his back Clive produced a small bucket and spade, and brought them to the car. Everybody laughed, though it was laughter with an edge, Emily couldn't help feeling, like razors among toothbrushes. Don joined in and reached for the ignition. He wouldn't have minded, if only the little bugger lifted a finger every now and then; or washed. Why didn't he wash, for Christ's sake? 'Bane of my life,' he said, too quietly for anyone to hear.

Neil Pattison's 'other' house lay near the village of Roussillon in the south-west of France. It had a turret,

cool tiles inside, a wide terrace, hammocks slung between stone pines, and a small hexagonal pool. Benjamin
was the only one of the children not to have seen it
before. The others were old hands and spoke, in the car,
of the house and who would sleep where. They shouted
when the hovercraft lifted its skirts and drifted onto the
sea. They camped on the way south as if they had never
known bricks and mortar, settling like nomads to life
in the plastic bubble that lost air during the night. They
counted down the endless kilometres on the autoroute
and yawned as Dad paid another toll, as if such things
were in the ordinary run of experience. For them, the
trip was by way of a prelude, whereas for Benjamin it
was the main attraction, a dazzling trek through Saharan
temperatures, insect percussion and sweet-cold sensations.
He had never tasted anything like Orangina before: it
sparkled without making you burp! He had not smelt
bread, or known that it could be long and stick-like with
such an odd combination of crusty outside and gluey
interior. Cheese was white and ran if you left it in the
sun. Pâté was a sort of slab, pink cement, quite nice if
a bit twiggy; and the shops in small towns where you
bought these things were dark like cellars, empty, until an
old lady – the one they'd already spotted at a table
outside – shuffled in through the strips of red, white
and blue plastic that formed a doorway. 'Je voudrais, je
voudrais . . .' he would start and then forget the rest and
listen proudly as his big sister gabbled in French. When
they left the shop, Benjamin noticed, Liz's flip-flops

smacked at the hard floor. She was even walking differently abroad; wearing a straw hat and dark glasses,
smelling of suntan oil, swigging from those little bottles
of beer his Dad bought in boxes and which he, Benjamin, secretly coveted. They ate in noisy cafes at night
and poured wine from thick glass flasks while the locals
looked on. There was a lot of sitting around to be done,
especially if you were old.

And plenty of that for the Alldens, too, as their
borrowed Toyota forged through the hot air with the
windows wound down. In the back the children lay
against sticky seats, grateful for the breeze. In the front,
their parents argued over directions. When they stopped
somewhere, they were careful to leave the car in the
shade, but the seats were always scalding by the time
they returned, the air unbreathable. The heat in England
had been freakish; in a mild, damp climate it produced
a gold-rush effect: lidos opened, families hauled folding
chairs out of below-stairs cupboards, beaches filled and
buildings emptied. Abroad, the heat constituted another
element almost, dry yet viscous. Like poured sand it
flowed over and around you when you left a cool, stony
interior, and anchored your ankles. It belonged to its
surroundings; the trees nodded slowly in its embrace.
The pulse of the heat was the rattle of grasshoppers and
cicadas and if you stayed in it for any time the pulse
grew louder, wilder, finally so dementing that you ran
indoors or under a tree, head bowed, never once looking up. From noon onwards the streets grew quieter the

further south the Alldens drove. Black shapes occasionally lingered in doorways, but the shuttered yellow
houses of every town and village they came to were otherwise motionless.

When night fell, stars filled the whole of the sky. They
were numberless and quiet, like handfuls of sugar strewn
over a black carpet, some grains sinking so far into the
pile that they ceased to sparkle even though you knew
they were there. Benjamin looked up at them, forcing his
head back until his neck hurt, scanning the heavens for
the ones that streaked across the void then winked out
of existence. He was supposed to wish for something. It
felt silly. He wished: for the top bunk, and maybe a small
volcano, nothing too threatening. Just a coughing crack
in a field, wide enough to show the lava speeding by
underneath. A book in the main library where Clive had
shown his pictures contained a photograph of a Mexican
church up to its spire in steaming black rock. They could
crop up anywhere, volcanoes. You never knew. Imagine
going to the toilet, here in France, and afterwards looking down that black hole in the floor and seeing the red
eye of the earth's core glaring back at you.

They reached Roussillon on the third day. While the
others were still coming round from the morning's ride
through hill-top villages and knotty vineyards, Liz leapt
from the car, grabbed the key from the generator hut and
ran up to the house. She wanted to be the first inside because

she liked opening the blinds and waking the rooms. She'd forgotten about the heavy wooden boards that sat on top of the sink and stove. They were quickly lifted and stowed. And the scent of untrodden kitchen tiles and the hot stone patio outside reminded her that she knew this place in a way the others did not. Clive could go on about Napoleon, granted, but *she* knew the language. In her heart she thought she deserved the privacy of the room in the turret – for Alan's sake as much as hers. She stopped at the foot of the winding staircase in the far corner of the open-plan front room, and listened.

Clive and Lotte, meanwhile, burdened by food boxes and luggage, were complaining about their grown-up sister's not having to unpack. Even as she told them not to be silly, Emily saw their point: Liz did have a knack for making her own way seem the only way, so she called out to her.

Liz strolled back to the car at a comfortable pace, like Brown Owl crossing the campsite to deal with some minor fracas.

'Hornets,' she said, picking up the biggest box with a practical groan. 'Millions of them, in the attic. We'll have to ring the *pompiers* in Apt.'

Emily gave a pained exclamation. 'Oh. *Would* you credit it?' Because she was frightened she manufactured another quick sigh of mere exasperation. '*Just* when we've arrived.'

The hut throbbed. Liz said casually, 'At least the generator's working.' The sound energized her. 'There's a massive nest in the middle of the room – it's actually very beautiful, sort of woven – and the air's black. It must take them ages to build. God knows how you get rid of them.'

'All we need,' Emily repeated, timidly.

Don, emerging from the hut, wiped his hands on already filthy shorts and listened to the news with satisfaction. He liked anything that involved a nest.

'Hornets, clever buggers – you don't want to mess about with them.'

'What are hornets?' Benjamin asked, and Lotte told him they were like bees only bigger. She spoke with a little too much confidence, however, which Clive, irked by his own passivity, couldn't resist denting.

'They're not bees. They perform *none* of the same functions. They're wasps on a prehistoric scale. Oh God, now she's going to cry.'

'Clive.'

'What? I'm just saying wasps and hornets have nests, not hives.'

Lotte stared at the ground for a moment.

'All right, all *right*. Lotte, they are like bees. They're exactly like bees, yes they are. And dogs are molluscs, I suppose.'

But it was too late. Off Lotte ran, weeping, into the pine trees and cedars to the left of the short drive. There she seemed to hear a sinister buzzing which sent her wailing back over the drive towards the dusty vineyards. His victory trumped by feminine emotion, Clive kicked the Toyota's back tyre.

'It's a trick, don't you see?' he raged, as Emily tried to quell the storm. 'She's wrong and she can't defend herself, so she blubs and scarpers.'

'It doesn't matter, Clive.'

'What d'you *mean* it doesn't matter? She's wrong. I'm not making a *fuss*, I'm stating a fact. She says hornets are like bees, and *that*—' changing tack, Clive pointed at Benjamin ' – smug little creep soaks it up because he doesn't know any better. Why should they be allowed to *get away with it?*'

Benjamin protested that he wasn't smug.

'Who asked *you*?' Clive exploded, and thumped his brother in the side of the head. It hurt his hand more than he'd anticipated. What he couldn't bear was that he'd won the argument, and now he was turning himself into the bad loser. Benjamin was too stunned to cry – another disappointment; so Clive, high with the horror of power, punched him until he did.

Clive's acts of petty violence had a mesmerizing effect on his parents; it was like watching a stunt motorcyclist plough serenely into the last bus. Not again, they were both thinking, *not again, please* – when the second flurry of blows finally broke the spell. Don half-led, half-dragged his son away from the car. Now it was Clive who looked white and terrified and miserable.

'What's the matter with you? We've been here five minutes, for crying out loud. I've just driven eight hundred miles so that we can be here for a nice holiday, and you pick a—'

72

Clive shrank from the suspected blow. Benjamin made a snivelling noise in the background and Don, dummying once, prompted more by his son's cowardice than by any urge to strike, cuffed Clive on the temples.

'What is the matter with you?' he repeated. 'It's a lovely day, we're in a lovely part of the world, and you have to start something. What is it that you want, dear?' The 'dear' sounded ominous. 'Do you want us all to cave in and bow down? Is that it? Is it? Or would you like to pick on someone your own size? Would that satisfy you? Tell me, for Christ's sake,' and now Don was properly furious, 'because I'm dying to know.'

The blanched adolescent pushed his glasses back up his nose, and retreated into the shade of a pine tree.

'Good,' Don shouted after him. 'And stay there. At least until you can bring yourself to have a wash. Christ alive, what a stink.'

'You're all right,' Emily was saying to Benjamin, her arm on his neck. You're all right. Try to forget about it now. Come up to the house and see the pool. Let that silly boy stew in his own juice.'

Don called over his shoulder as he returned to the car boot. 'The bloody cheek of it. We didn't have things like this when we were growing up. We didn't have holidays, in France. You've no conception. This is *paradise*. It's bloody paradise, man.'

'Particularly if you're a hornet,' Liz put in.

As she spoke, a cry of surprise came from the direction

of the pool. Lotte, apparently fully recovered, was pointing at the water's surface.

'They're *here*!' she said. 'One of them's in the water.
It's big and black. And juicy.' She stood back. 'It doesn't
look like an insect.'

An admiring 'Fat bugger, isn't he?' from Don verified
the find, and minutes later the Alldens were in the house,
clustered in the attic stairwell, whispering excitedly.
Higher up, where the white ceiling curved down towards
a thin lattice window, three of the inch-long creatures
shifted, buzzed and froze. Others slipped under the door,
unperturbed by the giant spectators, and launched from
the top step, making a falling noise like tiny crippled
biplanes.

'*Oh*,' Emily gasped, as another hornet spiralled past,
'they're not *human*.'

The insect landed a few steps down. With decisive
speed, Emily took off one of her espadrilles and cracked
it against the wall. The hornet fell bodily, like something
dumped over a cliff's edge.

Lotte shook with glee. 'Mum, you mustn't. You'll
make the others angry.'

'Great big ugly thing. It won't be the last.'

'The beast,' Clive intoned solemnly, 'turns on her own
kind. Now we see her in her true colours, the horned
one, Empress of ugliness—'

'Horrible boy.'

Don, with his eye against the keyhole, told them all to
be quiet, but Clive and Emily were locked in one of their

mutually reviling verbal embraces, where insults acted as endearments.

'It's the pleasure she takes in it. Look – the pure savagery.' Clive rested his hand on his mother's arm. 'She *enjoys* it.'

'That's right, I do.'

'If I were a hornet, crawling up the wall, would Beastie swat me like that?'

'Yes, I would.'

'Ugh.'

Don had decided to go in. 'I can't concentrate with you lot yapping,' he said, and reached forward.

'Oh, do be careful, Don . . .'

An incredulous Liz barred his way. 'Are you *mad*?' she said. 'The room's a swarm, for God's sake. You can't just waltz in and say, "Hi." ' Then, to Emily: 'Of course he's not going in. You two, honestly.'

'You went in. Why can't I?'

'Let Mum go,' Clive suggested. 'They'd never sting her. They'll probably start bringing her food. It's where she wants to be anyway. We should get rid of her now, before she starts laying eggs.'

'I'm only going to open the door and close it again.'

'I don't mind going,' said Benjamin, helpfully. 'Why can't I go?'

There was a general groan, several 'no dear's and one 'go on, then'. Don tried lifting the latch but the door was stuck. He pushed again. Waxy carcasses drifted down from the inside frame.

No cartoon cloud of insects rushed to the entrance. Instead there was a momentary lull in the activity around the nest. Benjamin, looking between his sister and brother and held by his mother, could see the hornets slowing down, their manic orbits plainly disrupted around the shadowy turban in the middle of the room. It was like watching the web in the spin-dryer coming back into focus. The nest droned pitifully, as if left behind by its squadron. And then the noise redoubled, got louder, higher. The insects sped up, cocooning the nest and flinging themselves about the attic.

Emily cried out: there was a bed, and beyond it chests of drawers, a mirror and a little window on the far side, half-obscured by gauzy material strung across the missing glass. That was where they'd got in. But it was the four-poster in the foreground that made her start. Its nets were neatly gathered up, intact, and the linen clean, a top sheet recently turned back. Someone, or two, some loving couple, had just awakened, gone to the bathroom, looked in the mirror and disappeared for ever. Or, spell-struck, they had come apart at the seams and dispersed into a million stitches.

'Call the *pompiers*,' Liz suggested again, over ham baguettes and Kronenbourg downstairs. Benjamin was allowed half a bottle and felt perfectly restored to happiness.

'I don't want to get into all that,' Don yawned. 'Let's just leave them where they are. Em and I will be all right down here. Clive and Ben can go in the generator and you and Lotte can share the tent. Easy.'

'What about Alan, when he gets here?'

'He's a grown-up. He can look after himself. I can't worry about that now.'

'I'll go in the car,' Lotte said. She liked being in the car: with the back seats down, the Pattisons' Toyota was like a small caravan.

Liz knew it was fruitless to pursue the discussion. Though her father liked to give the impression of being organized, the actual making of plans that suited other people, or achieved a compromise, bored him.

'When does Alan get here, Liz?'

Emily didn't like to pry, but it would help her to know. She was already worried about running short of food. 'Because I'll have to go to the market in Roussillon, and it isn't open on Tuesdays or Thursdays, Neil said.' She chewed and gazed at the shimmering vineyards. 'Then there's Neil as well, I forgot about that. Which makes eight.'

'He's just coming for lunch, Em. It'll be fine.'

'Alan's getting in tomorrow, Mum, at midday. If Dad can drive me into Apt, I can hitch to Aix.'

'Sure. Hey, look at that lizard! Quick!'

Don pointed between Clive's feet.

'Where?' Clive shifted one foot and peered down. Under his chair, the tiny arrow-headed creature slipped between two tiles with a flick and a gulp.

'Too late, slow coach. Missed it.'

*

So the hornets stayed in the upstairs bedroom and the Alldens learned to ignore the occasional hairy visitor to the salad-bowl or coffee mug. The family's arrival had been too sudden, too strange, too full of the anxieties of attainment that come with any migration, and it took a while for the sun and heat and their associated scents of thyme and toasted pine to smooth out the creases in everyone's mood. The older children were gratified by remembered novelties – the adventure of fine-mesh mosquito nets, the rediscovery of the hammock slung between two pines to the side of the house – and of course the pool. The sense of return was important: it gave Liz and Clive, in particular, a chance to display that nostalgia for their youth which was so impressive to the youngest.

'Do you remember the first time we filled it?'

'Of course I do. Lotte wasn't much older than Benjamin now, and Benjamin – well, Benjamin was embryonic. You were back in England, Ben. Hatching.'

'Now *that* was a hot day.'

It was a very small pool, not much larger than the inflatable ring they had at home, but the water here was cool on the surface and icy cold at the bottom. Benjamin was a little afraid: he couldn't yet swim, and they'd forgotten his armbands. He trod around the stone perimeter, stamping on puddles, until Liz, smiling from under a slick mask of brown hair, grabbed him by his ankles and hauled him in. The cold winded him; the noise of the element and its bright confusion turned panic into joy and back again. If you tried to float, your ears filled and the sun was a jittery coin. It took Benjamin back to some ancient time when people ate and swam on riverbanks and there were no cars or cod wars, or radios. Don, a little way off, was trying to tune in to the cricket coverage. He sat hunched in his canvas chair, still dripping, twiddling Clive's transistor from station to station. The clear voices were French, talking madly and laughing over each other while music cut in; the rest babbled in more distant tongues until static wiped them out. And every now and then, into these dark electric lakes of near silence, a single unmistakable syllable dropped like a smooth pebble: 'Played.'

'Useless,' Don declared, switching the set off.

When Benjamin clambered out of the pool, the sun clothed him. He saw his mother by the patio table rubbing cream into his brother's moley back while Clive taunted her with Beast language. ('Are you the ugliest thing in creation, Beastie? Or are there uglier things out there, more stupid and hideous by far?') Benjamin wanted to go to her and couldn't – she belonged to someone else – but then Emily saw him and waved him over, and he realized that he'd been waiting for a sign. The sharp dead grass and grit under his bare feet added to the excitement as he ran. He stopped in front of her, felt his ears pop, and jumped into his mother's arms. She turned him round, put a straw hat on his head, and began rubbing. Benjamin could see the sun picking little holes in the brim. Then he raised his head and looked out over the pool's erupting contents to the vineyards, planing away down and up towards the cluster of houses and the church on the hill. Roussillon's soft cliffs were clear bitemarks in a landscape that otherwise basked and rippled.

'Is there something like that—' He stopped and pointed. 'Does that happen in very cold places, Mum? Where it's very *cold*,' he said, before adding with the touch of ceremony Clive called smugness, 'I wonder?'

He was being held more tightly, he realized, and twisted in Emily's lap so that he could see her face. She was inscrutable behind sunglasses, yet he felt sure she was watching him. She gave another squeeze and said, 'You ask such good questions. I don't know, is the answer.'

Clive, sitting at the other end of the patio table, reading a thick paperback with his head half turned away, agreed that it was a good question 'in a sort of logically dim way. I take it you mean, "Are there mirages?", in the Arctic or Antarctic, and the answer is yes, but they're delusions caused by snow-blindness, not actual effects of light. I think you'll find.'

Liz stopped by the table in her bikini.

'Lovely,' she said, 'isn't it?'

'It's gorgeous. It is absolutely – well, it's heaven.'

'You realize the water's filthy. There's pesticides and oil and fuel—'

'Are there?' Emily said. 'I expect they'll wash off. Who wants to come into Roussillon with me and get an ice-cream?'

At five in the afternoon, the two shops – an all-purpose *epicerie* and a post-office-cum-*papeterie* – had re-opened for a slumbrous hour or so; and the bar on the corner of the square served an assortment of old boys at battered white tin tables, sultry teenagers staring at Liz, and thickset women with meaty ankles who fanned themselves like duchesses.

'C'est formidable, le châleur,' Emily ventured bravely, after Liz had done most of the talking and ordering. The others tittered, but the waiter answered, 'Oui, mais c'est normal, voyez-vous. Pour la saison.'

Emily couldn't tell if he was being polite or rude, and assumed she'd made a fool of herself, when the young man returned with the ice-creams in brown cones and handed her the biggest, saying, 'Pour la plus belle.'

A fly was bothering Clive. He took off one of his sandals to hunt it down.

'I'm forty-five – old enough to be his mother – *oh*!'

Clive banged the table so hard Emily shoved the cornet up her nose. Wiping herself clean, Emily noticed that the waiter was still looking at her, with a steadiness she sensed was significant. When had she last been looked at like that? Or did it happen a lot? Alarm created a surge of self-consciousness.

' "The maximum use of force",' Clive said, scraping his sandal on the side of his chair, ' "is in no way incompatible with the simultaneous use of intellect".'

'Catchy,' Don said. 'You hum it, I'll sing it.'

The sky above the square cooled now, became cloudy

violet and purple-pink with channels of blue. Don got
out his pad and began sketching. Clive stood up and
walked towards the shops. In the newsagent's he found
two hardback notebooks, bound in a kind of buff cloth
with grey end-papers.

'I'll get that for you, dear,' said Emily, coming up
behind him and picking up the plain book. 'As a treat.
You can borrow Dad's pencils.'

Clive was quiet for a moment. He took a breath and
held it. 'Not that one,' he decided at last, pushing his
breath out. 'I prefer rules.'

Of course when Benjamin saw the notebook he
was envious and ran into the shop himself. There were
smaller notebooks with blue covers; less expensive and
better suited to – to whatever it was he'd find to put in
them.

'Shh, Clive, darling, let him,' Emily whispered, as
Benjamin emerged with his new purchases. 'It won't do
any harm. He looks up to you, remember.'

Pacified by the appeal to his superiority, Clive could
afford to be amused. He asked Benjamin what he
planned to write, and Benjamin said 'some poetry'. Clive
made the face he always made when he wanted to crush:
a sort of supercilious downwards-pointing smirk with
raised eyebrows.

' "Some poetry",' Clive echoed in a piping voice that
broke off into cackles. 'And how long – how long—' He
stopped, tripped up by laughter. 'How long, Benjamin, I
wonder, have you been writing "poetry"?' He spluttered

again, and this time Liz joined in despite herself. 'About ten minutes?'

The sun melted behind hills, dragged down into the earth. After they'd eaten – left-over tongue, potatoes and salad – Liz produced a set of boules from the generator hut, and they played in front of the patio on a stretch of starved grass bounded at the far end by the Toyota and the drive.

They played to unorthodox rules in several sets, and like most family games this one ended in a state of amused disgruntlement. Emily threw the balls more accurately than anyone else, but kept giving her turn away to Benjamin, who was no judge of distances. There were mild arguments, too, about how far one could throw the jack. At one point Lotte hurled it into the pine trees. No one lost their temper. Even Clive seemed happy to let his father win; and with the first cool breeze of the day, as the village darkened against the western sky, the Alldens went inside.

Emily watched her family. Her awareness of what she lacked, call it romance, fought against a knowledge of how lucky she was. She did not want to idealize being a mother; she could put up with being ignored if she felt she was ultimately of use, if she knew a way to guide and to advise. What she wanted was her children's trust. She wanted it too much, now that Liz was herself a woman and disinclined to share her secrets or talk about Alan:

Liz, who had bought a bottle of cheap wine and was pouring herself a glass while sitting in the middle of the carpet, preparing to sew beads back onto a bracelet.

But Lotte came to Emily still, and asked for her arm and neck to be 'done' with calamine. The psoriasis came up in white spots, which itched at night. Benjamin was company, too, though apt to surprise one with flickers of rage and cruel honesty. ('I'm not jealous. *You* are.') He was standing at the closed French doors with his hands on the glass, looking fiercely at the hurricane lamp outside and the orgy of insect activity around it, blowing on the glass, watching his breath bloom and fade. He had the ability of young children to alternate between states of rapt scrutiny – staring at things, measuring his footsteps – and high, almost hysterical excitement. His brain was a furnace, consuming what it created. He could be angry or distracted, like Clive; quite unlike him, Benjamin could wait for his own mood to improve.

The glass cleared and he ran to Emily, burdened with a terrible secret.

'I haven't got a pen,' he said.

Emily went over to Clive, who'd set himself up at a little table in the corner of the room and was busy scribbling away. He was immersed and didn't notice Emily picking up a spare biro. Benjamin, however, was mortified.

'Not one of *his*,' he pantomimed. 'I don't want him to *know*.'

'Know what? It isn't his, darling. It's yours, now.'

Benjamin put his finger to his lips and hopped up and down.

'You're telling him. You're making a noise. I don't want—'

He followed his mother's eyes over to where Clive sat, the picture of concentration. It was like looking at a part of himself, someone he did, and did not, want to be. No one, not even Clive, who despised any lack of originality, would understand.

'Mum,' Benjamin began, seriously, 'what is the bane of your life?'

A family needs witnesses to its adventures to make them real, and the arrival next day of Neil Pattison happily provided one. Routine was setting in: Emily had mastered a morning at the market, Liz was on her way to Aix to meet Alan, and the others were jumping in and out of the pool or squabbling over the hammock. But when the kind, mildly stooping doctor stepped out of his car, the amazing fact of being abroad, in desert heat, among alien sounds and smells, presented itself in a fresh light. It was strange, in addition, to see the man they went to for official advice with his sleeves rolled up.

He greeted Emily with a kiss and a half-embrace, hands on shoulders.

'Hornets!' Benjamin shouted, before anyone could say anything. 'The tower's full of hornets. We can't go inside so I have to sleep in the hut. Have you brought your stethoscope?'

'D'you know, Benjamin, I do have my stethoscope with me. I always carry it in case of emergencies. It's a special big one you can use to check the engine and tyre pressure when it gets really hot.'

'I'm not silly,' Benjamin said quietly. 'I'm not five.'

The two adults made the noise Benjamin hated, and he wanted to run away. Clive poked him in the kidneys and Benjamin shoved back. ('*He* started it.')

'You know, you're right, Benjamin,' said Dr Pattison. 'And I'm sorry. Anyway, I'm glad to see you're better after that nasty cold you had.'

'My cough, you mean. That was ages ago.' An angry glance from his mother cautioned him. 'I am better though, now. I think.'

Neil grinned. 'Good. No lasting defects.'

Emily found that particularly funny for some reason and drew her youngest closer to her side. Benjamin was happy, too: whatever the spell the doctor used to make his mother's crossness disappear, he was grateful. Even better, Dr Pattison had gone back to the car to produce the stethoscope, in its velvet box, with the macaroni rubber tubes and steel fittings. While Benjamin marvelled at the sight and feel of this relic from a place called England, the car passenger door opened and a young woman got out.

'Since this is almost a surprise visit,' Dr Pattison said, 'I wanted to bring you almost a surprise.' The words came out in an awkwardly prepared rush. 'This is my wife, Nathalie, Emily, everyone. Emily, everyone – Nathalie.'

Nathalie gave the car door a satisfying slam and tottered sideways, as if her own strength surprised her. She was shortish, like her husband, and easily amused. Her hair moved to its own rhythm in a shiny bob and she wore a plain dark-blue linen shift that clung to her hips and belly.

'She's wearing make-up,' Clive sneered, when they got inside. Neil, Nathalie and Emily were talking in the raised kitchen, while at the far end of the front room the children pretended to play cards. 'And she's *French*.'

'She's beautiful,' Lotte said wistfully. 'She's got lovely teeth.'

'The hornets are an inconvenience, yes? But they are not *un fléau* – a disaster. Do not worry. We will ring the *vigneron*. He will use smoke.'

Benjamin peered over his hand of cards. 'Well, the rest of her isn't fat.'

His words, not quite a whisper, stemmed the flow of the adults' conversation. Lotte said 'um' but could not stop herself adding, 'So she *is*.'

To Emily's automatic apology on the children's behalf, Nathalie gave another laugh, her hands resting on the mildest of bumps. The two women kissed and Nathalie said, 'Thank you, thank you.'

Benjamin rearranged his meaningless hand. 'I told you.'

'It's still rude,' Lotte sniffed. 'You should say you're sorry. Mum lets you get away with murder because you're the youngest. I wasn't anywhere near as cheeky when I was your age.'

'Lotte's right,' Clive chimed in. 'You're insolent.'

'I don't care,' Benjamin said stoutly, putting a card, any card, down on the floor. At least *he* was pretending to play a game properly. 'Everyone's always saying sorry and they never are. I'm not sorry. And you're just as loud as me, Lotte. They heard you, too. Anyway, I've won so I can hit you both.'

Later, they sat at the dinner table with the windows open. Don had come back from Apt full of the news of the ochre workings in the area, where you could tap the rocks for coloured sands. Liz was quiet because Alan hadn't arrived and she'd waited for hours on the open platform before hitching home. And the boring talk – boring to Benjamin, at any rate – was about North Sea Oil and the Pattisons moving to France.

'If and when we get any of the stuff,' Don argued, authoritatively, 'we need to make sure it's ours, and not just creamed off by business.' He swallowed a chunk of bread, and the effort cued a further digression. 'I mean, how much further down can they go? Do they even know the oil's there?'

Benjamin said: 'If they go down too far, they'll reach the mantle. The lava will come up and everything will explode.'

A part of him was worried he'd done something

wrong, earlier, or behaved badly: one look from his mother could turn his stomach at ten paces. Had he been insolent, or bumptious (another Clive word)?

When they went back over to the generator room, he and Clive spent an hour swatting mosquitos. It was addictive work. The legs stirred even when the body and head were mangled. Benjamin hated the red stains they left on the white walls but couldn't resist adding to them.

'Smite the mite,' Clive said sombrely as they swished and slapped.

'I hate them. But I love doing this.'

'*You love to hate the one who loves the one you hate to love to love, Roger. It's a perfectly natural reaction. It's nothing to be ashamed of.*'

Benjamin was too absorbed to notice his favourite Pete and Dud routine, which Clive had on a record. 'I know,' he said blandly. 'But they can get through the holes in my net so we'll have to kill them all. Don't kill any spiders, though. They're nice.'

Back in the main house, because she sensed anxiety on her daughter's part, Emily was trying to offer consolation. Not directly – that would be an imposition – but through an appeal to Liz's maturity.

'I'm so pleased Neil brought Nathalie,' Emily said, wiping away crumbs from the stove's edge. They'd washed up and were both leaning against the cabinets in the galley. 'She's quite a catch. Not that he isn't attractive in his own way, but you know – *she's* remarkable. Don's eyes were out on stalks!' She trilled nervously, knowing that she'd already put both feet wrong. 'Mind you, being pregnant is good for you. It brings out—'

Liz tried to cover up her groan with a shift of position.

'But it's true. She's . . . so full of life. You only have to look at her: she's blooming. Her skin, everything about her . . .'

Why, Liz wanted to scream, do you insist on defending people who don't need defending? She felt the inevitable frustration of dealing with someone whose anxiously glistening eyes signalled a desire to be offended. 'I agree, Mum. I do,' she ended by saying. 'We both agree: she looks marvellous.'

Instead of walking away, Emily stayed by the cooker, bitter with a sense of rejection, and faintly suspicious of her own motives for inviting it.

'One day, I hope, you'll know what it's like.'

Liz ground the heel of her palm into a chopping board. 'What is this all about?' she shouted, suddenly. 'Why am I your opponent? I haven't said *anything*, Mum. I don't know why you do this. You wait until everyone's gone so that you can get me on my own. It's like you want me to collapse or have some extreme emotional reaction. Why? It's not about Nathalie, is it? Last year you were telling me sex would be the ruin of me because the coil wasn't safe and I'd wind up pregnant. Now it's the best thing a woman can ever do, apparently, and it does wonders for the skin.'

Emily put her hands almost over her ears, but took them away again.

'One day, if ever, I *may* have a child and then we can congratulate each other on God knows what, but until then, for pity's sake, give it a rest. I have no intention of having a baby with Alan or anyone else. Sorry if that upsets you, though I can't imagine why it should. Anyway, in case you hadn't noticed, the bastard hasn't even shown up.'

'Darling,' was all Emily could say. Her love for Elizabeth overpowered her. Everything her daughter said was unfair. Everything was true. She held herself below the stomach with one hand.

'If it's so bloody amazing,' Liz went on, 'why has it left you like this? I'm not blind. Every period is agony, you bleed everywhere, Benjamin practically killed you and still you go *on*. No one asked you to be such a martyr.' She breathed in, while Emily merely registered the shock. 'I'm sorry, Mum. But it's just too – much. You want it all ways.'

At the bottom of the drive, a late moped drilled its way into the now dark night, some teenager no doubt, revving up for the ascent into Roussillon. The irony was that Liz had been thinking fondly of her mother all day. The unsheltered railway platform at midday, and then later at three o'clock, and finally at six – after which she gave up – reminded her of the good things about Emily, which as children they were apt to forget: the things of which other kids, including Alan Rowe and the students at the university, declared themselves envious. *They* couldn't imagine a parent sitting down with them at midnight, when they were half-drunk, and making coffee or sharing a cigarette. In the instant of Liz's rage, memories jumped out at her like spurned cassettes: this was the woman who had taught her to sew and knit, who had let her make an endless mess in the kitchen; who stayed up nights in a row when Liz was a little girl so that she would have a beautiful green-and-purple patchwork dress for her ninth birthday.

Half a bottle of wine stood next to Emily now, and Liz glared at it. When she was fifteen, and heavily into home-brew – gallons of the stuff bubbling away under the kitchen dresser – Liz tried a batch of elderberry one morning before school and was frogmarched out of assembly by the headmistress.

'Elizabeth Allden,' the gloating spinster said, 'is that *alcohol* I smell on your breath?'

'Yes, miss, it is,' Liz replied. 'We always have wine for breakfast.'

The Alldens had no phone so there was no efficient way of disproving Liz's blithely Continental explanation for her drunkenness. Miss Knight wrote a letter inviting Emily to corroborate the story in person, accompanied by her daughter. Which, with impressive presence of mind, she did.

'*Mrs* Allden,' Miss Knight squeaked, 'I hope you realize that I take an – *extremely dim* view of this matter and that I am considering expulsion.'

And Emily had paused before crossing her legs and

saying, with her own not-unfriendly but somehow threatening emphasis, 'Are you? Really?'

Afterwards Liz doubled up and Emily whisked her into town for a victory lunch. She wished they could be like this more often.

'When you crossed your legs, Mum, Miss Knight was staring right at you.'

'Oh, that.' Emily fluttered her hands. 'Good job.'

The noise of the moped receded and in its place a softer crackle seemed to blow the kitchen window open: a car's purr as the wheels turned and stilled, an engine's surreptitious sweet nothings over dried grass and insect casings.

In a second Liz was coolly – not that coolly – kissing her boyfriend and waving goodbye to the driver. Words were exchanged, and Emily fantasized that the car contained the young man who'd served them ice creams the day before. She watched her daughter and Alan Rowe saunter back up the path, towards her. She felt pain down below but waved anyway, because this was what she always hoped for, a magical restoration. 'Don't go,' a voice called to her. 'I mean it, Mum, don't go. Stay here, and keep us company.'

The Emptying Nest

'Right,' Liz said to herself out loud, 'less than twenty-four hours to go before the commencement of Operation Southampton and what have I achieved in the packing stakes? *Pas de grande chose*.' She dabbed some more clear varnish on her toes. 'Just another coat.' The nail glistened. 'Just a little more,' she added, 'pointless distraction, here and there, and I'll be ready . . .'

Replacing the brush in the bottle she appraised her feet, trying not to notice the mess that spread beyond them, the clothes and knickers, the cards and letters, most of which she was tearing up lest they fall into maternal hands. They contained, well, intimacies . . . protestations. Nothing serious.

Sadly that was the problem, Liz reflected. Emily took romance *terribly* seriously and couldn't be light-hearted about it. She saw the boys not as the friends they were but as a line of suitors – Alan, with his motorbike and rock and talent for handling Clive; Tom Periss, neat and deferential; his brother Raf, the suave, gorgeous one; and Ollie Smith, who played bass in Alan's band and spoke Spanish with a Bristolian squeak, so that *qué tal?* became

K-Tel?, to the particular dismay of Tom, correct in all things – and half-Spanish.

Liz smiled. You'd never think it to look at him. Well-spoken Tom, who ironed everything, even his underpants. Always in a clean shirt with a bunch of flowers for Mum, who adored him. Would she adore him so much, or in the same way, if she knew the . . . extent of his hidden talent? Liz's smile broadened: Tom liked Emily – 'she's a fine-looking woman, dammit', he'd say, like the Marquess in *Upstairs, Downstairs*. Now there was a thought. If only . . . if *only* he could; if only *she* could. And why not, after all? Why ever not?

Liz surveyed the fantasy with generous circumspection. Mum'd feel so much better if she just went ahead and had an affair or two – it would even things up a bit, release so much inner tension – and, look, plenty of young men had the hots for older women, didn't they, so it wasn't that strange. Well, maybe slightly odd, seeing as Liz had got there first, but Mum didn't need to know that.

Possibly not a great idea to have invited them all round for a party the night before leaving for university. Should she have warned her parents? *Peut-être.* 'But there's always time,' Liz said, unscrewing the varnish bottle to effect minor repairs on her squashed little toe – an inherited trait – 'for one last dereliction of duty. Before I get my act together.'

*

It was Sunday morning and Liz had the room she shared with Lotte to herself. Lotte had got up early to do her weekend job at a tea-shop in town – a nasty chintzy place, Liz thought it, full of underage waitresses and ogling tourists. Still, it gave Lotte the chance to earn some money, look angelic and gossip with Robert Naish's girl-friend, Suzie Osborne, who also worked there. Robert was a shy, blond, porky type, the kind whose tops were always a little tight under the arms. According to Lotte, Suzie was 'breaking him in', which made even Liz wince: Suzie was but fifteen, and in her elder sister's mould – a minx, in other words. Poor Robert. Poor *kid*. Life was difficult enough for him, right now, and he never com-plained, never once cried, not even at the funeral. OK, she wasn't his real mother, but Julie was a good woman and they'd been close. Liz hoped Robert wasn't bound for a disappointment. Hoped, too, that Lotte, still only fourteen, wasn't taking all her cues from Miss Osborne, whose appetites made Liz seem strait-laced by compari-son. Enormous teeth, Suzie had, and green eyes. Green eyes, green eyeshadow, square head. She looked like a hedge with tits.

No, well, Liz sighed, Lotte would find her own way and in any case seemed happy enough with her doting boyfriend, Marc Dupont, he of the velvet jacket and pretty face. They were only kissing – *with* tongues, Lotte squealingly confided – although Marc had apparently cupped one of her breasts and gone red. She also thought she'd seen a twitch in the corduroy department. And was waiting for him to suggest . . . *no*, that wasn't quite right (Lotte said): she wasn't *waiting* for anything; she wasn't *impatient*. He was just a slow starter.

But how did she know, Liz wondered? She'd wondered the same thing last year, in France, when after a couple of glasses Mum made her tight little speech about their father's virility. What was it she'd said? 'Certainly no *shortage* there.' If he was the only man she'd slept with, how could she tell?

Liz smiled again. Interesting, she considered, how difficult it turned out to be to believe someone else capable of the guile one dreamed up for them: how the guile was exactly a property of one's own imagination, the sort of thing only a bad version of oneself could conceivably *do*, and therefore hard to attribute to another. Liz was pleased with this thought. She had similar ones on a regular basis and occasionally got as far as writing them down. Her eyes wandered the room. There was a pad in here, somewhere, very probably.

The sound of the Hoover knocking against the banisters was Emily's way of informing Liz that she'd now been in her room too long and that it was time to show her face. Step by step, the knocking and the Hoover advanced to the half-landing, then up again, nearer and nearer. Soon the usefulness of the ruse would be spent, with no more surfaces to be vacuumed, and Emily would be forced to knock on the door or just barge in and say, 'Oh! Liz! I didn't think you were in. I thought I heard you go out. (Pause.) I said to myself, "She can't possibly still be in . . . *on such a beautiful morning,*" ' and so on.

To her amazement, Liz realized she was crying. She checked herself for feeling and then remembered she'd been staring at one toe in particular for so long her eyes had begun to water. 'Thank God for that,' she muttered.

The Hoover's whine became a shriek, which happened when it stayed too long in one position or when the pipe gorged itself on a bit of carpet fringe. Emily was no doubt wondering what to say, how to gain entry. In irritation, Liz rose from her bed and opened the door to find her mother kneeling down, as if in prayer over the vacuum-cleaner, her hands spread on top of the complaining machine, her teeth bared, eyes closed.

Liz called to her father in his studio, and he said, 'Yeah. I'm here.' Jazz – Miles Davis, Coltrane, someone – burbled away in the background.

'Dad.' Liz paused. 'It's Mum.'

'I'm all right. It'll go in a sec.'

Liz said nothing, wanting to concentrate on her mother but instead noticing the sampler Emily had bought in a car-boot sale and put up on the wall above the top flight of banisters. This one had a pious sentiment in the centre, daisies around the edges, and a thread hanging from the last line. It was almost entirely without merit, Liz decided, an echo of some other anger helping to focus her mind. She switched off the Hoover and ran downstairs.

'I'm going to Gran's to ring for the doc. Mum's bad.'

Liz waited for her father to react. He was in a fugue of concentration, sanding the corner of a box frame.

'Oh for Christ's sake,' she yelled above the noise of the music. 'She's upstairs. Go upstairs, Dad. I'm getting the doctor.'

'Coming, Em.'

Having grasped the situation, he moved quickly.

'I'm all right,' Emily said.

'You two,' Liz said at the front door. 'I'm not having a bloody argument about it. I'm going now . . .' Her frustration faded as she ran. 'I've never known anything *like* it, honestly. What a pair.'

Caught by a gust of wind, the door slammed behind her.

'Can you get up?' Don said gently. 'Dear, or do you want to wait there?'

Emily repeated that she'd be all right. The pain was severe and she found she didn't want to make it worse by speaking.

She was on her side now – propped up on one arm – her legs around the Hoover so that it nestled in the crook of her knees. She wore a black-spot-on-white skirt and a black T-shirt, the skin on her arms and legs tanned a healthy brown, her face the same colour but greyed from within. Dark blood dripped from between her legs and pooled on the checked linoleum.

'The car's down the back,' Don said. 'I'll bring it

round. I'm taking you to the hospital.' He had been going to ask, 'Do you think that's a good idea?' dreading the inevitable denial. But Emily nodded and said yes anyway.

From reception, the nurses took her into a cubicle, rang for her notes, and wheeled her into Gynaecology for another painful examination, after which she was told she could have the operation the next day. She'd been down for November in two months' time, but the doctor shook his head.

'My eldest is leaving for University tomorrow,' Emily said.

She had many concerns and not enough breath. It wasn't the hysterectomy she feared, it was the hospital itself, the surrender. Don had his arms around her, perhaps to impress the doctor. He was saying he'd fetch her clothes and not to worry about Liz – 'You know her. She won't even notice.'

'Which university is it?' the consultant asked, smiling.

'Southampton. She's going to read – French. Uh. Ohhh. And philosophy, I think. That's right, isn't it?'

'Ah, well,' he said, between the groans, 'Southampton is a very good university. I went there myself and my younger brother is still there.'

Ordinarily, Emily would have exclaimed and made enquiries.

'He is studying Politics and Economics, although I think he will be a photographer. That is where his heart lies.'

'Goodness,' Emily said. 'Well . . . I shall tell her.'

'Tell her to look out for Dev Dasgupta. He is just like me, only not as handsome or clever,' the doctor laughed.

Don, who was worried, gave a disengaged chortle.

'I'll try to remember that. Dev-das.'

Lotte's cheeks flushed with alarm, and with the self-consciousness of the floored adolescent. 'Three weeks, that's ages. I want to see her now.' She sounded alone and on the verge of tears. 'Will you be cooking, Dad?'

Clive thought this very funny and hugged himself.

'Army rations,' he said. 'There'll be no mucking about, Lotte, Benjamin. You'll eat what you're given, *if* you're given it.'

Don rubbed his eyes. 'It'll be fine. We've done it before. When Em was in bed with you, Ben.'

'When *I* did the cooking,' Liz said, slyly.

'I remember that,' Lotte confirmed, digging at her younger brother. 'You wouldn't. You weren't even born.'

Benjamin rolled his eyes. 'Obviously,' he piped. 'That was *why*.'

'Just don't poison us with the porridge, Dad,' Clive said. 'Let's aim to get over that first hurdle: breakfast. A *pinch* of salt, not a packet.'

Clive's guffaws set off Alan Rowe – Alan, who'd just roared up the hill and was leaning back on one of the kitchen chairs so that the chair rocked on two legs and creaked in time to the creaking of his jacket.

'So. Don,' he said. (Alan could call him Don.) 'The situation is . . . you like some porridge with your salt.'

Don smiled wanly. 'They can make their own bloody porridge.'

Lotte giggled and stopped. 'I want to see her *before* . . .' she glanced at the clock, 'she has her operation. I don't like her being in that ward, Dad.'

'How do they take out your womb?' Benjamin asked. He had a vague idea of the thing that carried a baby, and knew that it wasn't really the stomach. So what was it? 'Is it big?'

'Actually not that big,' Liz said. 'But it's a big operation, because there are lots of bits attached to it. Lots of, y'know, vessels. It's quite dangerous.'

The word failed to impress Benjamin. On the contrary, he had the idea that hospitals were supremely safe places. His mother wasn't in one of Clive's battles, or climbing Mount Vesuvius.

As Don explained off-handedly that they could see her the day after the operation, Lotte burst into tears and Clive said, 'Don't worry, Otta.'

Fumblingly he rubbed her shoulder, though it was more of a shake than a rub. 'Don't upset yourself, Ottalotta.' He made a here-we-go face over the table at Alan, to whom all eyes suddenly turned.

'She's going to be just fine, Lotte. You'll see,' Alan said.

But when Tom Periss and the others arrived, with cans of beer and bottles of wine, Lotte remained red-faced and nervous. She felt squeezed by the others, neither a child like Benjamin nor a person in her own right.

Liz said: 'Change of plan, guys. Mum's ill, in the RUH, but come in. I'm making a thing, yeah?' A thing was a delicious meal. 'We'll have a bite and then we can zap down the road to the pub.'

The pale students murmured soberly, with the exception of Raf Periss, coolly inscrutable behind his sunglasses. Liz saw that she'd been wrong to confine interest in her mother to Tom alone – they all looked crestfallen – though Tom handled it more personally.

'Dammit, Liz,' he said, holding a spray of carnations he'd bought at the petrol station on the London Road. 'It's jolly serious. I mean, it's no joke for a woman, having her uterus removed. I should know. My mother had it done and it didn't improve her humour one little bit, I can tell you.'

Catching sight of Lotte's expression and trembling lip, he went on: 'But your mum's not like my mum, Lotte. You're very lucky, because Emily is a wonderful woman. She's going to be right as rain. In fact . . . why don't we go to the hospital now, and give her the flowers? We'll pop in and out. They won't say no.'

Lotte cheered up immediately. Tom was kind to her. They had two cars, their father's Mini and Ollie Smith's turd of a Cortina. On the way to the Royal United, Clive asked Tom why he didn't get on with his mother.

'To tell you the truth, Clive, she didn't like me, or Rafa, very much.'

'She prefer me.' Raf grinned.

'She did prefer Rafa, that's true,' Tom said, calmly. He wrestled sometimes with the propriety of saying what he felt strongly about. You could care so much that in time you ceased to care. What good did it do?

They were not safer days, but they felt safer. Just because a child had once been strangled in the woods, or a woman stabbed, did not mean you should fear the worst on a dark night. Benjamin walked to school and back on his own and made the longer trip out to Weston to visit his mother without the others. He didn't even tell them he was going.

He found the ward and walked down it with the primness of the boy who is pleased to be thought bold and independent. They'd moved her. He frowned. The other night, before the operation, she'd been in this bed at the end, laughing surreptitiously, afraid of what the ward sister would say. Tom's carnations were still lively enough in their plastic jug – but who was this, the limp creature with thin hair, shadowy eyes and the hanging mouth, where Benjamin's mother should have been? The creature registered his presence and moaned a greeting on two separate outbreaths, *ohhh*, and *buhhhh shuhh*.

'She's very tired,' the nurse said gaily, 'that's all. You come back tomorrow and see what a difference there is. Once she's come round properly and had something to eat.'

Benjamin nodded silently and left, even said goodbye and thank you to the nurse because he did not trust her and had the strong sense she did not like to be put to any trouble. His one thought was to get home. He would have to tell his father that Mum was dying. He'd feared for his own life before, when the van crept up behind him, but this was a deeper threat. This was Liz's careful phrase: 'quite dangerous', which, he now saw, meant 'very' dangerous. This was the menace at the back of words when adults pretended you weren't there, this watery dragging in your legs from which you couldn't run away.

The boy recovered from his shock, as Emily recovered from her operation; and yet he remained impressed by the memory of her vulnerability, on a ward bed surrounded by other women and visiting men.

She was soon his mother again, and full of vigorous surprises, like the day she took him to Weymouth to ride the donkeys and go trampolining – a perfect day. He was aware of it happening, that was the difference.

Benjamin had not considered the idea of personal luck before; now he did, albeit in brief flashes. It introduced a fuzzy note to happiness, like the bumbling of one's head against the sunny train window as you bowled along and all the bridges and signals in Somerset and Dorset whipped past.

Liz was equally concerned, though at a distance – from Southampton – and with her usual feeling that Emily liked to put herself beyond the reach of sympathy. The refusal to have a phone installed was one aspect of this: Liz couldn't just call from her new digs and say hello. The message had to be relayed via Irene, whose transmissions were not reliable. Nor did she want to be lured into a written exchange with her mother. That would merely feed Emily's love of the epistolary-dramatic – her peculiar belief, discernible in arch diction and hollow satire at Don's expense ('I think I may say *normal* service has been resumed!'), that she alone had been trusted with keeping the art of the letter alive, as though oceans and aeons separated the correspondents.

'Why don't you just come down,' Liz said finally, at Christmas.

'Oh, well, I don't know,' Emily said. 'I don't want to be a nuisance. You want to be with your friends . . . and you're busy. I don't expect it.'

Liz blinked. 'It's up to you, Mum.' (And Emily had pursed her lips.) 'There's a perfectly good sofa-bed, or you can have mine. I don't care.'

It wasn't quite the open-armed summons Emily had been hoping for, but it was better than nothing.

'Perhaps I'll come for the day. Would that be all right?'

'Whatever you like. You know where I am.'

So later in January Emily went to visit her daughter in her shared house in Derby Road, in the red-light district where rents were cheap.

She bought an ordinary return and packed a sponge-bag and change of underwear, in case she was made to feel particularly welcome.

The house contained a number of sleepy young men, much as Emily had anticipated, and they were nice to her – Liz's friends always were. One of them, whom Liz called Fint, ate cereals for lunch and had no shoes. His conversation was affable but limited, as if he didn't fully understand what she was saying.

'Well, yeah,' he said, answering Emily's attempts at light-heartedness. 'Yeah, you could say that. Definitely.'

Liz thrust a very large square brown-paper parcel under her mother's arms and said, 'This is yours. It's a thing.' A thing was a gift. 'It's your birthday, isn't it? Around now?' She knew she'd missed it by a couple of days: it fell exactly two weeks after her own, which she did not forget.

They went to the pub on the corner, where the smoke was so thick it all but concealed the pool table. At the bar, Liz discovered she'd come out without any money. Before Emily could stop her and retrieve the pound notes in her own purse, Liz had sailed out of the pub, back to the house. It was twenty minutes before she returned, a little smirk at the corners of her mouth. They had a round of cheese sandwiches each and a half of ginger-beer shandy. 'Pretty revolting,' Liz admitted. 'Sorry about that.'

A walk along the dock front, where she sometimes came for a run, was more successful; and then back through the eastern terraces of the city towards the centre and the Art Gallery. Emily enjoyed the fresh, cold air and the industrial expanse of freight and storage. It made her think of hard lives and big cities and of her father, who'd sailed from Southampton, or was it Liverpool, to Canada.

'Liverpool,' Liz decided. 'What have you done with your present?'

'My present?' Emily looked dumbfounded.

She'd left it in the pub.

'Doesn't matter,' Liz said, while her mother was apologizing. 'Don't worry. We can zap back to the pub on the way to the station.'

They broke their trek in the Art Gallery cafe, without bothering to look at any of the paintings. Above the central staircase, a society portrait of Lady Darling glared at them disapprovingly.

'I didn't realize it was for me,' Emily said, pleased and confused. 'You should have said.'

'I did. I asked you about your birthday, remember?'

Emily did remember, and laughed it off. What she couldn't tell her daughter was that she hadn't believed her. Since when was Liz in the habit of buying large gifts and wrapping them up?

She paused to reflect.

To her alarm she recalled that of course Liz *made*, rather than gave, things all the time – cooked, ran up a skirt, sewed a bead bangle – and presented them with a fling of the hands, as if no effort had been involved: she lived in a ferment of facility, or perhaps liked to be thought of in that way. The danger lurking for such careless achievers, as Emily well knew, was that people soon took you at your word – for granted – and then you resented them.

'It didn't cost me *nothing*,' Liz was saying, grumpily. 'I'm not that mean.'

'You're never mean, darling!' Emily said. 'Now I feel dreadful.'

The object was retrieved from the pub, which had just reopened, and Emily was on the point of suggesting that they go out for dinner or order a Chinese in, when Liz said, 'Mum, would you mind very much if I didn't walk you all the way to the station? There's this photography thing on at the union tonight and I'm going – I want to go – with Fint. I'm sorry. Would that be okay?'

'Of course. I'll get the bus. I'm quite happy.'

It wasn't far to the bus stop and Emily saw a cream-and-burgundy single-decker almost straight away. She felt bewildered, as though she were being evacuated all over again. She put the square parcel down with a bump in order to give Liz a kiss, and Liz said, 'Careful, it's glass. If you don't like the frame, get Dad to change it.' The out-of-service bus rattled past.

'Bastard,' said Liz, adding swiftly, 'it doesn't matter, they come every five minutes. You won't have to wait long. When you get to the station, walk over the bridge so you're on the right side, yeah?'

'Oh yes,' Emily replied. The sea was in the air, just a few drops flung across the street, as if a wave had crashed invisibly around the corner. 'I can't believe you're at university already. It's gone so quickly. Are you enjoying it?'

Liz inclined her head, as if she didn't understand the question.

'Are you enjoying your course?'

It was cold now, and dark. Liz said tiredly, 'Everything's fine, Mum.' She gave a low chuckle. 'I'll let you know about the course when I've done some of it.' They kissed. 'Nice of you to come down, Mum. You're looking well.'

'Nearly fifty, you know. Not far off!'

'Love to Dad and the others. I'll write soon.'

'Yes – and, oh Liz, thank you so much for such a lovely day. And for this.'

On the bus, Emily clasped the drawing or painting, or whatever it was, to her chest, though what she really wanted to do was smash it over someone's head and cause an accident.

'How old's your mum?' Fint said, over his evening bowl of cornflakes.

'God knows,' Liz sighed. 'Forty-seven, forty-eight. Something like that.'

'Looking pretty good for someone that old, isn't she?'

'Is she?'

'Yeah, she is. I can see where you get it from.'

Liz picked a hair out of her cleavage. 'Get what?' she said suspiciously, chin thrust down to inspect her bosom.

'The charm,' Fint said.

'Oh, she's all right,' Liz allowed. 'But she drives me mad.'

Fint grazed contentedly.

'I know exactly what's going through her head. She wants to check up on me, but she won't ever *say* what she's thinking. She's constantly angling for me to be nice to her and for some reason, I don't know what it is, I just can't. Which she knows. And then I get the look and the whole story about her mum and how poor they were, just like the poor people here. You should have heard it.'

'Probably feels a bit left out.'

'What's it all about, anyway? She's as middle-class as they come. Look at where she lives. It's so fucking patronizing. I don't even want to go into it, it's so tedious. Is that all you're having, cornflakes?'

When Emily got home, she tore the wrapping off her present, angrier now than she'd been on the train. As the paper came off, she gave vent to her feelings, shouting at Don, 'I think it's a bit much, that's all.'

'What is?'

'Leaving your own mother at the bus stop. She couldn't even be bothered to walk me to the station.'

'Well, you know Liz. She's got ants in her pants.' Don sniffed at the local rag. 'S – E – Q – U – O – I – A. Tell her. Tell her you think it's not on.'

'Imagine me doing the same to my mother,' Emily fretted. Liz had used a great deal of strong Sellotape and beneath the wrapping paper was another protective layer of card.

'I know you wouldn't,' Don agreed, lamely. 'Anyway, your Mum's half-blind. She'd never see the bus.'

'The thought would never have occurred to me. I'd never have dared—'

She held Liz's gift and as she stared her grip tightened, shifted.

It was a sampler, intricately worked in dark imperial purples and greens, the lettering quite small in the centre, but distinct: a verse in French Emily could understand. The poetry fruited inside a tree, within a garden she recognized as her own. The borders of the sampler formed the borders of the garden; two large birds tended a nest on top of the tree, one with a stick in its beak, the other flying in, laden with worms to feed her young.

Three mouths strained open at her approach. Another bird, the fourth youngling, flew happily in the opposite direction. Leaves fell beneath the tree and made a signature – Elizabeth Allden, 1977 – alongside a dedication, also in French, which read, 'Un cadeau pour ma très chère Maman'.

The essay in self-confidence and effrontery that was Liz's independence pleased her mother as much as it distressed her. It must reflect well on some aspect of her upbringing, she supposed. Of course, Liz took the occasional knock – she cared more than she let on about others' good opinion – but, wisely perhaps, she refused to dwell on her failings, or at least concealed her hurts.

Clive gave Emily no such peace of mind. Always an awkward child, he grew more awkward as he grew taller and thinner. Clad in a dandruff-speckled polo neck and heavy tweed jacket, he lurked in the recesses of the common room at school, speaking to no one, the captive of his promise and his disdain.

Emily wondered sometimes if she had played some part in this: for Clive was shy and easily discouraged by failure or criticism. After hearing that it was no good just having talent, he'd put down his pencils for good. Her frantic response had been to praise him for the things he could still do, for his writing, most of all. Except that it wasn't ordinary praise: it was a sort of whispered exaltation within the family circle of a special child, whose sensitivity was a proof of abilities in other directions. The world of compromise, of mistakes and muddling through, was not for Clive, this praise implied, and he believed it.

The obvious rift opened up between aspiration and reality. To write something brilliant one had first to write anything, but perfectionism is a ditherer, and at the blank page of his future Clive stared with mounting apprehension. Arsenal lost to Ipswich, Geoff Boycott broke his finger; distractions turned into omens.

He did anything to avoid work – in particular the

work he had to do to get into Oxford. He knew in his heart that his father had been telling the truth, that talent is an abstraction unless applied to the possibility of failure. But it seemed easier to assume that his father didn't understand him. He preferred his mother's trust in expectations alone. He preferred, greatly, the words of his headmaster, elated to think his comprehensive might at last send someone to Oxbridge, who'd vowed to eat his hat 'if that boy isn't worth an exhibition'.

Clive sat the entrance exam.

He rarely enjoyed tests but this time he turned over the paper, saw straight away that it could have been written with him in mind, and came home elated: 'There was a question about Milton and the Civil War. And one about *Macbeth*.'

He was called for interview two weeks later.

'He's been called for interview,' Emily told Maggie Cooper, the imposing owner of the local shop. The phrase sounded promising, so she tried it out on everyone she met. Maggie offered her congratulations, and asked Emily if she wanted to pay for the sausages now or put them on the book. Even sausages were getting pricey. 'It's the inflation,' Maggie said, tapping the counter.

Then, at home, on the day of the interview, while Benjamin was doggedly practising his scales on the piano, Emily unburdened herself to him.

'I do worry about that boy,' she said. 'I've been saying my prayers – I know it's silly, but I have been. It means so much, to him. He's so difficult. Well – you know, don't you?' She paused. 'If he could just get over himself, I don't know. I told you what Mr Batton said, didn't I?'

Benjamin liked E flat. Two in the right, three in the left.

'He said he'd eat his hat if Clive wasn't worth an exhibition.'

'But he's already had one of those.' Benjamin frowned at F sharp minor. Only three sharps but tricky to finger. Starting on the fourth in the left.

'What d'you mean?' Emily snapped. She flinched at the image of a row of half-eaten hats. 'It's not that sort of exhibition.'

'Oh. What sort is it, then? What other sort is there?'

Emily sighed. 'I suppose it's a scholarship,' she said eventually, over a scramble of missed notes. 'Fat lot you care.'

'Fuck,' said Benjamin, before he could stop himself.

Emily simply rewrote the word in her head.

'I *do* care,' Benjamin pleaded, a little terrified, and waited until his mother had thumped down the stairs before whistling with relief.

He stopped playing when the key turned in the front door.

Lotte got to Clive first, said a cheery hello and asked him how it had gone. The weary traveller exhaled dismally. Emily's cheeriness was even more forced, and Benjamin, sensing disaster, stuck fingers in his ears.

'There he is, there he is,' called Don, emerging from the studio. 'The Man of the Hour. Cometh the Hour. Cometh the, yeah. *How. Did. It. Go?*'

To avoid the family, Clive sought the refuge of his room. Ashen-faced, he pointed at Benjamin on the trunk that served as a piano stool.

'What's Benjamin doing?' he said. 'Why has he got his fingers in his ears – your playing's not that bad, is it, Ben?' Collapsing on the bed, he added, 'Or maybe it is. What the hell do I know?'

The indications throughout dinner were that Clive would soon blow his top, signals that Benjamin and Lotte had long ago decoded.

He began to breathe audibly, occasionally producing a fully-vocalized moan as though this, the toad-in-the-hole he usually loved, were real toad; as though he chafed under his family's respectful silence and longed to banish the lot of them to some remote and shitty eminence with one sweep of his arm.

His brow darkened, he dropped his knife and fork, he ate – in his mind and in actuality – like a Saxon overlord, pulling at fragments of fatty batter and sausage, jabbing the plate with his fingers, running them forgetfully through his hair.

'Don't do that, dear,' Emily said. 'It's not nice.'

Clive lifted his plate and pitched it at his mother, who ducked in the nick of time. The plate broke against the fridge and a fork stuck in the door where it twanged briefly like an arrow.

'You *witch*,' he shrieked, knowing that Don would now wade in.

Lotte and Benjamin ran for cover, like civilians under

siege, half-expecting the stairs to collapse under them or the banisters to explode. They got into the street, where the three combatants could be heard fighting fire with fire, Clive's rattling invective blocked by Don's counter-aggression, by quick stabs of mockery and condescension, and by his mother's too-articulate weeping.

Don would give up soon and storm out. Clive and Emily would go on for hours, following each other about the house, compelled to hurt and be hurt.

'They love it,' Benjamin said, who'd heard Irene say as much.

Lotte gasped excitedly: 'He's an animal. Did you see the way he was eating? It's not normal.' At sixteen, she still put her thumb in her mouth. 'I don't bring friends round because of the smell.'

'You bring Fraser round.'

'Yes, but Fraser knows Clive.'

Guilelessly, Benjamin said, 'Is Fraser your new boyfriend?' Marc, the forlorn ex, had been hanging around in the street at night, dolefully serenading his lost love, and waking Benjamin up. 'Have you told Clive?'

Lotte let her thumb cool in the air. 'Tell him what?'

Benjamin didn't know and perhaps didn't want to. He only sensed, vaguely, that Fraser and Clive had been friends first, and that Lotte and Fraser were now going out together, which meant that they stayed in, playing records.

Fraser towered over petite Lotte, who simpered in the shade of his red hair and heroic chest. It was a cartoon pairing: Benjamin saw his sister sitting in the palm of

Fraser's hand, like Tweetie-pie. Whenever Fraser called at No. 2, Benjamin cheerily said, 'Ho, ho, ho.' 'Fraser is here, Lotte, ho, ho.' But secretly he liked the music that came from Lotte's room and sometimes spun around to its echo, even though boys weren't meant to like disco, because disco was for poofs.

They walked the rest of the way to their grandmother's house in silence. The only other person in the street that evening was Paul Addicott, the Christian son of Benjamin's piano teacher, who wore a shirt and tie and a yellow badge that said 'Smile! Jesus Loves You!'. Paul was an illustration from a book. He had his hair slicked back twenties-style, called everyone Mr This or Mrs That in an old lady's voice, and seemed oblivious to the effect he produced. Did he know what he looked like, Benjamin wondered? Did he care? Or was he slow?

Irene and Arnold were sitting in front of the television after their tea. One bar glowed on the electric as usual and Arnold had fallen asleep with the *Daily Mail* tented over his belly. He awoke to the news that Clive had gone berserk.

'We came here to get away from it,' Benjamin said.

'Good job,' said Irene, who was knitting another scarf. Her glaucoma meant she couldn't read, and telly was only radio with shapes. But she could knit.

'Oh, I am sorry,' Arnold said, with a jovial sincerity that made the children feel better. 'I expect he was nervous. It can be nerve-wracking. Poor lad.'

'Do you think he'll get in?' Benjamin asked.

'He certainly ought to.' Their uncle smiled a little sadly. 'But it may not make any difference in the long run. To what he wants to do, I mean.'

'He wants to be a writer, doesn't he?'

Arnold agreed, as if Benjamin had gifted them a startling insight.

'Yes, *yes*. You're *right*, Benjamin. Exactly that. He does. And, well, he *is* one already, in my opinion.'

'Em should leave him be,' Irene clucked as she clacked. 'He doesn't have to go to university if he doesn't want to. I left school at twelve.'

'Oh, Mother,' cried Arnold.

Irene tittered and told them the one about her stingy parents and the watered-down ink, all her lovely written work drying into invisibility, *Oh, what a waste!* Lotte laughed until she choked while Benjamin seemed to see the words' grappling outstretched hands disappearing in front of him.

The story Emily fashioned from the scraps Clive fed her was that he'd got to St Catherine's and been disappointed to find that it lacked spires and quadrangles; so disappointed that he'd clammed up before the interview even started. After that, the placid unfriendliness of his two interrogators finished him off. They weren't interested in Milton or *Macbeth*. Instead they asked with a mean emphasis, 'Which *living* authors do you enjoy reading?'

In reality, things had been more complicated. To begin with, Clive got lost in the maze of 1960s corridors and stairways, and arrived slightly panic-stricken but just in time to see another candidate, a girl, leaving the interview room with a spring in her step. As she closed the door she turned to say goodbye with an annoying familiarity. 'They're really nice,' she whispered to Clive.

Uncomposed and tense, he walked into the dons' study only to be asked to wait outside for a minute. Were these the same nice people she'd meant? The two young, trendy lecturers wearing wide collars and smoking roll-ups? They looked like students. And something about the man, in particular, the predatory glance he shot at Clive before speaking, the superciliousness of his hesitation, the little mental strut it revealed, made Clive suspicious.

Which 'living authors' did he enjoy? What did they want him to do, name-drop? Since when had William Hazlitt become David Niven? Clive's two papers on Milton and Shakespeare, his poetical views on the building – the *exhalation* – of Lucifer's Pandaemonium, on equivocation and military strategy, lay open on their laps: what stopped them from asking him about those? The man made no eye contact, but simply sat, legs crossed, chin supported on one hand, swinging his right foot from side to side.

She, the woman, was more attentive. Sitting forward, and looking directly at him, she seemed to Clive to want to get things started.

'For example,' she said, 'what are you reading at the moment?' The man lifted a sheet of Clive's examination papers. 'Just to give us an idea.'

The two books in Clive's school briefcase were *Somebody Up There Likes Me* by Rocky Graziano, the great middleweight champion, and *Death to the French* by C. S. Forester, both of which Clive instantly rejected as inadmissible. Behind the bored man was a narrow window, a modern architect's idea of an arrow-slit perhaps, with anti-nuclear stickers on it. To the woman's left, in a wall of metal shelving, Clive could see nothing but the great Europeans, Zola and Hugo and Goethe in particular, about whom he was ignorant. His thoughts settled and concentrated furiously on the irrelevant fact that on the way to Egypt Napoleon warned his men not to poison their minds by reading novels, before retiring to his cabin to devour the latest potboiler. Everything was more or less a bluff in life, it sometimes seemed to Clive; the double-sense talked by the three witches, the Napoleonic pincer-movement, Ali's brilliant psyching of Foreman. The more examples of it he found, the more he wondered at his own foolish transparency. What was he reading? He had no idea. His mind was empty.

Or, now, not quite empty, as the woman firmed her lips in exasperation. Because part of the bluff of real life was that mysterious quality of *likeableness*, which gained other people's confidence and gave you some of your own in return. Into Clive's thoughts came the cheery girl candidate, his father's easy social manner,

Fraser's popularity. It looked simple enough, this affable induction into adulthood and adult plausibility. They all managed it – why couldn't he? You just had to borrow the style of the age, play at being self-assured and soon enough you were – stylish enough, confident enough, likeable, no matter that the plumes were borrowed. That was how one grew up. That was how you met girls. So what was he, Clive, doing, in the middle of an interview for Oxford, thinking about Fraser having sex with his younger sister? About being left behind – what on earth did he think he was *up* to?

'I don't know,' he said.

The man suddenly grinned and scratched his head. 'You don't know what you're reading at the moment?' His hand plopped onto Clive's essays, in a way Clive felt was deliberate. 'Listen, look . . . it's not a trap. It's a friendly question. We can both see you're nervous, but there's really no need to be. Why don't you go outside, take a break for five minutes and come back? We're running late anyway, we always do, so it makes no difference. OK?'

He was right. It made no difference, either to them or to Clive.

But he went to York the following week and in the middle of a dull day found himself chatting to Hermione Lee about boxing and literature.

'The thing about boxing, the thing you have to remember,' the pugnacious eighteen-year-old said, 'is that it's *in* the head and *to* the head. You don't have to be intellectual; you *do* have to be smart. And that's what boxers have in common with writers, I think. Well, the writers I like the most, at any rate. The ones who can move, who can dance, who have fast reflexes.'

'Interesting,' Lee said. 'Would that include Milton and Shakespeare?'

'Shakespeare, yes. Milton, no.'

'Why not?'

'Well, he was blind for a start,' Clive said, seriously, because in his mind's eye he could see Irene poking dimly at her stove. 'Couldn't find the ring, let alone get into it.' Lee nodded. 'The whole thing was a disaster.'

Redemption for Clive, largesse from Lee: an unconditional offer.

The turbulent spirit inside Clive was not appeased, however. Truth be told, he didn't want to leave home, was scared and unhappy. But knowing he must go, and too afraid to appear afraid, he fashioned his own expulsion.

A few days before term was due to start at York, Clive asked Lotte if she wanted to play tennis. They went to the park and Lotte returned an hour later in distress. She'd played gently but accurately, while Clive whacked the ball around the court with thunderously misplaced conviction. It was like being stuck behind a slow driver, he complained; they weren't playing the *same* game. She won the first set and Clive threw his racket at her. It wheeled through the air and struck her edge on. Winded, and lucky to escape with bruised ribs, Lotte ran shakily from the courts, not wanting the other players to notice her, hating her brother. As she passed the benches where pensioners sat in the September sun, resting their hands on sticks, clearing their throats, a kind old man said concernedly, 'You shouldn't let your boyfriend do that to you, my love. You're too good for him, all round you are.'

When the door shut on Clive the following Monday, Emily exclaimed, 'And a good riddance, that's all I can say.'

The cost of this judgement was some grief later on and in private, but for now the hush of the house returned the three of them, mother, son and daughter, each at a different height on the stairs, to a sense of what they might do, and who they might be, in a world beyond constant agitation and threat.

Months, terms, seasons went by in relative tranquillity. Liz moved from Derby Road to Marseille, for her year abroad, and back again. Except for rare postcards, Clive dropped from view. 'Your room feels so much bigger now, doesn't it?' Emily once said to Benjamin, who answered unregretfully, 'Yes.'

Because naturally it was thrilling for him to have his own room at last. To be able to practise the piano whenever he wanted, to put up posters, colonize his brother's shelves with his own books, and play records. Liz had bequeathed him some of her LPs and introduced him to a record shop in town, called Cruisin', where a tribe of punks and mods and highly coiffed New Romantics assembled on Saturday mornings to scry the blue and pink columns of the Charts.

Saturday mornings! The extravagance of their freedom, the energy their white-yellow light and simmering sound imparted from the moment Benjamin awoke and made tea to the last tricky bit in the Bach at Mrs Addicott's.

And then, the real morning – the pocket money from Irene and the lovely limestone expanse of town with a visit to every bookshop and, finally, Cruisin', solemnized by ritual. 'Beethoven is hewn out of rock, Mozart is gossamer silk,' he heard his piano teacher crying thinly on the wind. Poor Ludwig, dragged out of the ground like that. Poor Wolfgang, forced to wear pink. *See ya!*

Benjamin was twelve and ready to buy his first album. The process of selection had taken weeks. It wouldn't be the soundtrack to *Grease*: he had that on tape. Or Kate Bush (Liz had given him both of her records). No, it had to be something individual, he felt, but not too rude or shocking; something of which his parents might tacitly approve without saying too much and spoiling things.

It wasn't easy. Benjamin's best and oldest friend, David Fowler, a thirteen-year-old dude with a second-hand mustard-coloured waistcoat, looked aghast at the mention of Joan Armatrading and a band called Darts. With confidence, showing Benjamin how it was done, David flicked through the racks in Cruisin', stopping at Blondie (becoming uncool) and The Jam (not so popular now but still cool), then pausing again to inspect *Quad-rophenia* before settling for *What's Going On* (timeless) by a singer whose name Benjamin thought quite funny.

'It's got an "e" on the end,' David remarked acidly. 'It's his *name*.'

Benjamin flicked on. 'Yes, well . . .' he said, sensitive to his own air of imposture. 'He still sounds like a . . . like a bummer.'

David lowered his voice: 'Do you know what that word means?'

Benjamin shrank from the direct enquiry.

'Do you?' He shrank further. 'You shouldn't go round calling people that. A bummer is a man who puts his knob up another man's bum.'

'Oh, that,' said Benjamin in double-sided terror of detection, both as a naive youth who could be pitied for not knowing and, more unsettlingly, as someone who realized he did. 'I'm getting this,' he announced quickly, and held up *New Boots and Panties* by Ian Dury. 'What d'you think?'

'Get what you want,' grumbled David, still hurt by the slur, which was absurd. His brother would have told him if Marvin Gaye was a bummer. He glanced at Benjamin, paying for the record. Christ, what a sight. When would his balls drop? Look at the bowl-cut on him.

'Good one,' said the hairy man in the AC/DC T-shirt behind the counter. 'Very decent record. And a great *band*.'

That's what my dad says, Benjamin thought, and

took his new possession out of its bag to feel that it was really his.

But in the end it was Lotte, not Ian Dury or the boy in the waistcoat, who found and turned the key to Benjamin's musical soul.

For his birthday, and for Christmas a few days later, she bought him *Aretha Franklin's Greatest Hits* and *For Once In My Life*, by Stevie Wonder. (They were on offer.) Benjamin knew neither singer and put the records on, with low hopes. He would have preferred the soundtrack to *Jaws*. And then, without meaning to, he found that he was playing them all the time, on the mono turntable in his room and on his father's stereo, mostly when Don was out delivering or drawing, but sometimes when he was in, and didn't mind.

Over the sanding and hammering, Aretha's voice uncaged itself, soared free while Benjamin sat in his dad's falling-apart armchair, looking out at the city. The music beat the view into different shapes – the house that Jack built, a climbing rose in Spanish Harlem. It shimmered with the sun.

Lotte was gratified, and amused. She knew that otherwise she did not have much in common with her younger brother, who scampered about in his own climate of intense daffiness. Or perhaps it was that he exhibited such a strange combination of traits – Liz's appetite for social display, Clive's argumentative prowess, her own

secretiveness and pride. What she hadn't previously observed was his capacity to be absorbed by a passion for
hours, for days at a time, and with a romantic diligence
that was new, for him at least. It found its way to a deep
place in her own fond imagining, that she would one day
make such pleasure possible for children of her own.

'*The moment I wake up*', she could hear him singing,
'*before I put on my*, mmm . . .' Benjamin fudged the
inappropriate admission, but joined in with the chorus:
'*For ever and ever, you'll stay in my heart and I will
love you!*' To her diary, Lotte confided that it was really
'a mad thing for a thirteen-year-old to be singing! Not
entirely normal! It has been Aretha and Stevie Wonder's
blimmin' "Shoo-Be-Doo-Be-Doo" every evening this
week! What have I started! Fraser thinks it is funny! Oh,
Fraser . . . . He wants me to give him blow-jobs all the
time and I am getting bored. Suzie's awful! She said, is it
more than I can handle?!! And I said, quite the opposite
problem actually!!!'

Lotte sometimes read her diary back to herself and
vaguely detested the salivating creature she encountered on the page, the person the world did not see.
She craved what she saw as normality, but of course
the craving begat other desires and these worried her.
She was Head Girl. She was the willing vessel of her
mother's ambitions for her: to find happiness by being
conventional. She so wanted to be *good*; to marry someone she absolutely loved. Already she thought about it a
lot. The difficulty was that she'd spent most of her child-

hood being good, merely by playing second fiddle to the noisy duo who went before, and half of her was sick of it. She *was* good, she decided, and it was her goodness that entitled her, occasionally, to be bad. At parties, in cars, after work . . .

Looking at Benjamin, in one of his musical reveries, she felt suddenly envious. Enthusiasm possessed him and bore him far away. He listened for hours. Time meant nothing and he didn't care if you were there with him or not. It was as if he'd attained some state of self-sufficiency she lacked. His world expanded inwards, whereas hers was simply what she did and said.

'I don't mind being ordinary,' she told Fraser, who shook his head.

Lotte was ordinary, then. The problem was that she wanted recognition for it. This brought her into conflict with Emily who, being brazenly ordinary herself, had one eye peeled for signs of unorthodoxy in her daughter.

'I like you in that top, Lotte,' she said artfully one morning. 'So hard to find that shade of pale blue – plain, pale blue. It's lovely with your hair.'

'Thanks, Mum. I got it yesterday in M&S.'

'Oh! So it's new.'

Lotte felt her psoriasis itching down the length of one arm.

'It's only cheap – I worked the extra day last week.'

Emily pretended to look closely at one of the seams in

the patchwork quilt she was making. Presently she raised her head.

'No, I like it. Really I do.' The needle went back in. 'It's just that I wouldn't have thought you needed another one yet. Still – no, no. Don't get upset. I have to be so careful, dear oh dear. It's your money.'

'Yes, it is.'

'It is. That's what I'm saying. Goodness. I'm glad you've got enough to spend on something you like. Truly I am.'

'You're always doing this.'

'Doing what?'

'Making out I spend a lot. It's just a blue top.'

'I know, and it's very nice,' Emily insisted. 'It makes your hair really shine. Well, of course, *your* hair's beautiful anyway, not like my thin stuff . . .'

They were upstairs in Don's studio, drinking milky coffee while Stevie sang 'God Bless the Child' and Don concentrated on the difficult corners of a mount. Lotte gazed out of the window at the house below theirs in Bellevue Crescent. The children used to play games to see if they could make poor Mrs Millard come to the upstairs toilet. Only the bottom bit of her lavatory window was frosted so you could see her come in. In the toilet she was bald. But if you knocked on her door, she had a set of iron-grey curls.

'She's doing it again, Dad,' Lotte said, banging her cup down on the armrest.

'Doing what?'

'Fishing for compliments.'

'Fishing for—' Emily tried to sound nonplussed. Where had Lotte picked up such a cutting phrase? It sounded like Suzie Osborne, or Suzie's mother.

'You two,' Don said, who wasn't listening. 'Give it a miss, whatever it is. Don't make everything a competition.'

Emily was outraged. 'I like that. Who's being competitive? I know I'm not. I'm the *least* competitive person in the family.'

'Oh, Em. *Em.*'

'No, but really,' Emily snapped. 'I'm sitting here, minding my own business, talking nicely to Lotte and all of a sudden I'm accused of being – oh, I can't even say it, it's so ridiculous.'

'Competitive,' said Benjamin.

'Ha ha ha. Ha ha *ha*. It's a great big joke, isn't it?'

'Now come on, Mum. Don't be angry.' Lotte had quite recovered her humour by seeing Emily lose hers. 'And mind where you stick that needle.'

The quilt was a composition of black and white hexagonals.

'Anyone would think I didn't know how to sew.' Emily flourished her thimble. 'As if you've ever seen me nick myself with a preedle.'

Lotte screamed with merriment, but Benjamin had news to trump it.

'Mr Millard is coming up the garden path.'

'Is who?' Emily said in a smaller voice. '*Ken* Millard?'

'Look for yourself. He's coming now. He's at the back door.'

Emily was wary of people who dropped in, unless they were the children's friends of course – unless they were, well, family, or as good as.

'That's funny,' she said. 'I can't recall him ever coming round before.'

No one could. Don darted down the stairs, two at a time, to greet their neighbour. Ken worked in a gentleman's outfitters in Northumberland Place and wore a cream polyester shirt to work every day. He wore one most of the rest of the time too, with the sleeves rolled up. He remembered the children's birthdays and always stopped to chat if he was strolling back from work in the evening, or gardening, or sweeping out the yard. He stood now, ill at ease, Benjamin thought, with one hand on the back of his neck and another on his hip, waiting for the door to open. Benjamin pressed his face to the cool glass to see the moment of transformation, and there it was: a toothy smile, both hands going to the hips, eyebrows lifting, some nervous laughter.

They heard Don say, 'Hi, Ken, hi, hi, come in,' and Ken, politely, refuse; Don offering tea or something stronger, laughing; Ken trying to insist, saying, 'I only came to thank—' but not finishing.

Beneath the music, which Emily now turned down, they could detect a change in pace, no more bluff masculine greetings; and Ken not fully in the house but on the doorstep, then the door closing; their father, in a voice that was at once wise and kind, gently protesting that it was no bother, he wasn't doing anything.

They went into the sitting room.

To cover her interest Emily plucked from the air a hardly neutral query about Fraser. 'How's he getting on, Lotte? He must be at the end of his first year.'

'He's fine. Last I heard.'

'Didn't you speak to him last night?'

The Alldens had bowed to fate and put a phone in the kitchen.

'For two minutes,' Lotte said evenly. Her mother was scared by the prospect of bills and liked to interrupt conversations as soon as possible. She did this by wandering into the kitchen, saying, 'Now, where did I put my . . . ?'

'I expect you're looking forward to seeing him next year.'

'Next year? I start in October.'

'Next *academic* year, I mean.'

Lotte rolled her eyes. Fraser was a medic at UCH, while Lotte had opted to do nursing. She'd wrestled with the choice, and Emily approved it at the time. She understood her daughter's concern that she was not an intellectual. Then Lotte got her A-level results, and Emily, bursting with pride, balked at the thought of UCH not appreciating how bright her daughter really was.

'I think perhaps I'd better go down,' she said, setting aside a portion of the Giant's Causeway.

As she got up, the two men came out of the sitting room. Ken was saying, 'And thank Em, too, won't you? I'm sorry I can't . . .'

'Oh God, sure, sure. That doesn't matter. I'm just so

sorry for you. For both of you, I mean. You know what I mean.'

'Well, I'll be all right. It's Millie I'm worried about.'

'Sure, sure. Obviously we'll keep an eye out.'

'Thank you, Don.'

'Thank *you*, for telling me. Us. Can't have been easy—'

Ken's voice hit a different register. They were both quiet. Then Ken continued: 'You're so lucky to have . . .' he said, 'someone . . .'

'I know.'

' . . . Bye.'

'Bye, Ken.'

'Love to Em. Bye-bye.'

He left and Don came up, white in the face.

'Ken can't come to our twenty-fifth,' he said. 'He wants children.'

From the studio, Benjamin watched their neighbour walk down the path, stopping halfway to pinch the top of his nose.

Across the road, Ken's front door opened and Millie appeared without any hair. She was dragging a suitcase which she emptied out onto the pavement. Clothes, mostly. A few heavier objects that clattered on the concrete. Ken knelt and stuffed everything back in, watched by his expressionless wife. He hauled his suitcase to a car the children had not noticed waiting, with its indicators faintly winking, just visible. It wasn't a taxi. It wasn't Ken's.

Millie leant out in her housecoat and bellowed: 'Have him, then. Go on. Have him, he's useless. He'll be back. Don't even think of coming back.'

The car was at the top of the rise leading out of Bellevue Crescent before she stepped into the street to shout: 'This is your last chance, Kenneth Millard.'

Goodnight Penwithick

Like another child, the house absorbed years of offer-
ings, of cleaning, mending, cooking and silent forgiving
without a word of thanks. And as the children left, even
these daily contributions faded into the background, to
be replaced by Don's material demands – mouldings,
glass, Perspex, a new mount cutter for circles and el-
lipses – things which created more work and more dust.
More paintings and drawings appeared, some of them by
Don now that he no longer taught at the Tech, and on
their framed edges more of the sinister grey pollen. When
she cleaned, Emily saw little balls of fluff, small crests of
filth falling from her fingers onto her cushions' careful
seams and embroidery.

People noticed his frames because of their valuable,
often antique contents, whereas they simply sat on her
cushions, taking them for items of the present, which
they were not, or not merely, their flowers and birds and
curlicues all decorative virtues born of necessity. Only
Emily knew how much energy and devotion it took to
make things last; inventiveness, too, in the service of a
thrift that by definition concealed its own workings. The

black-and-white patchwork quilt on which Emily had laboured every evening for nearly a year had hung on the walls of the American Museum for three weeks, in a display of handicrafts. A lady from the repository of the Victoria and Albert took a picture of it and made enquiries. The moment passed. When it returned to Bellevue Place, the quilt was unpicked to make a bedspread and the remaining fabric reconstituted, for the second time, as cushion covers and rag dolls for Oxfam.

The process of recycling recalled Irene – and one pair of socks in particular, which Emily had worn on the hockey pitch during the war. These started life in 1939 as a pullover for Arnold, becoming next a winter cardigan for her, then two pairs of socks and finally one, before disintegrating to Emily's joy and relief on the field of play. From experience, she knew that there was an art to this economy, though it was not perhaps Art. Rather its satisfactions were invisible and came from seeing useful life prolonged, or Benjamin pull on a pair of mended jeans without a second thought. But if Emily wanted visible rewards for her sparing ways – and a part of her did – she had only to step into the garden.

Here were no mistakes that time and chance, maybe a bit of craft and luck, could not correct. Plants mostly mended themselves. Shrubs took off from the bare, wintered root, dark borders sheltered a shade-loving leaf. Even Don, in his zeal to cut back, could not mow her plot into submission, however hard he tried, however unconsciously.

Probably he was a little jealous of the garden, which

flourished under Emily's guidance. Perhaps that was why he mowed it so stroppily, beheading and uprooting on all sides. Probably he felt neglected; doubly so now that Benjamin was volunteering away from home, getting interested in the countryside.

When the mower rammed and broke their old whirly, Benjamin suggested they get rid of it and plant a tree. They didn't need a whirly any more.

'A *beech*, in that space?' Don said. 'What are you going to do with a beech? Bloody great thing. They're forty feet high.'

'They don't get that big overnight. And you can hedge them. That's what we've been doing in Cornwall.'

'Fucking beech, all we need.'

'Don.'

'Why don't we get an apple tree? Cox's. Lovely.'

Benjamin decided it wasn't worth arguing. It was their garden.

'Don . . .' Emily was standing at the open sitting-room window, squinting. The other two were on the lawn. 'What's happened to the clematis?'

'The what?' Don's eyes darted. In one hand was a pair of shears. 'The creeper, you mean? All that stuff hanging over the garage? Yeah, got rid of that. Bloody nuisance. Make room for the tree.'

So they got an apple tree – it was March – and after its first uncertain blossoming Emily made sure that Don saw her snap off all the cherry-sized apples and throw them into a sad little heap.

'Em, *Em*,' he yelped from the first floor. 'What are you doing? Are you mad? Jesus Christ. They were just coming on!'

'You have to do that the first year or the tree doesn't fruit properly afterwards. They'll be the better for it, you'll see.'

'Not this year they won't. Fat lot of use they are now.'

He banged the sash down. Emily looked guiltily at her son. 'I've done it now,' she said, making a tragic face. 'Another thing. I don't know. If it's anything of his, he always makes such a fuss. I can't win, can I?'

Happily, they were both wrong. The late blossom that year meant that several apples had yet to form and these fruit were therefore spared. Don was appeased, Emily relieved, and then the cat died.

She was old and tired: pungently half-feral, an unreliable visitor to her food bowl, and a worrier of mice she couldn't finish off, like a great lady with a piece of cold toast. Don doted on her. It was a family joke that he showed the cat more affection than the rest of them put together. The cat, in turn, sought him out as he dropped off in front of the news, and shivered in his lap. When Tabitha stopped coming to him, he took her to the vet, who told him it was cancer. Don shrugged his shoulders and said, 'Well, that's that. Put her down.'

'Now? She'll be all right for a couple of months. These pills will help.'

'No, do it today. Get it over with. She's had a good innings.'

Far from making a fuss, Don seemed almost to revel in his unsentimental practicality. ('I said to him, get the needle out. Djoonk, djoonk, djoonk.') Except that, as Emily correctly perceived, such candour masked a truer feeling, which was that he didn't want to see the animal suffer – was squeamish, in fact, about inarticulate injury, and had cried pitiably when their first pet, a kitten, tumbled under the wheels of the Mini.

The swiftness of Tabitha's despatch brought Emily and Don closer. The night of her death, they laughed in bed, Emily taunting him with visions of what she *knew* he'd do to her if ever she got too decrepit to have sex, Don sniggering and saying that she must be a terrible person to imagine him capable of such a thing, before edging up to her in the darkness and stroking her arm.

'Shhh. Go away. Get off me. Get *off*.'

'You're the one making the noise. Let's just test your theory—'

'Oh no, you're awful. I don't want *anything* to do with you. Don. Stop – oh—'

' – and I'll tell you in the morning if it's the knacker's yard or not.'

Afterwards, they talked for longer than usual, and with an ease the source of which was a mystery. There was agreement – they'd get a new cat – and, for Emily, consolation in the midst of her continuing anxieties about Clive, and Irene, to whose end Tabitha somehow pointed the way. The news would come soon enough. Only here and now, Emily felt that when it did come it need not be so dreadful; that her mother's illness, and resentment of illness, were temporary afflictions in the deepest sense. All losses had their compensations. In a few weeks Benjamin would leave No. 2 for good: but so be it. It was time.

'You can't turn back the clock,' she said, looking straight up and wondering why it was so much easier to be honest while lying down. 'I'll miss him when he's gone, won't you, Don? I shall miss – well, there's the piano, I'll miss that. And, you know, having him around. He's – got so many interests.' She paused to yawn. 'Fatima seems very keen on him.'

'Fatima?'

'Mrs Khoury's eldest. Oh, Don. They did music together at Brougham Hayes. You've met her – here. She's been here with all the others. They're such a nice crowd. So nice with each other. So *sociable*. I wasn't a bit like that. At least I know he'll always be all right on that score.'

'Fatima? The one with the – the tall one?'

'Trust you.'

'Yeah.' Don turned over. 'He wants to keep on with the music, if he can.'

'But he does!' Even at her most relaxed, Emily couldn't resist taking sides. 'He's got the organ. He enjoys doing that. He's always beetling down to the church and practising—'

'I know. Sure.' Don was ready for sleep now. The effort it took him to make his point made him even more sleepy. 'I didn't mean that.'

' – and he's going to the right place, I should think. Plenty of organs up there, in the wintry fens. Aren't there?'

'Be good if he could join a band or a group. That'd be good for him. It's not all about doing it on your own.'

'But he doesn't! He's got a whole gaggle of friends. That's what I'm saying. They're always doing things, going to . . . hear, you know, all sorts of . . . oh, you make it sound so lonely, but he *likes* it.' Her defence was directionless because unnecessary, and now she was tired too. 'He *likes* doing it in groups.'

Don opened his eyes into the pillow.

Emily slept. When she awoke in the near dawn, there was a man standing by her bed dressed in some kind of uniform, with his cap in his hands.

She gave an inward start and looked around, but there was no one else in the speckled darkness except the calm stranger, gazing down at her. She steeled herself to look more closely and decided that it couldn't be Neil Pattison. What would he be doing in uniform, tired yet proud, as if the news he brought at this absurd hour were so important it couldn't wait until morning? Then the soldier introduced himself, gently and without ceremony. He was with the Canadian Expeditionary Force. He said he was pleased to meet her, at last.

My Emily, he said, *I'm overjoyed.*

The room flared with words and exclamations, echoes of light. *Will you? It's strange. Let me just look. Can I?*

The disappointment on waking for the second time was less real than the encounter. It melted almost instantaneously into a sunlit conviction that her father had come to her in a dream. When she went to visit Irene later that day, she took a risk and told her story. Her mother listened, saying eventually in a voice not so different from the one she used to complain about her bag when it was getting full, 'I am glad, Em. I'm glad he found you.'

Meanwhile, on the other side of the city, Wally the verger, who didn't see why organs or pianos had to be practised, was letting Benjamin into the church on Jefferies Road on condition that he didn't make a lot of noise.

'I won't.'

'Only it's just been tuned,' Wally emphasized. 'And I won't be here for the next two weeks. I'm going to visit my daughter in Montreal.'

He grumbled his way out and Benjamin climbed through the dusty seclusion of the back stairs to the organ loft. He listened to the silence and looked down the nave at the polished wood and unvisited flowers. It was his favourite moment, before he switched on the instrument, kicked off his shoes (he pedalled in his socks) and picked a registration for music he loved but couldn't play.

There was nothing incorrigible about his technique. His hands and feet were capable of articulating Bach with reasonable accuracy, if he practised slowly enough, went over the tricky entries enough times and generally ground away so that the flame of frustration had a chance to burn itself out. And occasionally he did find himself playing well, embarking yet again on the St Anne Fugue, feeling his fingers establish a pattern of movement, and arriving at each note with the clear determination to be there and not somewhere else. It was just that the bits he most wanted to get right had a habit of piercing his concentration, and when that happened he began to make mistakes – not just skimmed or held notes but thwacking great avant-gardisms instead of major triads and runs that sounded as though he'd been electrocuted. It was infuriating.

Lessons were even worse. To Kieran, his teacher and friend, the problem and solution were obvious. Kieran was in his mid-twenties, a very good organist, very shy, though a hit with the ladies. He had a facial tic, which got worse when he tried to correct it and disappeared if he simply let it come and – go.

'You can't play when you're like this,' he said. 'I can't help you.'

'Fucking thing drives me mad. I can hear it perfectly well in my head.'

'What are you getting so worked up for, then?'

Kieran had a progressive view of morality, but he didn't much like swearing in church. It seemed excessive and out of character, not like the Benjamin he knew, full of laughter and ridiculousness.

Benjamin didn't understand either and was embarrassed. He found he didn't like being watched while he played. It was as if he'd been caught talking to a mirror; the music and the presence of another, close by, were exposing. Why did he care? He wasn't going to be a proper musician, so why did it matter? Perhaps because he heard one kind of emotion in the music, when Kieran played it – a sort of beautiful yearning to work things out – and something quite different when he approached it, and the notes played *him*, as it were, uncontrollably. He didn't make mistakes so much as feel deeply mistaken.

Liz diagnosed performance anxiety, during one of their weekly phone calls. She'd only just started teacher training after a long period of unemployment, and was sympathetic; well, sympathetic up to a point.

'Let's see, you're playing the organ and you say *you don't know what you're doing*.' She paused, amused, not wanting to be cruel. 'It's fear of failure.'

But Benjamin couldn't see that it was, not exactly. In what sense might he fear failure? He told Liz that he didn't have those kinds of expectations where music was concerned. Never had. Failure? (The word began to obsess him.) It wasn't fear of *failure* that plagued him, just a sort of adrenaline . . .

Why was he being so dense? Liz frowned into the phone. Was he having sex yet, or not? She hoped he knew he could always talk to her about anything. At the same time, she struggled to suppress her instinct to point out to people the clear (and instantly remediable) error of their ways. He needed to get away from Bath, for Christ's sake, and shag a few girls. Or boys, whichever it was. Benjamin chuntered on, and Liz nodded to herself. Come to think if it, that would make sense. Liz knew loads of gay blokes.

Whereas Benjamin did not, though he was clear about liking men. And he had already tried running away in an effort to embark on a sexual career – in France, in Cornwall – only to find that it wasn't that easy. He had himself to master first, wherever he went; or as Stevie put it, 'Everybody's got a thing but some don't know how to handle it' – and wasn't that the truth. He dreamed of sex, of course, but also of lovers who would make him feel at home, elsewhere. He sensed, too, that they were a long way off, and it was this intimation of life being held in reserve, of love and recognition waiting to be claimed, that tripped him up when he played, because like any teenager he was in a hurry and didn't want to have to wait for ever.

He wondered about joining a band, but he wasn't that kind of player. The blues chords he knew were ones he'd discovered by accident. Don thought he should 'play around' with them, and Benjamin hadn't the heart to explain that he didn't know how, or even what a blues scale was, really; or that it was also liberating *not* to be able to do what Aretha and Stevie did. They were brilliant and a world apart, utterly unlike the white middle-class boy he saw himself to be. The strange thing was that their remoteness touched him so nearly and freed him to be who he was. They spoke to him in the midst of his ordinary, piffling confusions and said: *don't you worry 'bout a thing.*

Don was very taken with the idea of the organ. He hadn't been in a church above ten times in his life, but the instrument impressed him. He came, cautiously, to a recital by Kieran, and listened to the recordings Benjamin had of organ music. His initial surprise – didn't sound much like Jimmy Smith – gave way to admiration and enthusiasm both for the scale of the sound and the engineering craftsmanship it implied. It was a feat, a dare.

One afternoon while Don was fiddling with a jammed mount cutter, Benjamin came into the studio and put on the 'Prelude and Fugue sur le nom d'Alain'. They'd heard Kieran play it at Jefferies Road to the usual audience: a loyal handful of the congregation, the wasp-waisted vicar, his sexually demanding wife, and Wally. The recording, made in St Paul's, was a hugely grand affair – and as the eight-second echo of the last chord rolled away, Don whistled.

'Amazing. *Romantic.*' He was silent for a time, moving things about on his desk. Benjamin gazed out of the window at the strata of buildings and trees. 'And that's the same piece we heard the other night?'

'The same.'

'How does that organ get to be so different? More

pipes? Isn't there a limit to what you can build? A stand-ard of some kind.'

Benjamin didn't really know how to answer this, and so passed on the one useful bit of technical knowledge he'd gleaned from Kieran. An organ was just wind pressure applied to pipes of various pitches, various widths and lengths. You could have any kind of com-bination, depending on your builder and the building, and how much money you had – and every combination was different, because the thing had to be built not just assembled, so no two organs were ever the same. There was one in America, at West Point, that went on grow-ing. A pipe was added every time a soldier died in action.

'Variations on a theme.' The record whispered. Don went over to lift the needle. 'Yeah. I get that, sort of.'

'Not that I know how they all fit together. It's, um, very painstaking. You have to have precision-tool manu-facturers. From Denmark, apparently.'

The moulding guillotine in the corner of the studio was from Denmark. Nowhere else were such things made. It was a unique design.

'But you've given me an idea.' Don returned to the cutting desk and picked up a pencil and straight-edge. 'I like the principle – as you say. First principles. Talking of which, have I ever taught you how to do *this*?'

And he showed Benjamin how to put an oval window in a mount.

Benjamin had never properly watched his father at work before, nor been invited to do so. Don claimed to have no head for figures, yet here he was using a compass, whisking his pencil across the card, taking measurements, making an individual shape. Quickly, too. He was completely absorbed by the process.

'You're high,' Benjamin said, as Don drew a horizontal line to meet the vertical one that divided the mount. 'That's above the centre. You've got more space at the bottom – quite a bit more.'

'It's the optical centre.' Don broke off and peered at his son. 'Your eyes place the centre of the frame higher than it really is. O ye of little.'

The next bit was in its own way a piece of magic. Don marked the top and bottom of the oval he wanted, and the width, along the lines he'd drawn, and then drew a tilted square – a diamond – in the middle of the board. Each side of the square was the radius of the oval, so that the diamond's north and south were about an inch shy of the oval's ends. Don tacked the diamond's north and south with pins and to these he attached some thread, just long enough to make a right-angle if you pulled it out to one side. Finally, he took his pencil, put the tip inside the thread at the top of the oval and pulled it around and down, keeping the thread taut as he went. A smooth curve appeared: half an ostrich's egg.

Don said: 'Your turn,' and Benjamin drew the other half. His was rather shaky; you had to draw lightly and confidently, pushing against the thread so hard but no harder. He apologized, dissatisfied, but Don said, 'Not bad. Hold the pencil nearer the tip and don't press. Bring it round and up in one go.'

He rubbed out the jagged line and Benjamin was about to finish his first egg when the doorbell went – *clang-a-LANG-a-lang-a-lang* – and it was Lotte, hot off the train from London, in a froth of excitement, wanting to tell them in person that she was engaged. In his mood of rapt distraction, Benjamin wondered where on earth the bell was. It was a real bell and he'd never seen it.

'Oh, Lotte!' Emily cried jubilantly from the kitchen. 'Lotte, I *am* pleased. Congratulations, dear. You're getting married!' She stopped. 'To Fraser?'

The two words fell like a match on the petroleum lake of Lotte's emotions. While the women fought – while Lotte blazed and Emily whimpered – Don and Benjamin retreated to the sitting-room to watch the telly. There, a foetal kangaroo oozed towards the teat in its mother's pouch.

'Disgusting,' said Don, fascinated. 'They should call it the *Unnatural World*.'

In the next shot, the pouch was occupied by an identifiable youngster, though one that still didn't quite resemble its mother. The physiognomy hadn't fully developed. The nose and face didn't protrude far enough.

'I tell you what I could do with.'

'What?' Benjamin was keeping one ear open for his

sister's choicest accusations. (*Why can't you both be more normal? I'm fed up with being different! Why can't you have a* normal *response?*)

'A bit of rabbit. I love rabbit. I used to catch them all the time.'

'You? When?'

'When I was a boy. I used to set traps. Catch a rabbit for tea, skin it. I'm not joking.' Don turned his head and smiled carelessly. 'You may laugh. Bloody hell, look at that one go. Cor!'

A frightened wallaby launched from a disused mineshaft.

'*Skin* a rabbit? You go green if your chips are underdone.'

'I'll bloody show you. If we go to Wales for that weekend, before you bugger off, I'll show you.'

'We could go this weekend.'

'All right.' Don bit his nails and raised his eyebrows. 'That's good for me. I'll tell Em.' He got up and went to the door, hesitated, came back and sat down. 'I'll tell her later.'

I don't know what to say, darling. I'm so pleased for you. I couldn't be more pleased. What can I say to make you see?

Lotte was by now ululating at a high, non-verbal frequency. The two men listened respectfully to the sound, which shimmered and looped.

'It's like that thing in that piece by Kieran's hero.'

'Zappa? The theremin. That's what I'm thinking of.'

'No, the – the symphony. Can't remember the name.'

'Amazing sound. Weird and spooky. Where does she get it from?'

Two full-sized adults boinged serenely over a parked car.

'That's that, then,' Don said, as the producer's credit faded. 'Time to face the music.' At the door he turned and pointed. 'Onde martenot. Gotcha.'

He went into the kitchen and Benjamin heard him say, 'Come on, Lotte, Em. Lotte, what are you so upset about? Never mind what she said. She didn't mean it. We're really happy for you, of course we are. Fraser is a great kid – *man*, I mean. Man, of course. You're a credit to each other.'

'It's true. I'm so sorry.'

'Oh, it's all right.' Lotte's voice was frail, exhausted. 'I don't know what it is. I'm so – I'm just so—'

A few comfortable stirrings in the room – Don opening the fridge, Emily pushing her chair back, Lotte blowing her nose – and the storm was over.

'Have you told Clive and Liz?'

Lotte hadn't, and was comforted by the idea. She picked up the phone.

But Clive wasn't in. He had evenings off at the nursing home, after all. One of the other carers at Camberley said he was away sailing with little Ronan, and Lotte laughed and said that sounded nice. 'It depends,' said the carer, who knew what little Ronan was like.

At that moment, in a squall somewhere off Broadstairs, Clive was stumbling out of a hatch with a catheter in one hand and a bucket in the other. He'd left little Ronan cackling in his wheelchair, roped securely to the capstan. But these three elements had separated from each other in the half-minute Clive had been below decks, and now as the vessel yawed into a trough, lightning revealed the tipped-over chair slamming into the guardrails and little Ronan, still cackling, shooting aft on a sheet of foam, like a gnome in petticoats.

Days passed. The weather brightened as Don and Benjamin made their way into Wales. They stopped twice, once on the English side of the Severn Bridge, where they poked around for lumps of gypsum on Aust beach, and once in Abergavenny to buy supplies. Bacon, eggs, sausages, ham, butter, cheese, longlife milk and tomatoes went into a variety of plastic containers in the warm boot of the Mini. Bread, tea and sugar could stay in their bags. The missing element was cereal, or more particularly *Force*, which Don said he remembered from childhood. *Force* was plain and brown, with a kink or a curl to it, like wood shavings. Benjamin suggested bran flakes instead and marvelled at his dad's persistence. The sun gusted outside. Light blew into the shop.

'Found it. I had a feeling they still made this stuff. *Force*.'

The wind and the sun ushered them like leaves along the vale of Ewyas. They listened to a sketch show on the radio as the hills rose. The show ended and Don switched off the radio, spotting in the same instant a large bird of prey beyond the roadside oaks. Benjamin fished for his seatbelt and Don accelerated.

'Buzzard – or a red kite. Buzzard.'

A car honked past, its driver shaking and opening her fist.

Don pulled over and got out his binoculars. Even in the distance, the bird looked big, tracking up the green mountainside into the blue. There it circled, floating, wings outstretched and riffling, tilting, rebalancing, preparing to dive. The swoop began as no more than a downwards reorientation, a mild drawing-in of the wings and shoulders, but if you looked too long at that you missed the speed of the body. The head never moved, never flinched, even when the wings lifted and the struck-out legs landed their prey.

'Gah! Merciless.'

The bird flew further down the valley and came to rest in the confused brown and grey of a distant outcrop. Don handed Benjamin the binoculars. It was only just visible, urn-shaped, with its back to the world.

'What's that?' Benjamin moved the glasses to take in a higher contour of scree and grass. On a tufted ridge, a bigger urn – a bigger bird – waited. 'It could be its mate. It's got a white crest and a black head. Here.'

Don panned right to find the ridge. 'Difficult to tell

at this angle. And it's so far away . . . it's not a buzzard, that's for sure.' He refocused excitedly. 'It could be a white-tailed eagle, though I've never heard of them in Wales. But they're really big, and it *could* be – there it goes! Oh. Oh no, not an eagle, no. Sorry . . .'

'What then?'

Don waggled his ear with his finger.

'It's a sheep's arse,' he said. 'Better push on.'

They returned to the car. Just before they set off again, a fighter jet lowered itself into the valley ahead of them and streaked past, the shriek of its turbines swallowed up by afterburn. The day's silence fell apart and put itself back together again. So massive an abnormality seemed not real, a trick of perception or a subject best avoided. The jet didn't come back and wasn't followed by others. The two men said nothing about it, though the restored calm of the field in which they later pitched their tent felt more extraordinary as a result; those trees, that gate on its loose hinge, this stream and the palpitant air.

It was just a field. The farmer let them have it for ten quid for two nights, and asked if they wouldn't mind doing their business on the other side of the stream. Don bought yet more eggs, and together he and Benjamin settled on a part of the bank that hung over fast water, where there were fewer midges.

When they unrolled the tent, the groundsheet was

found to be dirty and not quite dry on the inside, so Don wiped it clean with a wet sponge and left it in the sun to dry. While they waited, he unpacked the gaz stove and Benjamin took the mugs and all the perishables to the stream, weighing the tubs and containers down with rocks and pebbles.

'It's a fantastic spot,' said Benjamin with a kind of forced neutrality.

'Good tea. It's the enamel.'

'I don't know why we don't drink from these mugs at home. Everything tastes better off enamel. We should tell Mum when we get back.'

Don declined to say more than 'yeah'. He had a vision of Em's face as the two of them purged her shelves of crockery.

In the afternoon, with the tent up, they crossed the stream and climbed the hill, taking with them sketch books, pencils and a thermos. Don wore a flat cap and Benjamin a fatigued sou'wester he'd inherited from the conservation volunteers in Cornwall. The oaks grew scrubbier before they disappeared altogether, giving way to mountain ash and bracken, then bracken and bilberries, which the two scavengers picked and ate. The day was ticklishly hot.

'Got some beauties, here.'

'I think the sheep have been at them.'

'Not mine they haven't. Some real beauties over here.'

Benjamin looked at his father, scouring the scrubby

heath in shorts and sandals. His legs were so smooth they reflected the sun. And Benjamin was relieved, because though he didn't much like his own girlish legs, they were thick with pile compared to Don's burnished Twiglets.

At the top of the mountain, if it could be called that, they sat on the sloping coarse grass and drew what they saw. Don's was a confident sketch of the fields and woodlands below, on the opposite side of the valley, their lush solidity and contrast caught with short, selective dot-dash strokes so that the airier, upper reaches of the scene appeared in the white of the page. Benjamin chose a single rock much closer to hand, with bilberry and heather poking out of a cleft at the base. His view was smaller, his marks heavier. In the sun, the granite was a light grey, veined by quartzite, but Benjamin had made it stormy and dark, which left the problem of how to convey the darker foliage. So he used a rubber to widen the strip of quartz and imagined that behind the leaves instead.

For dinner they cooked sausages and spuds. Don laid the fire and Benjamin maintained it. They ate mostly in silence, nodding appreciatively. When they were finished, Benjamin burned the greaseproof paper and clingfilm. Mesmerized, he watched the plastic shrivel and run. At the back of his mind was the jet and the way he'd crossed his fingers when it shot past. This particular superstition he blamed on having once seen, at an impressionable age, a bleak documentary about the likely consequences of a nuclear attack by the Soviets. Pumpkins, standing in for heads, were shredded by flying glass. Dummy eyes rained down dummy cheeks. Doors slammed shut in refugees' faces. But the night, the real night, in Capel-y-ffin, was openly beautiful and still.

They awoke to heavy dew and far-off cows being milked. Sheep bleated thinly above the tree line. The stream was louder, nearer than before.

With more absence than presence of mind, Don decided to hike over the hill to Grwyne Faw Reservoir, about three miles away, in the hope of seeing more birds of prey and a Bronze Age cairn or two; maybe the odd panting soldier.

'This is where they do their endurance training,' Don said. 'The SAS, the Paras. Backbreaking stuff, man. Just imagine it – with a fifty-pound Bergen on your back all day. Fifty or sixty pounds those buggers weigh, at least.'

'What are they supposed to be enduring again?'

The sun was tolerable. How bad could it be? In his wandering mind's eye, Benjamin saw piggy-back races involving tiny Norwegians.

'You try it,' Don scoffed. 'No food. You've got to find something to eat.'

They gazed along the empty ridge.

'You've got to get served.'

'All that,' Don said, pointing at some confident-looking rabbits.

*

Benjamin didn't need to see soldiers in Wales. The next day he was off back to Cornwall to work with one – Colin Throsby, from Barrow-in-Furness, who'd served out his first commission in the army and then quit, aged twenty-five. Colin had roved the country – and, who knew, possibly the Black Mountains – for a while, before ending up in Penzance where he now worked as a Task Leader for the British Trust for Conservation Volunteers.

Don dropped Benjamin off at Bristol Temple Meads on the Tuesday and Colin met him that evening in St Austell.

'I asked Gray for help,' said Colin, as soon as he saw Benjamin, heavy laden with his own cheap version of a Bergen, weaving towards the van.

'Hello, Colin! Long journey. I'm knackered.'

'And he sends me you. Why am I not surprised?'

Colin and Graeme were friends who hated each other. Graeme was a committed, trained Field Officer, employed by Truro Council, with a girlfriend, Becky, whom Colin fancied. Benjamin was the unlikely peacemaker: they'd all worked together before, in a wood near Truro, on Bodmin Moor.

As they drove to the pub, Colin laid out their objectives.

'The week goes like this. Three days doing a fence on one part of this shit-hole site, two days burning the rest of it down. Your job, Tired and Useless, is one, not to get killed. And two, not to get fucking killed. What is it?'

BTCV 'working holidays' normally attracted a dozen people; but in remote Cornwall the figure dwindled to four or five. In truth, this suited Colin very well, as he found demonstrating the difference between mattocks and billhooks to an assortment of pensioners and mental outpatients, and Benjamin, tedious. At least he was polite to the old ones ('Not like that, love, like *this*. Away from your leg'). Scrub-clearance and fence-building were his specialities – but anything that involved axes, mauls, chopping, burning and barbed wire would do.

Graeme and Becky greeted Benjamin with handshakes and hugs.

'Great to see you,' said Graeme. '*Great* to have you on board.'

'The *Titanic*.'

But it was of course Colin who nearly got himself killed, within hours of beginning the task at Penwithick. The day was grey, the visibility poor – lights were on in the village – and a skittering salt breeze had soaked all four stoics by mid-afternoon. Their job was to fence off one side of a right of way, separating it from a private estate. They'd dug a series of holes and managed to ram a couple of posts into place using a cast-iron hood that dropped over the stake and forced it down. Graeme and Becky were doing their best with the third post, raising and dropping the hood with doting ineffectuality ('How are we doing, love? Are we there yet, are we close?'), when they encountered a tough root.

Graeme peered into the hole. The nearest tree was twenty yards up the hill.

'Yes, well, they spread a long way. There's not much topsoil you see.'

The post would go down so far and no further. Un-wiped spectacles cheery with defeat, Becky called Colin and Benjamin over. In the hole, Graeme was still scrabbling about with his hands an instant before Colin's spade fell, slicing easily through the root in one fluid movement. There was a loud jolt and a blue crackle. The lights in the village went out.

'A root,' said Colin, in the darkness.

'Oh dear,' said Becky. 'Dear, oh *dear*. And it was going so well. Are you all right? Are you hurt, Colin, love?'

'Am I smoking?'

'Yes,' said Benjamin, because Colin smoked all the time.

'Then I must be all right.'

Graeme, the good employee, was already worrying about costs. 'The bill, Becs, the bill. Sheesh. How much this is going to set us back, I *daren't* think.'

'Why break the habit of a lifetime?'

'You were lucky, Col,' Graeme said later. He was less anxious now that the electricians had been called. 'Thank God for rubber soles!'

'If I hadn't been wearing wellies, it would have been Goodnight Vienna.'

'And Goodnight Colin,' Becky added, sipping her lager top.

Colin looked at her expressionlessly, a fag bent into

the corner of his mouth. What did he truly feel for Becky, Benjamin wondered? Compassion? Pity? Lust? All three, possibly, or none. Colin's mood was like his fringe, a zone of listless defiance. It should have been inhuman; instead it inspired a sort of painful levity – and trust. Benjamin was in the company of experience, in the hands of a fighter and survivor, that much was clear, even if the historical nature of the fight was not. At odd moments he imagined a banal but professional ruthlessness, perhaps involving Northern Ireland or the Falklands, but Colin would not be drawn on the subject. He said only that he'd been bored.

'Bored', to Benjamin, implied 'worn out', fatigued or shocked. The truth was simpler. He'd left his posting, in Hong Kong as it happened, to look after his mum, who would otherwise have died alone in Barrow. There, on the Ormsgill estate at the top of Mill Bank, right op-posite the junior school where he'd been locked in the toilets, Colin held Darla's hand for two days.

There were low-flying planes in Cornwall, too, over Bodmin Moor, but their effect on Benjamin was differ-ent from that of the Welsh jets. They emboldened him, their tearing noise a fanfare of farewell. Not everything, but certainly this – this strange happiness he felt away from everyone he knew best – would soon end, and the knowledge was like a drug. He was reckless under its influence. He rolled bales of barbed wire downhill without checking to see if anyone was at the bottom. He attacked rhododendrons with a billhook and nearly took Graeme's arm off. He was unlike himself and more himself than ever before, with people who had no interest in his future. He was a tourist. They knew he was a tourist and, not being fooled, were nice about it. In the pub they played pool and drank the Supplementary Benefits version of black velvet – Guinness and cider.

'Come back soon, dappy,' Becky said, at the end of the week. 'Dappy' was Colin's word; she often repeated things he said. 'We love having you.' But of course Benjamin never saw any of them again.

On the long haul from the station, he met his mother coming down Margaret's Hill. She took short, almost tip-toe steps, holding a loose cloth bag. He was very pleased to see her, and immediately irritated by the depth of his feeling because he badly wanted her to see that he was independent and could fend for himself. Even if that meant leaving her and hurting her.

The flash of emotion passed, but Emily, nearer now, stared through him. Her stone eyes informed Benjamin that she did not care. The day was high and the sun was strong. She drifted closer without speaking.

SUNNYBROOK

Suddenly someone you know is wounded; then a shell falls among the staff. You notice that some of the officers act a little oddly; you yourself are not as steady and collected as you were: even the bravest can become slightly distracted.

Carl von Clausewitz, 'On Danger in War'

The Break

The phone rang at a quarter past eleven and it was Liz.

'I'm back,' she said, quietly. 'Oh, Ben. It's awful. We cannot – *I* cannot, I *can't* let her end up – it is so absolutely. I know about these places. It's one of these – it is. *In*describable.' There followed, nevertheless, a description of sorts, the threats of inexpressibility rising in volume, the nouns of sense – day room, strip lights, wing-back chairs – jerking like caught fish. At twelve, Liz's phone cut out, the batteries low because her son had left the handset lying around. Benjamin went up to bed and lay awake, considering.

In the morning, Liz rang again. She was feeling much better. 'I'm going for a swim. I don't suppose you've got time, before you go down?' He hadn't. He had a train to catch. 'Oh. Oh.' Liz sounded unconvinced.

The residents of Sunnybrook were having lunch when Benjamin arrived. It was a spacious, well-lit room of eight or so round tables, with wall-to-ceiling windows on one side and a hatch at the end. Some ate faster than others, sucking up big spoonfuls of mash and gravy and reaching wide-eyed for their squash, while a few seemed to have made no progress at all, and sat in front of full plates, looking slightly out of breath but not unhappy.

One troublemaker, her screwed-up face couched in a froth of white, yelled from a far corner. She pushed her food away, threw down her fork and daubed her neighbour with pink custard. The servers and care-workers, the whole lot of them, were buggers: she *wunt never coming back neither.*

'I wish,' said an elegant lady to one side of the hatch, 'that we could keep Doris in her room at mealtimes.' She smiled, one palm offered to heaven. She was wearing a worker's pinny and enjoying her break. 'But I'm afraid it isn't possible. We haven't the resources.'

Her regret led naturally to a discussion of what these resources were, Benjamin explaining that his mother was currently on the waiting list for a room. It was as he'd expected: the home was basic, comfortable, and stretched for staff because of its location, eight miles from the city on a failing rural bus route. A hard core of workers lived in Peasedown itself, on the estate next door, and could not afford to live elsewhere, the Health Service having discontinued all travelling expenses. The rest – the casuals – were drawn from a dwindling pool of nursing agencies and had to toil in from Paulton, on the outskirts of Bristol, or Frome. Violet herself had taught for years in Radstock, another old mining town along the Fosse Way, until her husband died in the 90s.

'The portions are good, though,' Benjamin observed, 'and people are allowed to do things at their own pace.

That's important.' As he spoke, a busy blonde with strong arms and understanding in her smile plonked a resurgent Doris back into her chair. 'I'll have you,' the coiffed monster shouted.

Violet drummed her fingers cheerily on the table and stood up. A few crumbs fell from her blue apron, which had come untied. 'I expect I shall be seeing you again,' she said kindly, and moved off, setting upright a tumbler as she went. Benjamin noticed that she was holding on to a book, and that its confident title, picked out in yellow on black, was *Mastering Arabic*.

Sunnybrook's manager, the woman Benjamin had really come to see, put her head in and out over dessert, nodded a few greetings and then retreated, waving; she hadn't much time to talk. Carla Rose, or Carl, was a compact, briskly pleasant, middle-aged woman whose gaze, because it recognized grief, refused to indulge it. Trays, faxes, files and phone directories filled her office, the door to which never stayed shut for long. Room keys were always being dropped off, kitchen supplies delivered through the back, drugs signed for, casuals signed out. Benjamin found the air of contained frustration soothing.

'What you have to remember,' she said, 'is that everybody's trying to do their best. You are, your family, your father especially. But it's what's best for Emily that counts in the end, and that's a different matter.'

She spoke with tired conviction. On other lips, perhaps, the same arm's-length formula would have sounded condescending.

'I suppose my main concern is that Dad gets a break soon, because he's not coping. And that's not good for Mum.' Benjamin was hot with relief at being allowed to say what he thought. Carla, acting on an ungiven signal, nudged the window open. 'He doesn't see that she's *responding* to his anxiety. It makes her far, far worse. Really, it's long past the point—'

Carla interrupted. 'You can't make the decision for him, Benjamin. He has to come to it in his own time. It usually takes a couple of little disasters, a few tries.' She let the word 'disaster' disperse gradually. 'Emily's coming in for respite in ten days, isn't she, so we'll see how that goes and take it from there. You know Callum, don't you?' Benjamin nodded. Callum was the Patient Service Co-ordinator at the hospital. 'Have another chat with him. He's very good. He knows what's happening and you can trust his judgement. We've been doing this,' and here Carla Rose laughed out loud, a girlish giggle on top of a cough, 'for ever, practically. We're old hands.'

Getting out of Sunnybrook was not as easy as getting in. The first set of doors had a combination lock. Armed with the code, Benjamin was about to punch his way free, when the blonde from the canteen came up to him and stayed his hand. The lift had opened and they were being watched by one of the residents.

'You have to wait till she's gone,' explained the orderly, 'or she might try to escape. Wouldn't you, Peggy? Because you're so determined.'

The neat, flat-chested seventy-year-old, emerging from the lift like the Oracle from her cave, rolled her eyes at Benjamin, and took his arm, still raised. It might have been the prelude to a put-down. The alertness of her face, the flutter of the papery mouth, suggested humour. It seemed appropriate that she should answer the orderly, and so he waited. And while he waited – for her to speak – Benjamin felt for the first time the effects of simple alarm, not at Peggy's impairment, whatever it might be, but at the idea of its being a fixed characteristic. Peggy remained *determined* in the midst of confusion. Like most young children, Benjamin had enjoyed pulling faces for the various shades of consternation it provoked in adults. The more medieval the grimace, the sweeter the assurance from his mother that the wind would change and he would, one day, stay that way. Probably that's what happened when you began to lose your wits. Your true nature, or some true aspect of it, consolidated while the illness divested you of nicer traits; or, if you were nice to start with, you lost whatever edge of rancour life had given you and became beatifically tractable.

'Are you all right now, Peg?' said the blonde, her eyes softening. She aspirated, touching her chest. 'Is life treating you well?'

Again, Peggy looked amused.

'I don't rightly know, to be perfectly candid,' she said, and gave Benjamin's forearm a reassuring squeeze.

'Then you'd better come along with me and let that man be, hadn't you?'

The old lady looked hard at Benjamin a second longer, as if to be quite satisfied, and finally linked arms with her guardian. 'Seeing as I haven't got any better offers,' she said, and was steered away.

On his way back to the bus stop, Benjamin tried to conjure an unbiased view of his surroundings and felt more than ever like an outsider. The sledgehammer tourist returned from Cornwall minus the sledgehammer. It was cold for June.

Not so long ago, quarries and mines had shaped the landscape around the village of Peasedown St John, but the village itself had no shape: it was a dribble of grey stone cottages on an exposed ridge. Wind funnelled into the High Street and made it feel claustrophobic, as do all exposed places where the sky presses down on the inhabitants. The path through the housing estate came out at some local playing fields and the bar of the British Legion; a little further towards the main drag you came across the Victorian school and village hall. Working men and women had given Peasedown a reason to exist, and now the reason was gone; greened over, like the cast of bumpy hills to the south-east, which Liz said were Neolithic burial mounds, not slag-heaps.

The mining families had stayed on. But what bound them to this bleak outpost, with its arrested housing development, coach-hire garage and – the only other person at the stop – silent priest? A few businesses survived, the ones that catered for spare time all the time, and Benjamin counted them as he waited. Here was the Ming-Wah Chinese Takeaway; next to Peasedown News ('Good News for Everyone'), West Country Vending, Aarleen Coaches, Witts End (the hairdresser) and a surely satirical estate agency. And a pub, the Red Lion, the sort of place, Benjamin guessed, in which the desire to blend in might one day lead him first to the pool table and, later, to the A&E unit at Frenchay.

Why did Peasedown linger? Because people have to live somewhere, Benjamin richly supposed; and because they lived here. Sunnybrook offered professional employment, albeit for the minimum wage, to a sorority of carers. That was what they did, these women, in spite of being ill themselves, some of them, and pitilessly got at by their own families.

At home in Bath at No. 2, Benjamin listened while his father sat at an uncomfortable, slouching angle on one of the kitchen chairs, rolled his head like a weary dog, bit his nails and talked.

Emily had been lured next door by the evening light in the garden, which thrived; Don took the opportunity to explain himself, his eyes creased shut or boggling in resentment of the effort involved. He seemed continually on the verge either of tears or a complete loss of temper, his normally low baritone strung out into a caricature of exasperation. Benjamin heard it most evenings, when Don rang to cite the latest signs of decay. These signs didn't change much from day to day, but Don repeated them anyway, clinging to the idea that he had not yet been heard, or properly understood. There was always something the rest didn't grasp, didn't appreciate ('What you don't *see*, what you don't *witness* . . .'). He didn't want Benjamin's sympathy, or Liz's, or anyone else's. And he certainly didn't want to have to listen to advice, even from Lotte, who'd nursed for years. What he wanted was to be looked after again – absolved of error, trespass, adultery, miscalculation. That was what his wife had done for him, for nearly fifty years; and he wanted her, or someone, to go on doing it. He had started to call her 'Mum'.

'She keeps putting her knickers on at bedtime, and I keep telling Mum to take them *off*.' Don wiped his mouth with the cabled sleeve of an ancient and filthy cricket sweater. 'You'll notice that. That's new. Maybe you'll have more luck with her. And, oh God, getting her to drink that stuff, the Fibrox, and take the pills. It just takes for *ever*. Goes on and on.'

Benjamin wondered aloud if a night away was really enough, holding up by implication the prospect of a week off in just a fortnight's time. Don's head lifted quickly as if stung, his mouth set in a line. He appeared to be holding his breath, a trumpeter without his instrument. Eventually, he let it out.

'Of course I can go on,' Don said. 'That's not the issue. It's just that I need a break from her every now and again. Every now and again.'

He was cheered by his own proposal of a meal in

town until Benjamin second-guessed the restaurant and expressed reservations.

'What's wrong with Pizza Express? Em likes it. It's all right.'

'Mightn't it be crowded, on a Saturday? A bit loud for Mum?'

The vigilant green of Don's eyes wavered. Around them worked the small facial muscles of incomprehension and anxiety. Benjamin saw how every decision was a precious territory to be defended.

'I think it's OK. I mean, everywhere's too loud come to that. Where do you draw the line? Unless we give up completely.' Don swallowed. His legs were getting restless. 'She doesn't have to have pizza. She can have cannelloni. She likes cannelloni, don't you, Em?'

In the kitchen doorway Emily fiddled with her hairband, which had slipped and caught on a silver-star earring. She gave a mirthless laugh and shuffled forward into her son's half-embrace, his arm around her shoulders.

'Hey, Ben,' said his father, almost excitedly. 'I tell you where they do great pizzas. Really great. Nowhere better.'

'Where's that?'

'Germany.'

At street level the restaurant looked inviting enough. Tastefully framed reproductions of Kokoschka and Matisse monitored the comings-and-goings of capable student waiters. It was busy, but not too busy; there were not too many tables and the relaxed posture of the diners suggested they were not all fighting to be heard. But this was the sunlit upper deck, reserved for a mysterious elite, their clothes unspotted by sauce and cheese. At the bottom of a spiral staircase lay a different pizzeria, to which Don and the others were led, crammed with tables and couples, inches apart, shouting at each other over fake carnations.

Benjamin guided Emily through the throng while his father bounded ahead, like a rock star on his way to collect a prize, broadly gesturing when they reached a free table from which the last customers' dirty plates had not yet been removed. Emily's mournful face turned to Benjamin and her lips moved, questioning. The waiter pulled back a chair and smiled. Emily approached and put out a hand to steady herself on a rail, or a bar maybe, that didn't exist. He caught her hand and gently reeled her in.

'Are you all right, madam?'

'Yeah,' said Don, taking over. 'She's all right.' With one brutal movement, he wrenched the chair away from the table into the back of another diner ('Sorry!'), and pushed his wife down into it. 'She's fine now.'

The young man stared. Benjamin knelt at his mother's side while the plates were cleared and murmured the usual encouragements, about taking her time, not worrying, there being no rush. Don, who'd sat himself against the wall, listened resentfully and glowered at Emily as she belaboured the menu.

When the waiter returned, he asked the lady first what she would care to order, and she replied, just audibly: 'Am I wrong?'

'No, madam. There's nothing wrong. Would you like me to explain the items?'

'Give her the cannelloni,' said Don, and leant across Benjamin to tap the waiter on the arm. A startled look passed swiftly across the boy's face. He withdrew his arm. Don leered at him. 'Hey. I'm interested. *What's. That. Accent?*'

'Sir?' He lowered his pad. 'I'm from Munich, but I've lived here—'

'There you go.' Don wagged a finger in Benjamin's face, his lips wet with triumph. '*What* did I say? How about *that* for a coincidence?'

Benjamin agreed that it was unusual.

'I was just saying to my son – just before we came out – I was telling him about the pizzas in Germany. And I don't know whether you can confirm this, but they are *great.* Terrific pizzas over there. Have you noticed that? Do you know why that is? Because I'd be *really interested* to find out.'

The waiter seemed to have regained his composure, and apologized for not knowing. He was still polite, but a new formality had entered his voice and bearing as he took their orders. Don played with the carnation, dunking it up and down. At the adjacent table, a woman talked into her partner's bald patch. 'He's been in textiles for years, and now he's a fishmonger . . . .'

They waited for their food, Emily holding on to her menu with both hands and cowering behind it in who knew what kind of fugue. All her life, she had wanted to be noticed, promising one day to write a book, to astound the world. It was a joke, and not a joke. Now, in the merciless clatter, Benjamin could feel eyes alighting on his mother, so unfairly gathered to the God she'd served, and wondered if he should just get her on her feet and take her back.

'So, what did you think of Peasedown? The Home?'

Don asked the question without looking, one leg pumping beneath the table.

'Well, I know Liz had reservations,' Benjamin began cautiously, 'but I think she was distracted by the decor, which is, you know, institutional. To be honest, I was impressed. The women I met were very nice. I mean, there's a fair bit of wailing and a few smells here and there, but that's par for the course.'

'That's *exactly* what I said. That's what I tried to impress on— it doesn't matter about the chairs and the bloody lights. None of it matters. What matters is the care. Have you met Carla? And Vikki – the little blonde one?' (Was it Benjamin's imagination, or did his father perk up at the mention of her name?) 'Vikki's fantastic. She's great, is Vikki. So nice, so – capable.'

Behind her carnation, Emily clung to the menu. Benjamin again saw that she was using both hands and had none free to steady herself at the table. Perhaps her wrists were doing the work – but the edge of the marble top was cold and sharp. Was it cutting into her? Was she uncomfortable? It was difficult to tell because she sat so low in her chair.

'Dad. Perhaps we shouldn't talk about this now.'

'Who? Because of Mum?' Don started, as if prodded awake. 'Oh Christ, that doesn't matter. I've given up on that. I mean, forget it. She doesn't care. Just get on with it – I do. She won't mind.'

Emily's eyes were where they'd been for the past five minutes, fixed on her son's face, searching not for pity but, so it seemed to Benjamin, for the simplest registration of shared meaning. *Give me a sign that you know I am trying.*

There, surely, in the flicker of one eyelid, that parting of the lips and upward deviation, was the beginning of a smile; the acknowledgement that Don's cruelty was no more than the perpetuation, in extremis, of a familiar trait. It was not even cruelty, come to that, which requires a degree of premeditation. It was simply that he could not bring himself wholly to believe in other people. It was a mystery to him that they should think differently about anything, or do anything he wouldn't want to do. In recent years, his youngest son had been twice to Australia, where he had friends, but when Don learnt of this rapport with the Antipodes, he remarked to Liz (who relayed the enormity with satisfaction), 'I don't know why Ben wants to go all the way to bloody Melbourne. Crazy! He could go to Darmstadt and stay with my friend Herta!'

There was a soft *thunk* as Emily knocked over her

juice, followed by a roll and a leisurely smash. The shaking in her fingers worsened as she pulled her hand back below the table. Her lips trembled.

'Oh, Em,' Don lamented, almost tenderly. 'What is it *now*?'

As he repeated himself and his voice rose, the couple at the next table stopped eating and looked on with helpless sympathy.

'Emily,' he screamed, banging the table so that the cutlery jumped. 'What is it? What is it, dear? *What is your problem?*'

The woman whose friend had turned fishmonger joined the waiter clearing up and asked, in a friendly way, if they were all OK. 'Because I can see that this lady's having difficulties. Is she your wife?'

Don looked into his emptied wine glass.

When the food arrived, it was hotter and more reviving that any of them had anticipated. A new waiter asked Emily if she was enjoying her cannelloni, and Emily swallowed before answering, 'Yes, I think so.'

Benjamin had a horror of waking up to find his mother drifting about in his room. Every closed door was now an invitation to her, so he wedged a chair under the handle, and then dozed twitchily, half-expecting to hear it rattle.

The three of them were up before eight, in time to see the city's church spires standing proud of a valley of

whipped mist. Don had been through the morning routine of pills and Fibrox, dressing and wiping, and packed
a small satchel with a change of underwear. He found it
hard to say goodbye.

'Really great,' he sniffed. 'Of you to do this, Ben.'

'I haven't done anything yet. Anyway, it's a pleasure.'

Don scoffed. 'I don't know if it's *that*.' He seemed
suddenly upset. 'But it's nice for me. And it's nice for
Em, isn't it, eh? Isn't it, darling?'

Benjamin wasn't sure if he had ever heard his father
call his wife such a thing before. He was a little ashamed
to find the expression so odd, so incongruous, as if
anyone cared what it sounded like. The truth was that
Don did not know where to go, or what to do.

'Are you going to see Alison?' Benjamin asked. Alison
was an affair of the 1980s, who lived near Barnstaple
and kept farm animals, eccentrically injured ones, as
pets. She had a goose with one eye that liked television.

Don bit into an apple and spoke while chomping.

'Yeah, maybe. I'll see how it goes. I may not get that
far.' He dropped the core back in the fruit bowl. 'Don't
worry about a bath by the way. No need.'

'Everything's fine, Dad.' Benjamin tried to sound
normal, in charge, perhaps not particularly attentive.
'There's no need for you to hurry back. Try to enjoy
yourself. Try to get used to, you know – the time away.
Being on your own. It'll be good for you.'

This was too much, and even as he said the words
Benjamin regretted them. To his credit, Don made no

reply but ducked out of the door and up the stairs. He had to leave before he grew fully conscious of being unwanted.

When they were alone, Benjamin winked at his mother, put the kettle on and gave her a damp cloth. They would find a routine together. He did not have the least idea what it would be exactly, or how long it might last. He simply assumed that the next day or so would be (as everyone else apparently already knew) like looking after a small child. With the difference that this particular child could learn nothing new; all she could do was go over old and failing ground.

But it would reassure her to be in the kitchen. Benjamin guided her towards the cupboard next to the stove and quickly emptied the shelves of their various jars and packets. The surfaces were jammy with dirt, seasoning and slow leakage. He put two spots of washing-up liquid on one stain and rubbed in circles, indicating that Emily should join him. They worked away and were absolutely quiet. Emily did not even mutter to herself, so engrossed was she in her task. When one shelf was done, she did another, less thoroughly. After that, she got shakily to her feet, thrust her J-cloth at Benjamin and said, 'Boring.' Her eyes had cleared. Then, as she sipped a half-cup of coffee (good for the constipation), something galvanized her into independent activity. Tugging at her son's arm, she led him into the sitting room, where inspiration, like the rising mist, deserted her.

'Oh,' she said. 'That's strange.'

She made her way to the good chair, with the faded pink upholstery and cat-savaged braid, and gazed out over a plastic table into the garden where, perhaps, the Sundays of her life still flowered. If you stood at this window, you could see the rest of Bath beyond Bellevue Crescent, waiting like an audience, and if you sat the audience obligingly disappeared.

'It's very strange,' she said again. 'It isn't very nice.'

She was like a pot-bound plant finding her roots in open soil.

'He's very good. It's horrible. I think it might be better if I was somewhere they could, you know, do it . . .'

The phrases were hesitant but at least they followed on from each other. Finally, some ease returning to the movement of her neck as she faced her son, Emily completed the thought: ' . . . and look after me.'

All she needed was time and the absence of undue interference. And this her husband, a creature of benign tumult, could not provide. His element was noise, and with his daughter Liz he shared an aversion to waiting and planning. Don could not follow the plots of films and associated delay with failure. As a boy he'd been so sick with excitement at the prospect of going to the circus that his mother had made him stay in bed.

Of course, Benjamin was only on duty for a weekend: he admitted, fully, the desperation he'd feel if forced to tend his mother permanently. There were difficult, long moments, cutting and feeding, pointing and soothing. And instant accommodations with taboo, when Emily, roaring and wailing in the upstairs toilet, had to have the shit pulled out of her. But none of it, in close up, appalled him very much. He discovered, to his surprise, that he did not shrink from her empty breasts in their stained singlet, or from the scar-white flap of her bottom. It was not in any way remarkable to see her hairless body in the bath, or to watch her flinch and whimper as he rolled a white nightie over her head. The one sticking point was getting Emily into bed, where the instinct for warmth and preservation snagged on her vulnerability. Clean and tidy, Benjamin's mother perched on the edge of her bed. He had his back to her for a minute, while he counted the pills and mixed the Fibrox; but when he turned around, he found her doubled over, trying to pull on a second pair of knickers.

'No,' Benjamin assured her, 'you don't have to have them on now. You can take those off. They're for the morning, aren't they?'

He reached round her waist to encourage her. She pushed him away. Some clotted memory of distress had taken hold, and Emily was now weeping, one hand locked firmly on the hem of her knickers, the other – with freakish strength – gripping Benjamin's forearm and resisting him.

'Oh, it's absolutely potty,' she pleaded. 'If I do, in the night.'

'You don't need them. You don't need another pair of knickers, sweetheart. You've been today.'

'You don't know. I don't do.'

'All right. If you think you'll be better off . . .'

What was the point of making a point? The extra pair were hardly clean, Benjamin noticed – he could just imagine his poor, exhausted father flinging them on the line – but they seemed to comfort Emily; and swaddled in stretch-elastic and grey cotton, she calmed down. She was too thin now to be on her side, so she lay on her back with the duvet flat across her shoulders, her mouth open, staring at the ceiling, skimming the surface of sleep. Benjamin stayed with her for perhaps half an hour, until the room, toasted by an ancient heater, grew warm.

Outside, over the dormant city, great tides of cloud retreated in a south-westerly direction, and an obol moon lit the way beyond forgotten mines to Peasedown St John. Benjamin was too tired to stay up – and too full of a private conviction that he must speak to his father as soon as he returned home.

The opportunity presented itself earlier than expected, at seven the next morning, when Benjamin made his robotic descent to the kitchen and there found Don carpentering away at some stale bread. He had been gone eighteen hours. 'Jesus,' he was already saying as Benjamin entered the room, 'it's not enough. One day is not enough. More hassle than it's worth.'

'You'll have a whole week soon, Dad. A week, and then you can relax properly. She's told me she wants—'

'Fuck *me*.' Don dropped the bread knife angrily, and picked it up again. 'Everyone knows what to do, don't they? Everyone's a bloody expert. But it's me who's left here every day, isn't it? That's what you *don't* see. Every day the same. In and out, in and out. Jesus.' He stiffened over the bread board, brushing away tears. 'It's not much fun, Ben.' There was a long pause. 'A week,' he said, eventually. 'A whole week. Big deal.'

'I *am* sorry,' called a small voice nervously from the passage. 'I wish I could make it better. I wish, I do.'

Ten days later, as arranged, Benjamin rang Sunnybrook to see how Emily was settling in. Carla Rose was busy, but he managed to get hold of Vikki, who remembered him from the business with the lift.

'Peg's been asking after you,' she cackled. 'You made an impression. She goes, "Where's that young man, then? Where's my young man?" Ha, ha, ha.' Vikki's laughter subsided. 'Did you want your dad, my love?'

Benjamin drew in his breath with a whistle – a paternal habit – and fought the pricking in his nostrils, the little sunspots of anger that clouded his vision. How long had he been there? Was she to have no respite at all? In the background could be heard two voices, a man's and a woman's, ministering to their silent charge. 'There you go.' 'Nearly.' 'Oh. Oh.'

'I can get him if you like, Benjamin,' Vikki offered, more gently this time, as if she guessed what he was thinking. 'Or your sister, Liz – they're both here.'

'No, I just wanted to check up on things. See how

they were going. How has Mum, Emily, been? I'm sorry I wasn't there to see her in.'

'Your mum's doing quite well, darling,' said the orderly, lowering her voice once more but still speaking brightly. 'She *has* been a bit tearful today, what with the visits. Your other sis – Charlotte, is it?'

'Lotte, yes.'

'Lotte was here yesterday. It's a lot to take on board.'

'I know.'

'It's a lot of – stimulation, I suppose you'd call it. But they're just getting their coats on, the others. Getting their act together.'

In his mind's eye, Benjamin could see the two of them, Don and Liz, doing the rounds, whirling their belongings in the faces of the bemused residents. What he could not see, however hard he tried, even as he looked at the pin-pricked photo dangling next to the phone, was his mother. She had vanished.

Vikki sounded positively conspiratorial. 'Yes, that's them done, my love,' she confirmed. 'I'd say they're ready. Almost very nearly ready now.'

Understanding Passback

Margaret's Hill, the steep and narrow lane pouring off Camden Road and down into the city, divided where the Georgian houses of the upper slopes ended and the new estate, Alpine Gardens, began. A low stump of a wall jutted out of the new build to mark the division. The right fork slowed its descent and took you past tilted forecourts and cars moored at an angle to the vast cedars of Hedgemead Park; the left fell fast into Walcot and traffic.

Emily approached the wall and let the luxury of having no important decision to make guide her. Her back and knees remembered toiling up these slopes weighed down by heavy shopping, but her eyes saw the pleasure behind the years of pain: her pride in the family to which she was returning, her delight in their high humour and ribbing; both proofs, it seemed to her, of a kind of distinction. The pride produced a succession of moving pictures, real phantom witnesses to her sacrifice. Here was the lamppost growing out of a privet, where she had caught Liz with her legs around an unfamiliar youth (Liz covered her eyes, the boy buckled under her). And here was the pavement, a black strip that went soft in summer and left tar on the white psoriasis scars of Lotte's skin when she tripped over in her sandals. Clive, too, stood in the middle distance, in the middle of the road, looking at her with his head turned away, as though trying to grasp something in his peripheral vision. Over them all glowed the milky light of September. The different notes of the children's cries filled the air for a moment, and in the silence afterwards she realized someone was missing – the youngest. Curious thing. She fancied he would appear if she concentrated hard enough, swinging his music case, feigning exhaustion as he reached for her arm, but it was an effort – for her – that threatened to tear the fabric of the dream.

It was pleasant to be on the brink of waking. Ideas, people and conversations beckoned on either side of the low wall, and if she chose one or some over the others, it wouldn't matter. In the lovely V-neck of the city, seen from Margaret's Hill, the amber terraces and purple roofs breathed deeply with sunrise. How the day advanced! The heat stirred the hairs on Emily's top lip and bore her leftwards, downhill, into the city centre.

Around the first bend in the road, she stopped again. There was a young man in front of her. He was crouching and tinkering with a motorbike. Then he looked up and smiled. Before he'd finished introducing himself, she'd said, 'Oh yes,' in a timid voice and was embarrassed – but he didn't react. His eyes were steady. He was somebody's son, he said, and a friend of Benjamin's, from school.

'Benjamin's homosexual, you know,' Emily remarked.

The young man made a spider of his right hand on the gravel and replied that, no, as a matter of fact, he hadn't known that.

In a letter written to Benjamin shortly afterwards, Shaun Bisdee reflected that he must have said something to Mrs Allden to lead them both out of this social cul-de-sac, because they 'parted on good terms, so there was no harm done'.

When she came to the bottom of the hill, Emily knew that she could go no further. Cars and lorries thundered past on the London road, inches from her face, the whip-lash of their passing so strong that it pulled her fine hair out from under the spotted scarf she wore every day. The strands flapping in her eyes made her lift her arm – and she saw that she was fully dressed. She had on dyed blue loafers, tights, a knee-length red corduroy skirt; best of all, the long Mexican sweater, from whose sleeves delicate hands and wrists like turtles' heads offered themselves for inspection. Across the busy main road was a furniture store. She had passed by this family con-cern at least twice a week for the past fifty years without once venturing inside.

The thought became a far-off shark in the glass of the shop opposite, moving steadily upwards, climbing through the heavy medium.

*

Her room at Sunnybrook was clean but spartan. It had a sink and a mirror, a hard washable floor, a large window and pale blue walls.

Clive, with his experience of Camberley and other Cheshire homes, saw only defects. The bed had no side-gates to prevent his mother falling at night. And he refused to acknowledge the contribution of the care-workers. Don was effusive in his praise of them, but it was an attention-seeking praise; and it drove Clive wild, as if his own history of working all those years with desperately ill, deformed people suddenly did not exist or had never been worth noticing.

'It's unbearable, Benjamin,' the older brother complained, in person and over the phone. 'It's excruciating and – and – patronizing, and yes I *know* I should be able to ignore it but I can't. It just gets to me. He knows *nothing* about that kind of life. He lives in a bubble of art and Bath and *jazz* and privilege.'

Clive talked through the foam that covered his teeth, which made him sound as if he'd been sick. He breathed hoarsely.

'It's a fucking awful job, Ben. I've done it, so I *know*. And what Dad, pathetically, doesn't realize is that they, those people up at the home, don't give a fuck about him. They're brutalized by what they do. They're not saints. They work in a death camp and that's it. Period. That's all there is to it.'

The other siblings were more practical. Liz and Lotte together had selected a few items of clothing, some jewellery (mostly beads) and photographs from Emily's dresser at home and arranged them at Sunnybrook as naturally as they could. There was a cork sideboard now, next to the sink, covered in pictures of children and grandchildren, some soft toys in a pile on the chair, and a few of Emily's last dabbled watercolours – purple squiggles – which Don had framed nicely in a lime-washed box made of ash.

'About time, too,' said Lotte. 'He never took any interest in her work before. What about those drawings she did on holiday? They were beautiful. I'd like one of those, if she goes. When she – oh, and her quilt! Do you remember that? No, I do. That was on display at the American Museum.'

Lotte was angry with her father for having put Emily in a home. She agreed that he was unable to go on looking after her, and that he had done all he could according to his lights; still, the way Lotte saw it, he had betrayed her.

'I don't care,' she said. 'I'm sorry, Ben. But if you really love someone, you don't . . .'

She took her mother's part now that Emily could no longer speak for herself, and with a persistence that voiced more than Lotte perhaps realized of her own grievances. She and Fraser led independent lives, he in London near his clinic, she in Oxford – in the house to which Fraser returned, and not merely dutifully, at weekends. It was a separation that struggled on, like a war with a forgotten cause, re-arming itself with hints and allusions to wrongdoing, comparisons, precedent. Her father's affairs were never far from her lips.

Liz's predicament was tenderly revealing, too. First impressions had been forgotten. Now she championed Sunnybrook as a model of care. She grew, quickly, to like the place and the people who worked there, and was liked in return. She was glad that her mother had found a kind of sanctuary; relieved that she was well fed and warm. But the fear of old age nagged at her: each visit, for Liz, was an immobilizing ordeal in which her own vivacity, however much appreciated in her other life – at school, by the kids – or by the care staff, could not reach, far less convert, the residents. When she sprang into the day room, they stared back at her, mutely wondering, or ambled away. They were not moved by her loud cheer or tears. They could not confirm what she felt. At a Christmas singalong, Liz sang and ate, acclaimed the doddery organist, husband to one of the residents, then dissolved. Benjamin found her bawling in a corner. One of the carers brought Liz a cup of tea.

It was so sad, everyone always said, about Emily. So awful to see her thus reduced. And the epitome of that reduction was her room, with its few trinkets stripped of context and only occasionally shuffled about by their owner in a thin echo of housework. The mementos were for the visitors, of course: a reassurance not that Emily had ever cared greatly for paste jewellery, but that she continued to care for them. Liz, Clive and Lotte sought recognition – Lotte most urgently of all. ('She knows me, she does. I'm not being funny.') Leaning in close, they found an image of themselves flickering in their mother's eyes and gathered what they could – a whispered word, a shiver – to its flame.

Benjamin felt differently. Like the others, he visited his mother every three weeks or so. Unlike them he saw little in her slow physical deterioration that shocked or surprised him. It was so secondary, the ageing, the weight loss, the caramel teeth. He knew that he had grieved most in the early stages, when he could see her pleading with herself, begging her mind to stay intact.

But now that it was gone, so was he. Emily regarded him with dim wonder. Was there something in the bearded man looking down at her that ought to excite her interest? No. He had vanished from the radar – along with the radar. What remained was memory-gas, like air trapped at the bottom of a pond, which every now and then came to the surface: filler phrases, deployed with accidental humour. 'I'm your youngest son,' he once said, when he stepped into her room too quickly and her face grew long. 'I don't think that's right,' she ventured before adding with an almost-smile, 'well, if you say so.'

Benjamin found himself looking forward to the afternoons he spent with Emily at Sunnybrook, strolling up and down the corridors, taking her to the kitchenette and back, singing a verse or two of 'Away In A Manger' from *Hymns Ancient and Modern* (there was a copy in the activities room, along with a dartboard). She was safe, and no longer at the mercy of her husband's infectious anxiety; except of course when Don came, as he did every other day, bearing fruit smoothies and bits of cake which he pressed on her. These she gulped down loudly, painfully, a mewling protest snuffled back into the bottle. Don was drawn in by this sad ritual. It composed him.

'She likes this. You like this, don't you, Em?'

The feed lasted five minutes at most, then he'd leave with a hand raised in farewell, not looking back, speeding head down towards the lift.

One afternoon, while Don's shouted goodbyes were still fading, Emily heaved a great sigh and batted a grape resting on the arm of her chair across the room.

'Come on, Mum,' Ben said, picking up the grape. 'He's doing his best. You know what it's like. He wants to show you how much he cares and it's too late. You're not interested – and, well, I don't blame you.'

Emily turned her head slowly from the door and fixed Benjamin with a stare. He was abashed. He could say things now, share stories and confidences, in a way he'd never done before, back when she might have responded. She had always shrunk from intimacy of that sort, and her body retained a suspicion of it.

The room was still. In the lucid distance, beyond elder bushes that marked the boundaries of Sunnybrook, children screeched in a playground; and beyond that, a train's rude horn tumbled into a gallop.

Tricia put her head round the door. She was one of the senior workers, a big woman with a thatch of black hair, large hips, gold earrings and a husband who played skittles. Jason, the chiropodist, had arrived. 'He'll be ready for you in ten minutes, my love. All right? Emily? Do you want to come now?'

Benjamin nodded. They were in a waiting room already, he realized. The home was really a waiting room, where conversations took on an inevitable urgency: there was so little time before the train pulled in and pulled out again.

He took a passport photo of his boyfriend, also called Jason, out of his wallet and showed it to his mother. He'd long planned a recap of the relationship, how they'd met (at a bus stop), what they did together (went to non-league matches, browsed in charity shops), why it went wrong (Jason changed his mind). But now it came to it, Benjamin saw there was no need. 'I thought you'd like to see this,' he said instead. 'This was the man I told you about. It's OK. It's no one you know. He made me very happy – I just wanted to show you.'

Emily dwelt on the thumb-sized portrait and handed it back.

'Are you ready, darling?' said Tricia at the door. 'For your golden slippers?'

'*Oh!*'

The exclamation was thin but fervent, full of sudden emotion.

'*Oh, it's wonderful.*'

Emily shook her fists up and down with delight – 'I'm so happy' – and tears flushed in abundance from an unknown source.

'I am really. You don't know.'

Tricia's colour deepened a little. She was fond of Benjamin's mother and had asked to be her key-worker – a difficult job, particularly at bath-time.

'Oh bless you, Emily, my love. She's that pleased to see you, Benjamin. You watch out now, Emma-lily, you'll get me going. Come on, then.'

The chiropodist had set up shop in one of the glass-fronted, overheated day rooms on the lower floor. A steady flow of residents were guided to his surgery to have their talons filed, but the queue was far from orderly. The stately Violet, whom Benjamin had met on his first visit two years ago, coaxed people in from the corridor where they lingered and muttered or fingered clothing and poked each other. Getting them to stay put was hard. They took one look at the bearish ginger man with the tray of shiny implements and lost interest; or were bemused and then frightened. The great thing with most of them, as with Emily while she had her strength, was to be on the move. Doris, Sunnybrook's one-woman louring cloud, had to be dragged in and held down in the chair so that Jason and Violet between them could prise the plimsolls from her surprisingly shapely little feet while she yelled and fought. Others wandered in, sat down, tutted at the racket, and left again. But there were stayers as well. Trombone Herbie, who had the room next to Benjamin's mother, seemed happy to wait his turn, as did a small, smiling lady with a face so compressed by laughter lines it looked as if it had been held in a vice. She saw Benjamin approach and began chattering.

'And people used to say, "Where did you go to get your hair permed?" Oh, he was a dear man,' the smiling woman confided. 'He was a lovely boy.'

'Bom bom bom,' said Trombone Herbie.

As Benjamin steered Emily towards a chair, Doris's incredible resistance resolved into a sustained, single-note lament. It was a piercing cry, in a register somewhere between soprano and smoke alarm – and Emily quailed before it. The note broke off and Jason pruned at speed, unperturbed.

'I don't want it,' Doris exclaimed. 'Where's my car?'

'Where does *that* come from?' Benjamin wondered aloud, and Tricia, sitting on the other side of his mother, comforting her, explained. The ones who still talked in sentences, however short and rude, usually ended up repeating themselves; what they said often made good sense, but it was on a loop.

'Look at Myrtle, there,' Tricia said, pointing to the woman who'd made the observation about hair. 'She's precious, bless her. All she wants to talk about is her husband and how happy she was. But with Doris, well – as you can hear –' the room's occupants cringed at another top D ' – it's all up here, it's all emotion, and that's what's left. She wants a car, you see, a taxi. She's never had anything to do with them, I shouldn't doubt. 'Smatter of fact, I know she didn't, 'cos she used to be a dinner lady at the quarry canteen and lived local. I don't know what it is. The taxi, the car. She *wants* it, see. Whatever it is,' Tricia sighed, 'it's what she really wanted.'

'All done,' shouted Jason cheerfully. 'Who's next?'

'Bom bom bom.'

Herbie was neat and spry with his green collar done up, a very youthful ninety-one. He hopped into the chair, where the sensation of being tended to quite pacified him, and his bom-boms softened to a whisper. Out went wicked Doris, with Violet for a guard, and Benjamin was struck again at how many of the care-workers themselves seemed to be nearing, or past, retirement. They seemed to understand their charges. There was affection, but not much pity.

He'd absorbed the idea from various sad-old-bag dramas on the telly that homes and the people who ran them were Victorian throwbacks, choked with misery, resentment and air-freshener. The reality was different. Instead of a workhouse of grotesques, he'd found at Sunnybrook a sort of stop-motion St Trinian's, stuck for ever in the occasionally hilarious doldrums of winter term, with both year's end and the Big Break a distant prospect. People died all the time, certainly, but no one made a fuss. Or rather the loss wasn't felt as relatives felt it, sorrowing over their own pasts with a mixture of guilt and relief, but as a trusted absence: all who came to Sunnybrook left school in the end. *So and so was a character. She's gone now, yes.* Tricia talked about Emily in this way, only ever having known her as a little wisp with a struggling but attentive family. The gas of communicable memory had evaporated and left behind 'a lovely lady'. So maybe the narrowing of her life into a single room, with a wipe-clean floor and some furry tigers, wasn't a tragedy. Maybe it was liberation.

'I'm the baby of the family,' Myrtle said, on Benjamin's left. She looked at him closely. Emily's head sank forward but Myrtle's was upright. When she spoke again, she leant over and patted his arm, beating time to mark her feeling. 'My father used to say, "And this is my baby," and I used to feel, oh, ten feet tall! My brother and sister were twins and I was the baby. Are you married?'

Benjamin said that he was not.

'Do you have brothers and sisters?'

'I do. One brother and two sisters. I expect you've met them. They all come to visit. Well, not all at once, but—'

'Oh yes.' Myrtle seemed tired of the idea. 'How did you get here?'

'I got a train from London, where I live, and then a bus from Bath, out past Combe Down—'

The smile on the old lady's face broadened.

'Combe Down was where we lived, my husband and

I. And people used to say, "Where did you go to get your hair permed?" Oh, he was a dear man.'

The tape was back at the start. Emily meanwhile, muttering to herself, slumped forwards, her head hanging lower than ever. Benjamin wiped her lips and helped her to sit tall. With this action came a flicker of awareness. On a mealy outbreath the drivelling stopped. Emily looked around, a little contemptuous, perhaps, of the company she kept. It was the same look that she used to fix on the children when Don began talking politics; or when she saw that they were listening to him and not bothering about her.

' – and a bus,' Benjamin said to Myrtle, while still watching his mother, 'is where I met my boyfriend. Well, a bus stop . . .'

He faltered because it had just occurred to him that the old lady's gaily uncomprehending questions and reflections were mad, yes, but utterly without guile. She said what she meant, though she may not have known she was saying it. Self-awareness had become a very minor part of being true to oneself.

'Bom bom bom. Bom bom-ba-bom bom.'

'OK, Herbie. And the next,' Jason called out above the buzz and tick of his clippers. 'That's *you*, my love. Every one a winner.'

Before she went to the chair, Myrtle patted Benjamin's arm one last time.

'I don't know how, but he knew he wasn't going to live long. And he used to say to me, "If you see anyone you like the look of, I'd be very pleased for you." But I never even looked, no. Because I often think, well, if I hadn't been so happy, I'd be thinking only – when I look back – I'd only have miserable thoughts. But I was very, very happy.'

Alone on her island paradise, Myrtle looked out over sunny waters. Her breezes were warm and sweet, even the ones that carried the crispy whiff of athlete's foot when she shook off her shoes. The occupants of other islands, a way down the oceanic corridor, called and hooted in states of lesser perfection, none so stridently as Doris, who could be heard terrorizing the TV in the day room with threats and oaths. Her bleak atoll had no shelter, and its unique inhabitant lashed out at the waves in strange defiance.

Myrtle's son and daughter came out regularly, Tricia informed Benjamin, unlike Doris's family, by whom the ferocious old bat had been abandoned.

'Emily's one of the lucky ones,' Tricia added. 'There's a lot here don't get to see no one from outside. It's very sad.'

Emily scowled and winced before the nail clippers. 'Ooh – ooh, it's terrible,' she whimpered, her skinny arm braced on the chair's red leather, the lower lip sucked in, her eyes sharp then dull again with the passage of fear.

'Were you frightened?' Benjamin asked afterwards, when they were back in her room, doing the usual tour, looking at pictures of Lotte and Liz, of Clive aged ten in uniform with a big black busby and tin drum. He held his mother as they shuffled round the room together. 'Is it very frightening?'

'Yes,' said Emily, and was still for a second or two. Quickly, but as clearly as he could, Benjamin told her that he loved her.

Don had slept with other women in the 1970s and 80s, and Emily had not married a man she wholeheartedly wanted. Or not at first, and not without some Cokerish resistance to the idea. She had been looking for a father as much as a husband. There were betrayals and self-deceptions enough between the two of them to explain the kind of docile mistrust that exists in many long unions: but nothing, so it seemed to Benjamin, to account for the determined melancholy of Emily's later years, except perhaps determination itself.

On one occasion, Benjamin remembered coming home from London to find his mother sitting by the gas fire, making cards. For the last fifteen years of her life, before she became ill, Emily made birthday cards for everyone she knew. They were collages of black-and-white photographs, newsprint, pictures of mosaic tiles, flowers and wallpaper, even rubbings of the marquetry designs on the battered old piano in his room, all ingeniously folded together and enclosed by hand-drawn Roman lettering, with comic verses inside. The best of these were acidly funny, powered by an ill-concealed impatience with her husband's chat about art. 'Out with the Potorowski and Tower / In with the gaudy and unreal flower', she wrote, memorably, above one sparkly pink chrysanthemum. The words on that card – for his thirtieth, Benjamin recalled – spilled out of the mouth of a piebald kitten, because it was the card-maker's conceit that the whole enterprise had been secretly undertaken by the cat, Kodak. The animal authenticated each finished work with a pawprint and signed herself 'Me'.

After paying Emily a genuine compliment on the latest design (a grey plaid version of the Batmobile for Liz's son, Matt), Benjamin watched her eyes swim and lips purse. He knew that she was saddened by news of Liz's dissolving relationship with Matt's father, and said neutrally, 'What's the matter?'

He knelt by her chair and rubbed her arms. She stiffened, sniffed and denied that she was upset. Don had gone out to a party with two old marching-band pals; she had refused to go with him.

'I don't want to be dancing around at my age. Going everywhere, all smiles and *hee-hee-hee* all the time. I'm sorry, but I don't.'

She set aside the card and scissors and gripped the handkerchief Benjamin had pulled from her sleeve.

'I know what they think. They think I'm this silly person just sitting at home – well, I don't care. I brought up four very individual children. I—'

'Who does?' Benjamin asked, before she became too involved in her own distress. 'No one thinks that.

They're not standing around talking about you, Mum. If you didn't want to go or weren't feeling up to it, that's fine. But they're your friends too, remember. You shouldn't judge them so harshly.'

He had tried to speak sympathetically but Emily was resolved to hear only his frustration and to magnify its effects. She looked annoyed.

'I expect you're right, as usual.'

At that Benjamin had to laugh. Emily immediately became animated. 'No, but you *are*,' she insisted, and pushed at him, quite hard, with her elbow. 'I can see that now. Really I can.'

The last thing she wanted was sympathy, he realized. Sympathy meant understanding, and a part of her was adamant that she had been – had to be – misunderstood. It was like watching someone tunnel under an open door.

'I just wish I'd been more loved,' she said simply. She picked up Matt's card and flashed it at Benjamin, with a defiant levity.

'Mum,' said Benjamin. 'What on earth do you mean?'

A contributor to the paper for which he worked had once said to him in the course of a rambling discussion that the more anyone wanted something from you, the less able you were to give it to them.

'For goodness' sake, don't go on, Clive. Don. Oh! *Benjamin*. I've accepted it, I have. It's over now. I am perfectly all right. There is *nothing* the matter.'

*

He told her again, even giving her shoulders the mildest shake. Emily looked as if she were considering the matter, but not favourably. At last, her fingers sweeping over the sink-top's laminate, she replied: 'Clever dick.'

It wasn't the response Benjamin might have hoped for, though he wasn't much surprised either. Each family has its peculiar way with meaning, and the Alldens' was never to take things at face value.

While Benjamin was still making his way back to Bellevue Place from Peasedown, his brother arrived on the family doorstep. Clive was paying regular visits these days, turning up unannounced and haggard. Since leaving Camberley in the late 90s, he'd drifted, ending up in a flat in Hastings. Don suspected a difficulty at work – Clive now did shifts at a meat-packing factory a few miles outside the town – but knew better than to sound alarmed.

'Hey, Clive!' he said, smiling quickly. 'Great to see you. What a surprise . . .'

Clive's stubbly face snapped backwards as if the Invisible Man had just taken a swipe at him. Don put a hand on his son's arm. The touch was well intended, but Clive felt it repel him.

'. . . what a *fantastic* surprise!'

They went downstairs and Clive dumped a thin, dirty rucksack onto the kitchen floor. He passed the sleeve of an even dirtier anorak over his liverish brow, looking for a way to avoid further physical contact with his father. They both went for the kettle at the same time, a sort of reflex gesture of conviviality – and Don, with his greater coordination and birdlike ability to move in fits and starts, got there first. He grabbed the flex an instant before Clive reached it, and unconsciously turned his back into his son, knocking him out of the way. Clive swore and tottered into the gas stove. He was a large man who trembled a lot. Neither Parkinsonian nor alcohol-related, his shakes were nonetheless constant and real, symptoms of some bottle-necked vital force, prevented – but by what? – from spending itself in anything other than little ripples of anguish and fury. His hair clumped; his spectacles were chipped. He was forty-five.

Clive had something in his throat and cleared it with a bout of expressive hawking. He pointed at the boiling kettle and said, 'Let me do that.'

'No!' Don shouted. 'Hey, no way. Just relax. Sit down. Take the weight—'

'Fucking hell,' Clive said, collapsing into a chair. 'What a mistake. I should never have come.' He shielded his eyes. 'I don't know why I . . . . What's the fucking point of being here, of trying to help, if . . .'

Clive withdrew his hand and saw, momentarily, the equivalent frustration of his father, an awful complex of grief and bafflement. The smaller man's shoulders were drawn up into an arrowhead of tension. It always shocked Clive, to see his father struggle so with feeling, but it was strangely important that he did see it.

In a calmer voice he asked, 'How's Mum?'

'Yeah, she's fine.' Don dropped spoons into cups. 'She'll be – yeah.'

He straightened up, poured milk, breathed in.

'Is that a cricket jersey you're wearing, Dad?'

'She'll be really pleased to see you.'

Don took a second to register the question, the new direction Clive was indicating. He looked down at his old Somerset Cricket Club souvenir.

'This old thing, yeah.' The business of the tea put him more at ease. 'But you've seen it before.'

If he had, Clive didn't say. The jersey, with its cabling and purple stripes, spoke of the past, and the past spoke to him. It wasn't what you remembered that mattered, it was what you could lay claim to remembering, and what that said about your ability to endure. It was classy just to have been around.

A conversation between the two historical witnesses began, and Benjamin let himself in upstairs halfway through it. He shut the front door quietly and listened to what sounded like a radio discussion.

'It may be before your time,' Don was saying, 'but Fred Russell came here once or twice. To *this* house. And Russell gave me this jersey.'

'Didn't he bowl for England?'

Clive had used the jersey as a sort of diplomatic gambit: he had no actual interest in its sentimental value, but the connection to Russell was promising.

'Very fast. And I met, well I *knew* John Hammick.'

'Ah,' said Clive. 'Now he was a batsman's batsman—'

'Right. Exactly.'

' – but he never really built on his reputation. I seem to remember,' Clive said, hesitating over the implied feat of embryonic recall, 'that he was always getting out – but I suppose it was that kind of era.'

'Yeah, people took their knocks, didn't they?'

Don met Clive's unstill eye and hurried on. 'Half the injuries they get now weren't even classified as injuries back then. They players took them and went back to the crease. No one made a fuss.'

It was a different point, which Clive let pass unchallenged because it married with his own train of thought. Don meanwhile wondered what sort of meat-packing plant employed people like his poor son. What, apart from anything else, happened to the meat? A noise. Upstairs. That would be the door – or, no, maybe it was the wind in the boarded-over fireplace. Clive was arguing that the injuries themselves were the same – 'hamstrings, tendons, ankles'.

'This is football,' Don confirmed.

Clive nodded vigorously on the other side of the table. 'This is football.'

Upstairs in his old room, the one he'd shared with Clive for seven years, Benjamin sat on the low chest that had once served as a piano stool.

It held paperbacks and letters, boxes of lead soldiers and hardback notebooks – the ones containing a whole history of the Napoleonic Wars – that belonged to his brother. Most of the other items in the room evoked Clive, too: the neat rank of Penguin Classics above a new desk (at which Don now worked), the set of Hardy novels, the larger shelf of books on boxing.

Next to these outsize volumes leant a stack of LPs, to which the boys had listened on Friday nights, arguing the relative merits of David Munrow, *The Six Wives of Henry VIII*, Tchaikovsky's *1812 Overture*, Geoff Love's *Big Bond Movie Themes*. Each week a different record prevailed. Later, Benjamin joined Aretha's chain of fools, but the nearest Clive ever got to pop music as a teenager was the soundtrack to *The Graduate*.

In the bed nearest the window, the glass so cold during winter that it frosted over on the inside, Benjamin lusted after a few boys at school. He'd made rather a meal of this in his first book; in reality, the martyrish sensation had been quite enjoyable because he knew that it wouldn't last for ever. Now, though, what struck him most was that he had not cared much when Clive left for York University and a life of catastrophic independence. Had he even noticed his brother's absence? And did that make him a callous person?

Don and Emily visited Clive once, in his second year. Benjamin went with them. Clive's hair and nails were very long. He took them to the canteen on the campus, where he duly scrabbled for change. Emily cried but did not return to York. She wrote one of her letters to Clive's tutor, pleading for some sort of mercy, and got a tough-minded reply.

Another, more recent letter lay on Don's new desk, this one from Clive himself. Benjamin picked it up and read it, backwards. It contained an amusing postscript about the film of *Casino Royale* ('Daniel Craig pretty good in a muscle-bound – oh dear, Benjamin might like it! – sort of way. But putting real dirt under Bond's fingernails just makes the things he does even more absurd') and an arresting account of Clive's last visit to Sunnybrook:

> *. . . the highlight of the afternoon was when Mum hauled something quite extraordinary out of her mental ragbag. She did her Duck Face (actually an impression of the old Naish crone, Jeremy's Mum, I think). As I recall it, whenever Mum performed this frighteningly accurate imitation, which came complete with spittle running down her chin, it meant that she was in an excellent mood. With me, I suppose – I'm fairly sure I was the only one who asked her to 'do her Mrs Naish'. The others may not even have been aware of who she was. Anyway, there it was again, along with signs of an improved appetite (I am told that Mum is especially fond of her semolina and has been seen attempting to relieve other residents of theirs!): crumbs of comfort, for us, from a pretty bare table.*

Far below him, it seemed to Benjamin, the conversation between Clive and Don was speeding up, its skewed harmony moving faster and faster as it approached a cadence. He put the letter down and went to stand at the top of the stairs.

'A long-standing problem exists,' Clive declared, 'at the highest level of English sport. Passback's become an awful kind of – I don't know—'

'Defeatism? Sort of, oh, here-we-go-again.'

'That's right. It's part of our distrust of creativity. Why we produce defender after defender.'

'After defender.'

'I can't stand that.'

'No, nor can I.'

'Simply can't understand it.'

Someone moved suddenly in his chair and presumably spilled the contents of a mug. Something rolled and broke. Don said, 'Shit.'

'And Beckham should be dropped,' he added.

'Yes, yes. Get rid of him.'

The voices tailed off, Clive humming ruminatively.

'Changing the subject entirely,' Don said, in a tone of royal confidence, 'would you like a *nice* cup of coffee?'

The Vigil

'I've got a key,' Liz said cheerfully, on perhaps the third or fourth morning of their vigil. 'Vikki's given me the key to the kitchenette so we don't keep having to go downstairs. There's a kettle and cups and a fridge, milk, everything. I'm going to make some tea. Who wants some tea?'

Lotte eyed the plate of Jaffa Cakes by Emily's sink but smiled her refusal. 'I didn't mind going downstairs, to be honest. There's such a wonderful atmosphere down there.' She seemed to require a word or gesture from Benjamin, who nodded. 'Vikki and Tricia. And Elaine – *she* writes poetry. Tricia's husband, I think, or is it Vikki's—'

'Vikki isn't married.'

'Yes she is,' Lotte insisted. 'She is. But they're separated, very amicably. And I think it's Vikki's husband who's gone to Chilcompton to get the syringe.' She swallowed knowledgeably. 'The doctor came in the night because Mum was in a lot of discomfort, and he gave her something to dry her secretions, but they need a special syringe for the morphine drip and they've had to go to Chilcompton to get it, would you believe.'

215

In the doorway behind Lotte, Liz drew her finger across her throat. Benjamin realized he was frowning and blinked away his cross face. Like Lotte and Liz, he'd been in the home all night, dozing some of the time by his mother's side and for a few hours in a spare room. He'd missed the doctor's visit; while Emily was being pumped full of antihistamine, he was fending off a naked Peggy, who'd gone for a wander and decided that his room was hers. He woke to find her toddling towards him, fingers plucking and grooming the air.

Peggy was tractable – mad, but calm and happy to be redirected; Lotte less so, and firmly resolved, in a sort of crooning empathy with her mother, to maintain what she felt was the appropriate tone of self-denial. When asked if she couldn't at least manage a slice of toast for breakfast, she again shook her head: 'Ben, I'm fine. I have plenty to eat. Don't give me that look: I know what you're thinking. I eat plenty; I'm little. I've always been small.'

As Benjamin rose to leave the room, Lotte recalled his attention to Emily's shallow breathing and to her hands, which she held and stroked: 'All those lovely things you made, Mum, those lovely dresses. You had such beautiful hands. Oh! She looks so peaceful.'

Benjamin agreed about the hands, though his powers of recollection were weakened by a sense that Lotte had somehow confiscated them. Run off with the ball. She remembered these things; he did not, or was not supposed to. In the background a turned-down CD of Jim

Reeves duetted with Emily's soft hissing. She lay with the covers up to her shoulders, eyes two-thirds closed, oblivious to Jim's entreaties. *Welcome to my world. Won't you come on in?* But there was something wrong with the soundtrack to this dying, Benjamin felt, and it wasn't just the words or the fact that his parents had never in their lives listened to Jim Reeves or anyone like him. (Whose CD was it, anyway?) It was the idea, disturbing once it got hold of you, that you could be lulled to death.

'Here's a good one,' said Don, in the corner. He'd stopped sketching and picked up the free local newspaper. 'Local ads,' he announced. '"Molecatcher – no mole, no fee". How about that?'

Lotte made no reply, choosing instead to greet the two carers, Vikki and Tricia, who knocked on the open door and said it was time to turn Emily. They did this every two hours to keep her from getting sore. They changed her once a day, too, although Emily no longer soiled herself. It was just a relief to witness activity of any description – and the air of the corridor and kitchenette felt fresher as the Alldens filed out.

In the kitchenette itself, Benjamin and Lotte found Liz with Peggy, now decently clothed and at her ease in a thick grey cardigan.

'How are you, Peggy?' he said, not sure if she'd recognize him or not. The old lady's face lit up with pleasure; she turned, like a mother breaking off an adult conversation to greet her two young children.

'To be perfectly candid,' she said, 'I'm right browned off.'

It was a wise move, on Vikki's part, to give the family the run of Sunnybrook's upper floor. They couldn't sit cooped up in Emily's room all day, and they had to have somewhere else to go, even if it was only for ten minutes. The difficulty was time. Each of them had asked her the same question: how long? And to each of them, though in different ways, with more or less reassurance according to their needs, she said what she knew to be true: that death was a process; not in most cases a sudden wrapping-up, but an unfolding.

The children – all except Clive – arrived in the middle of the night, an age ago, expecting their mother to die at any minute. She'd gone to bed on Tuesday and changed colour on Thursday, which was when Vikki called Liz.

But Emily's last silence would not be hurried, not now that she had their attention, and the family was caught, Vikki could well see, between pity and screaming frustration. Did they want her alive or dead? Of course it was not just Emily who detained them; it was the consoling idea of her tenacity. If she clung to life, if she was at heart a fighter, as Lotte claimed, then it was largely because they would not have it otherwise. Each made the other hang on.

Such stalemates were not uncommon in Vikki's experience; a lot depended on what people understood by loss, and on their willingness to concede. The more people involved, the longer it took, usually. Families seldom knew how to say goodbye – but encouraging them to leave the sick room, so that Emily could unconsciously prepare herself, was a start.

To begin with, the Alldens – Lotte especially – were reluctant to go from their mother's side for fear of missing 'it', the moment. Then, as it dawned on them that her silence, like the silence between strikes of the clock, was not yet empty, they ventured out for little walks and chats, gentle conspiracies of irritation with each other in which the main topic of roundabout conversation was their own necessity: who could plausibly stay, and who should go.

'Is Clive coming this afternoon, do you know?' Lotte asked her sister.

Liz slopped boiling water into four mugs. 'I think so, yeah. Ask Ben, he spoke to him last night,' she yawned. 'I just hope he holds it together. We'll have to be on our guard – you know what he's like.'

Lotte didn't like the suggestion she was unguarded or not careful enough in Clive's company. Did his behaviour have to be her responsibility?

'I think he'll be OK. Surely he will,' she whispered, 'for Mum's sake.' She paused. 'I don't know what I'd do – what we'd do – if he blew up. It's just such a lot – no, no sugar, thanks, Liz – such a lot for us *all* to deal with. I'm like a – like a zombie, what with the kids and Ade's trip to Portugal. It's full on.'

She looked hungrily at her brother.

Benjamin leant against the threshold of the kitchenette as Liz finished stirring, and turned to stare out of the window. Her reflection there wavered faintly in the dull morning light but clearly enough for Benjamin to see that she was trying not to smile. Between them, Lotte spoke into her mug.

'I'm not joking, the three of them, teenagers. It's a lot – obviously, I'm not *complaining* – they're fantastic kids, and Ade's tournament's a big thing. It's a big thing for him, I mean. He's really good at his tennis, Ben. And the drums. And Yasmin's got a lovely singing voice – and Anna's just been in *Pineapple Poll.* Do you know it? She's only fourteen, it's quite good. But I can't just leave them all to it, they're not old enough – not yet. So I've got to get back, even if it's just for a night, because there's only me at the moment.'

'Join the club,' Liz said bluntly. 'I've already taken a week off.'

Lotte, who didn't have to work, sipped her tea in silence, until Liz repented: 'I can look after them if you like, Lotte. If you want to stay with Mum this weekend, I'll go up. If she's still alive.'

'Don't say that,' Lotte said, while over her head Benjamin mouthed to Liz, *Why not?* They waited, brooding, behaving – but it was Lotte who laughed first. 'I know you, Ben. You're terrible. She's got a strong heart, though.'

'That's what worries me,' Liz said. 'She'll have the

last laugh on Dad. He'll have a coronary and she'll still be here in a sort of suspended . . . *thing*.'

At the mention of her father Lotte turned solemn again. 'He'll be all right,' she muttered. 'Don't you worry. Now that he's got Sally.' She nodded to one side of Liz and pointed down at Sunnybrook's forecourt, where Don could be seen smoking and gesticulating. 'I bet that's her on the phone now.'

Sally was their father's new girlfriend, a business analyst for a wind-and-wave energy company in Cardiff. She was also a printmaker and photographer. She and Don had met in a gallery while he was hanging another artist's work; she'd asked him to frame six of her collages and a friendship had developed.

Liz, in whom Don had confided, blabbed to the others and declared the friendship to be sexual. Reactions varied. Though the children were all mildly put off by the affair, and by its timing, the girls found it hardest to stomach. They couldn't get past the age difference. Benjamin, too, shied away from the thought of his seventy-seven-year-old father in bed with a woman barely half his age, younger than both his own daughters – but it was Clive who put the problem in its proper abstract context. And in the abstract (which a phone call always was), he grasped the situation's banality.

'We have to remember,' he began, with his usual air of disappointed patronage, 'that this is a kind of emotional wartime. That's how Dad is treating it, consciously or not. And people were at it like rabbits during the war, because they felt they had nothing to lose.'

'Yes,' said Benjamin.

'Add to that the fact that Dad doesn't really dwell on any of this anyway; isn't *aware* of his own feelings, much less those of other people, and you can even make the case that this Sally woman, whoever she is, is his solution to a fairly fundamental *animal* despair. It's – she's – almost an inverse proof of how completely at sea he is without Mum.'

Benjamin wondered whether Clive saw anything of anyone else in this portrait, but he knew better than to interrupt.

'I may be sentimentalizing somewhat,' Clive admitted, his voice becoming gruffer and shorter-of-breath. 'I certainly can't say I'm *at all* comfortable about this relationship, if we can call it that. I suppose it's typical Dad, though, isn't it? The usual flouting of proprieties.'

Benjamin waited before making a cautious advance.

'I don't know,' he said. 'I think doing the right thing matters a lot to Dad. He's very aware of his obligations and does his level best to live up to them, but that part of his brain isn't in touch with the part that craves comfort and the company of women, you know, and someone to look after *him*. I don't . . . I think maybe some people just *can't* help themselves, whatever their sense of duty. Which was your point, wasn't it, so . . .'

'I see,' Clive said distantly. 'Was it? *Well*, Benjamin.

Thanks for spelling that one out!' He laughed – a laugh close to expostulation. 'Thank God *you're* on hand to put us all straight.'

On the edge of his guest-house bed, Benjamin gulped.

'I meant—'

'I know what you meant,' Clive said angrily. 'Just don't even *think* of trying to lecture me.' He paused long enough for Benjamin to register the racing of his heart, the B-movie drums. 'So,' he resumed, 'have you met her?'

'We said hello at his last exhibition. She seemed perfectly nice, I thought.' Even the 'I thought' was potentially inflammatory. 'She's got a daughter, so she has responsibilities, you know. She's certainly not hanging around, waiting for Dad to be free or anything. Anything like that.'

'A daughter?' Clive was struck by the idea. 'Do you think he's met *her*?'

'I've no idea. Possibly.'

'Christ almighty. Where will it end? Doesn't Sally realize it's the slippery slope? The *daughter*.' Clive groaned. 'He'll be going out with a foetus next.'

'We should try to get Mum on the morphine before Clive gets here,' Benjamin said. The girls were silent, at a junction of the tactless and the true.

'I'll ask Vikki,' Lotte said. 'It may have come this morning. Actually, that's a thought. It might be downstairs now. I know they had to send off for it. Apparently the nearest place they could find the right syringe was—'

'Chilcompton,' Liz nodded, adding hurriedly: 'Let's hope they brought back more than one, then we can all have a shot.'

They went back to Emily's room, where the carers were still turning the wisp of a body that had cooked and sewn and laughed and walked everywhere. Lotte asked about the syringe and Vikki said that they were going to fix it up next, just as soon as the nurse from St Martin's arrived. 'We're not nurses, see,' she said, cradling Emily with both arms while Tricia pulled the sheets out from under her, dusted the mattress protector with talc and wiped it away again. Then a new clean rubberized blanket went down, more talc, and two sheets over that. Lastly, they inspected Emily, as the three children covered their mouths.

'She's dry as you like,' pronounced Tricia, to her satisfaction. 'Aren't you, petal? But we'll give you a new pair just in case. And a fresh nightie.'

The new gown was primrose-yellow with a pattern of small white roses. Vikki whispered something to Lotte, who stood closest to the bed, and Lotte, misunderstanding, began to bundle the others out of the room.

'No, darling,' Vikki said. 'You don't have to go – it's just we don't know how much your mum can see and feel so she needs a bit of privacy. You just stay back a bit, that's all.' She held Emily still in her arms, one hand supporting her head. 'As long as you don't mind, that is.'

Off came the old gown and the knickers, and for no more than ten seconds they saw Emily as she was, the skin drawn over the rack of her ribs, the whole body a membranous sac. There were no marks on it, no bruises, although she had been motionless for two weeks. Lying back on the new sheets, in her new gown, she held her breath for five, six, seven seconds before letting it out with the faintest crazing in her forehead, a tiny pulse in one of her eyelids.

'You still with us, Emily, my love?'

Tricia bundled the dirty sheets together. 'She's with us. Not going anywhere yet, are you, Em? Not while there's all this lovely attention.' She winked at Don, who'd just put his head round the door.

Vikki gave Benjamin a squeeze on her way out. 'I expect she'll have a sleep now. You been getting much, darling?' She raised her eyes and pinched the back of his neck. 'Sleep?'

Benjamin said that he did, or he could, but that he had Jim Reeves on the brain.

'That's nice,' Vikki agreed, glancing at the ancient CD cassette player on Emily's sink surface. 'I'm more of a Ronan Keating fan myself.'

The two carers left with their arms full and moved next door to Trombone Herbie. They knocked. No answer. 'Herbie, love, you in there?' They waited. Benjamin stepped out into the corridor, saw the door open slowly and Herbie standing on the threshold, burbling a little, crestfallen. 'Oh, Herb, pet' was all he caught as the women moved inside.

Peggy was next on the horizon, stepping from the lift and approaching Benjamin with her usual look of amused circumspection. A shadow passed across her face, some objection, some rejected possibility.

'I've come up here for a bit of peace and quiet,' she announced before the pout of her lower lip disappeared beneath a slick of bile. She grabbed Benjamin, who caught her with difficulty because her head lolled so extravagantly. He tried to imitate Vikki's firm but cushioning clasp, afraid the old lady might twist her neck. It was like holding a parody of a baby.

Lotte appeared at his side. Together they guided Peggy to the bathroom and Lotte helped clean her up with towels and wipes and toilet roll.

'It's the bug,' she said. 'Carla says they've got it downstairs. You'd better wash your shirt, Ben. And keep using gel on your hands. I've tried to tell Dad, but he won't listen.'

He did as he was told: put on an overnight T-shirt and laid his other shirt to dry on the radiator in the spare room. Nine days of knickers and socks and vests sprawled on the backs of chairs or hung from sagging wire coat-hangers, forming a small army of the missing, the vaporized.

When Benjamin went downstairs to fetch more paper towels and alcohol spray, he saw the scale of the problem, and why it was that the young and the old get the runs so easily – all those fingers wandering into mouths not their own.

The healthy residents were in the dining room, where a frantic male orderly, assisted by Carla Rose, did his best to serve mince, wipe tables and clean hands at the same time. In the corridor a tense silence punctuated by cries did battle with the telly. The home was understaffed, as usual. Between them, Vikki, Tricia, two temps and Carla had to cope with forty residents, half of whom were ill, until other local carers could be found to work an emergency shift. On the inside front doors they posted a warning to visitors – keep out. Vikki and the others ran from room to room with buckets and mops; a faecal stench mingled with the sharper pH of disinfectant. The Alldens' vigil seemed to have taken on some of the qualities of the virus, spreading outwards, expanding until it became a full-scale siege. Returning from the store room, Benjamin found Doris, slumped by the lift, being tended by the reliable Violet – though here, in one stroke, his normal sympathy and pity failed him, quashed by the fear of some deeper contagion. Violet's eyes were knowing and sad.

'I'm going to drop these off upstairs, and then I'll be straight back,' he said, feeling his legs soften and his skin prickle. As the lift doors closed, Violet raised her intelligent face. From the pocket of her orderly's overalls peeped the familiar copy of *Mastering Arabic*.

'Mumma,' she said, a voice on the line from Old Europe. 'Puppa.'

He returned directly, as he'd promised, only to see Carla shepherding the stately teacher around a far corner. Doris had disappeared altogether, leaving behind a few fast-evaporating smears on the linoleum.

To the children of war, it had always seemed natural to help others. Necessity, defined by bereavement, injury and separation, prodded the social senses. But the generous impulse faltered closer to home, where stoicism bred a distaste for weakness, a deep suspicion of incapacity, a hatred of fuss. For this reason the Alldens slept all of their married life on two army beds pushed close together; Emily washed all their clothes by hand for eighteen years; heating was not installed until Benjamin was on the point of leaving home; towels smelt. What didn't kill you made you stronger. If you were still weak after that, or tired, or upset, or needy in any other way, then a strange thing happened: the hand of friendship curled into a fist and resentment found a voice. The self-deniers became the hard-done-by.

'What about me?' Don said, biting the ends of his fingers where his nails should have been. 'Christ, Liz. If you go, and Lotte goes, it'll be just me and Clive, won't it?'

'And me.'

'Yeah, and Ben.' Don's eyes widened as he contemplated the floor. 'It's the same thing, the same thing,' he said, mysteriously. 'Piggy in the middle.'

Lotte reminded him that their uncle Arnold was also

due to visit his sister, at which news Don crumpled in his wing-back chair.

'Oh Jesus, not Arnold too. I'll have to drive him; get him up, get him into the car, get a chair for him here, get him upstairs. It just goes on and *on*.'

'There's no need for any of that, Dad,' Lotte said, with the placidity she reserved for people she considered outrageous. 'No need, now really, is there? He's ordered the ambulance-taxi and the driver will help him in and out. We're his family and he's entitled to see his sister.'

Liz stood on the far side of Emily's bed with her arms folded. She looked at her father impassively, too exhausted to be impatient. 'Anyway, Clive might not get here until tomorrow,' she eventually pointed out.

Don studied Emily as she absorbed her morphine.

'I tell you one thing,' he said, 'it won't be those bloody Church friends of his who step in, when Mum's gone. It'll be me, won't it?' He seemed on the verge of tears. 'He's always telling me how marvellous they are, Geoffrey this and Rachel that. If I've heard it once . . . But where are they when he has a heart attack? Who is it who takes him to St Martin's or ferries him into town to see his friends? Bunch of creeps. Creepsville.' His voice broke. 'That's what gets me. He just expects it. He's not even my brother. Muggins here turns up and Mother Church gets all the thanks. Fucking useless, the lot of them.'

Billy billy bayou, watch where you go, sang Jim.

'I bet you anything you like—' Don continued, before Lotte stopped him, trying to impress on her father the fact that, in this case at least, no one was asking him to drive anywhere.

Don gazed at each of his children in turn, his eyes watering. Ordinarily, they knew, he would be the first in line to offer lifts, but something about his brother-in-law nettled him beyond words, and when the ambulance-taxi bearing Arnold arrived later that afternoon, Benjamin thought he glimpsed it in his uncle's pained expressions of gratitude – 'thank you, yes, yes, oh *thank* you, that's *so* kind' – as doors opened, chairs unfolded, drivers niftily departed and the whole world extended its reverential welcome. He was a devout and loving man who delighted in his family. He had nothing but praise for his nephews and nieces – for Liz's craft and energy, for Lotte's devotion, for Clive's restive intellect and humour, for Benjamin's dogged industry. They were children he loved as his own – and of course it was this, on the face of it, unimpeachable fondness that got Don's goat. Because it made him look small. It even implied, in some weird way, that the children were more Arnold's than they were Don's.

Lotte wheeled the old man out of the lift and into the room, sprayed his hands and bustled about. Liz disappeared to make yet more tea. When she came back with two cups, she offered one to her silent father, the other to Lotte.

At the prospect of refreshment Arnold's loris eyes came to life. He raised one hand towards the tea as it passed in front of him, and mewled.

'Yours is coming, Arnold,' Liz said, hurrying away.

'Yes,' he murmured without lowering his arm, so that Don, at whom he gazed next, was more or less required to say, 'Have mine.'

Benjamin watched in fascination. The morphine would dry up the rest of Emily's secretions, Lotte had begun to explain, though it was all mouthcare now. Don leant over his wife and tried to get a few drops of smoothie past her lips. Her lower jaw clamped upwards in refusal, the reflex movement somehow serving to emphasize a deeper rigidity. Stronger lines now etched themselves in the cheek sockets as Lotte dipped a swab in water, pressed it to the corners of Emily's mouth and drew it across her forehead.

Arnold extended his other hand:

'Yes,' he exclaimed. 'The feminine touch!'

It was the hand not the phrase Benjamin found funny. He wished for a moment that Clive had been there to witness it. He recovered with a cough and Lotte did the same. Their uncle's hand meanwhile stayed where it was, not helping, not assisting, simply indicating. Benjamin realized what it was he had always found odd about crucifixion scenes and pietàs: no one did anything useful in them. Or intervened. They just stood around, hearkening.

Don had begun counting out loud, one, two, three. He meant to mark the intervals between Emily's breaths. The actual effect was a subtle increase in tension within the room. *One, two, three, four . . . thirteen.* 'It's thirteen

now. Getting longer. One, two . . .' Each time the counting restarted Benjamin felt a stab of panic. He realized
he wasn't breathing either; and wondering, as Clive
surely would have wondered, what his father hoped to
prove. The maddening intimacy of the vigil made logic
precious. Benjamin could hear himself (or was it Clive
he heard?) objecting to some internal court of inquiry:
*He's counting at different speeds. She doesn't breathe
evenly. There's no mathematical control. You need to
take samples and average them out as you would with a
pulse. What if she's asleep?* Benjamin's own pulse raced.
He'd laid two fingers on his left-hand wrist. The pulse
disappeared. Arnold's arm was still raised.

The dark shape behind Arnold's wheelchair came from
nowhere. One minute that part of the bedroom was
empty, the next it was full of Clive.

He wore a dirty brown fleece inside a torn anorak, his
hair was long and wet though it had not rained in days.
His eyes were small, quivering. The hard pupils found
Benjamin first, then Don, counting; then Benjamin again.

'Why is he counting?' Clive said. 'What does he think
he's doing?'

Benjamin led a chorus of uncertain greeting.

Ignoring them, Clive asked again, 'Why is he counting?'

Don's voice became a whisper and Clive left the room
as silently as he had entered it. But he didn't go anywhere. The rest of the family could sense him just outside

in the corridor. Benjamin fancied he could even hear his brother huffing, shifting his rucksack from shoulder to shoulder, stopping, cursing.

Before he could stop her, Lotte was out of the room, too, chattering quickly and pacifically, leading Clive away. When Benjamin caught up with them outside the spare room, he saw that Clive was listening with grim intensity to the story of the secretions, the quest for the syringe. His silence penetrated the babble; but the more he listened, grunting here and there in what Lotte mistook for assent, the less sense she made, the more naked her appeal became.

Now she was apologizing, actually saying that she didn't know what she was saying; that she was like a zombie what with the lack of sleep, the kids and the worry, because she *was* a worrier, just like Mum. Clive winced at this piece of unconscious point-scoring while Lotte, feeling his reproof, churned the wheels harder and deeper, insisting that she *knew* Mum knew they were there.

'And how do you know that?'

'I don't know, Clive. I don't *know* how I know, but I just do. I don't know what it is. I've always had a strange feeling about Mum. It must be – I don't know exactly, of course. Something,' she paused, 'in my gypsy blood.'

Benjamin was walking away from them towards the kitchenette. Had she said that, or had he misheard? He looked back and saw Clive with his head bowed and one hand pushing and pulling at clumps of hair.

'It'll be soon,' Lotte assured Clive, 'now that we're all here. I know it.'

'Yes, well . . . it could be any time.'

'Probably as soon as tonight. I wouldn't be surprised.'

'No. Well, you . . .'

'It could have been last night, but something told me . . .'

'Something?'

'I thought "not yet", that's all I can say. She was very weak, and Tricia and I sent for the doctor and he ordered the syringe from Chilcompton. But I thought, no, it won't be tonight. She's a fighter. She's been a fighter all her life.'

Clive seemed to want to grab his own head and tear it off.

'She had to be, didn't she?' Lotte said. 'Being married to Dad.'

If her powers of sympathy were so pronounced, Benjamin wondered, how could Lotte read the situation so badly, make such gross tactical errors?

Now she was embarked on the latest enormity in the Book of Sally, and gaining rapidly in confidence until Clive interrupted her with: 'I can't listen to any more of this rubbish, Lotte.' And steered her into the spare room.

He used no obvious force. He merely stood very close to his tiny sister so that she tottered and swayed in retreat.

'No . . . no, Clive,' she pleaded in vain.

'That's enough from you, bossy-boots,' he snapped,

the childish reprimand a galvanizing mishit. 'Who made you chief carer? Who appointed *you*?' An alarm went off in another part of the building. Voices called and laughed and buzzers buzzed. 'You. You fucking—' The spare room rang with obscenities.

Liz appeared in the corridor and gazed along it, at Benjamin. They were mirror images, each standing trying to work out what to do. The miracle of it was that Lotte didn't run as soon as Clive started, and that neither Liz nor Benjamin felt able to intervene. The outstretched hand is helpless, Benjamin thought belatedly. The truth was that they were both afraid. Clive came at you in waves. They stood like passengers on a boat watching someone in the water.

Lotte tried to remonstrate but her words turned to high-pitched mush. She let out a squeal, though the squeal wavered under the influence of half-formed syllables, a choked sob. Clive was repelled and excited in turn.

'"I'm like Mum" – what a pile of crap,' he spat. 'What fucking rubbish.' He had her cornered now, and knew it. 'Well, I've got news for you, Lotte – though I suspect it isn't news and you're perfectly well aware of it, which is what galls me the most: the person you're *really* like, in *fact*, is Dad.'

Liz folded her arms.

'And if Dad is the feckless adulterer, what the hell does that make you?'

Lotte's meek fury changed register. She howled while

Clive grew imperious. In the kitchenette, Benjamin's arm trembled as he poured hot water into a mug.

'*You*,' Clive said slowly, '*bitch*. Mum may have struggled but the one thing she didn't have to struggle with was her conscience. Don't tell me—'

Benjamin walked up to Clive, smiled and gave him the cup as if he'd heard nothing. It gave Lotte the chance to flee and forced Clive to respond. He took the cup and said, 'Thank you.' Tea bounced out and scalded him. He dropped the cup, as if rocked by an exterior force; and then he began hawking, coughing and gagging as though a gigantic furball had formed in his throat. Benjamin asked him what was the matter. Clive stumbled about the room, knocking into furniture, his head dropped forward like a hanged man's.

He stopped abruptly, shielding his eyes.

'I don't know,' he said. Water filmed every part of his face. 'There must be some kind of – evil welling up in me.' Clive rested his hand on a radiator covered with Don's rinsed-through underpants.

'I thought I heard you, Clive, darling,' said a kindly voice at the door. It was Vikki, who as usual seemed more amused than surprised. She pointed at the knickers in Clive's grasp. 'Don't do that, mind, or your Dad'll love you.'

Clive stared at the Y-fronts.

'Just to let you know the priest is here. Liz thought it would be nice for him to come seeing as he's local and it's no bother. He's signing in now.'

'You go,' Benjamin said to Clive. 'I'll clear up – it's fine.'

'Both of you go,' Vikki said firmly. 'It's only tea.'

They returned to find a tallish young man shaking everyone's hand, waiting for the stragglers to arrive, Jim Reeves playing the congregation in. A little way off down the corridor, Lotte could be heard saying tearful farewells to Liz, who joined them presently. Don, seated, gave Benjamin and Clive each a black look and said out loud: 'Don't ask me. *I* didn't invite him.'

'Dad,' Liz hissed. 'He's in the room.'

The priest smiled. 'So, Emily and Don, everyone.' He stopped, briefly menaced by the silence. 'May I just say what a special privilege it is for me to be here now, as Emily prepares herself for the next stage in life's journey.' They all contemplated the motionless figure. 'Which is the death of the body.'

Clive turned his head to one side and studied the priest.

'But not of the spirit. The spirit which returns to God who gave it.'

'Amen,' said Clive and Arnold.

'And how wonderful it is, Don, Emily, that your three children can be part of the family gathering today.'

'Four children,' Don corrected him. 'There are four of them.'

'Four?' the priest repeated dully. 'Gosh. Even better.'

Arnold lowered his arm.

For some reason, this took the heat out of the exchange. Liz cleared her throat. No longer helpless with each other, the Alldens had a new arrival to inspect; and reason to thank the nervous cleric, as he made signs and said prayers, for demonstrating the calming effects of good behaviour.

'Calming' in a relative sense, of course. To an outsider, Clive's agitated request for the one about 'miserable sinners' might have sounded aggressive – but it was rather the antidote to aggression, Benjamin reflected; the carefully plotted occasion for some fresh demonstration that kept him off boiling point.

The young priest wanted to be obliging.

'You mean, the General Confession?' he said. 'Of course, if you like . . .' He sought approval elsewhere. 'If I can remember it. It's a little – ah, strong.'

'But beautiful,' Arnold suggested. 'Like the "Deus meus".'

'"We have erred and strayed from thy ways like lost sheep. We have followed too much the devices and desires . . ." Isn't that right?' Clive enthused. 'I can remember Hodge saying that and my shoes being covered in spittle. Fatty Hodge. Let's have that one, Vicar.'

The Rev V. W. Hodge had been Clive's primary-school headmaster, an orotund immensity with overactive glands. An ogre in a stained waistcoat.

The reddening stranger now said, 'I have to disappoint you there, too, I'm afraid. I'm not a vicar. I'm only the priest in charge.' He closed his eyes.

'"Almighty and most merciful Father. We have erred and strayed from thy ways like lost sheep. We have followed too much the devices and desires of our own hearts. We have offended against thy holy laws . . . "'

When he got to 'have mercy upon us, miserable offenders', Clive shifted noticeably, repeating 'miserable *offenders*' to himself, as if he didn't believe it. And at the end, while the others murmured their thanks, Clive said:

'I forgot about the offenders. I forgot it was "offenders" not sinners. Sorry about that. Can't think how I got that wrong. But I'm pretty certain it's "spare thou *them which* confess their faults", not "spare thou *those who* confess their faults". No? And "restore thou *them which* are penitent". I'm not sure about the modernization. It's weaker. *Thou them which*, you see. Much stronger. More atmospheric.' Clive gave an ecstatic shudder. 'Terrific words, though, aren't they? The Book of *Common* Prayer. What a great title.'

'They are beautiful words, it's true.' The priest laughed generously. 'And I must say they've stayed beautiful.'

'Apart from the meddling – yes,' Clive said, irritated by the priest's feeble rebuttal. 'Though, on second thoughts, I'm not sure about the *sparing*.'

The priest opened his mouth and shut it again. He didn't want to take part in an inappropriate discussion. People behaved oddly in the throes of grief. One had to make allowances and keep one's distance.

'The point being,' Clive continued, 'that if you're

God – or Henry VIII – you want people to grovel even when there's no hope of a reprieve.'

'Ah. I'm not sure that's what the author meant, but it's a thought – I'd—'

'Oh, but it *is*, Vicar,' Clive said, raising his voice. 'That is *exactly* what Cranmer meant, even if he didn't say it.'

The priest looked at Liz and then at his watch.

It was too late. Once started, Clive had to finish. And, as usual, a part of Benjamin, perhaps a part of everyone else who was present, wanted him to – because if he was shredding someone else, he wasn't shredding you.

'No one knew better than Cranmer that the business of sparing is frankly whimsical. Appeals are neither here nor there. They cut no ice with absolute power.' Clive paused for effect. 'Which is absolutely without mercy.'

'OK, Clive,' said Don. 'Good point. And thank *you* – I'm sorry, I didn't catch your name?'

'Terry.'

'Terry, really, thanks for coming. Super stuff.'

Clive was too interested in his own peroration to mind that people were trying to get away from him. He addressed his last remarks to Arnold, who met his gaze and listened unperturbed as the others let the priest through.

'In fact, the more I think about it,' Clive said, pointing at the priest's departing back, 'the more it seems to me that the text is corrupt. What it should have said is: "Spare thou them . . . for as long as it pleasest thou to prolong the agony.'" He almost laughed. '"Then watch the bastards fry."'

Benjamin had a waking vision of Emily rising from her bed, sitting bolt upright and exclaiming: 'Four children and I've got one of each, haven't I? One married, a single parent, a homosexual, and a black sheep.'

The taxi came for Arnold soon afterwards. As the driver helped Liz and Benjamin manoeuvre their rigid uncle into his seat, Arnold said sadly, 'You'll look after him, when Emily's gone, won't you? Won't you, you two especially?'

'We should talk about this another time.' Liz sounded deadly.

'Because he loves you,' Arnold added. 'And he hasn't got anyone else.'

Liz slammed the door and waved goodbye.

Well, they'd wanted something to happen, and lo, it was happening. Someone, the priest perhaps, should have warned them: be careful what you wish for.

Now as they went back inside and gelled their hands, Liz asked Benjamin if he was planning to return to Jennifer Clay's guest house in Bath overnight. He said that he was, and she pleaded with him: 'Don't. He's completely out of control and I can't face him on my own. Please.' Before Benjamin could think of the right response, Liz said: 'This once I'm asking you. I know you don't want to. I understand, Ben. Do this for me.'

Reluctantly Benjamin agreed to stay and they traipsed up the stairs, listening for voices. They trod more carefully as they approached the room, slip-sliding like the lost residents, arms almost touching.

It was quiet. Clive, leaning over the far side of Emily's bed, tried to angle a small bottle of juice over her famished lips. Don jittered in his chair, eating his fingers. Clive pulled back.

'She's a graven image,' he said helplessly.

Don stood up and almost shouted, '*Hey*, Ben.'

Clive's attention turned to his younger brother.

'How are you getting back to Jenny's?'

Benjamin said that if he was going back, it would only be for a couple of hours.

'Yeah,' Don said, in a panicky voice, 'but let me – I can take you. I can take you back. I've got the car. It's no problem.'

Clive breathed heavily, a mixture of sighs and hoarse rumblings. He was sitting back down now, curled in on himself, a permanent grimace on his face. 'Why?' He spoke with peculiar intensity, not quite to himself, not explicitly to anyone else. 'Let the little shit find his own way back. What does he need a lift for?' His voice came out of hiding. 'He can walk, can't he?'

Without looking at Liz, Benjamin said that he'd prefer to catch the bus and left. It came to him as he went that no one could help anyone else now and that nothing made any difference. People lied and accused and ranted in the face of death because what they did, in the end, made no earthly difference; and because they wanted other people out of the way. That was what it always came back to. At the core of the anger and enmity burned the question: how much did she love *me*? Equally, would have been the living mother's frightened reply. I love you, all of you, equally. But the child's heart is unique, and knows it.

After five freezing minutes at Peasedown's bus stop, Benjamin saw a blue Ford swing out of the lane that led from Sunnybrook. The car jolted to a halt in front of him. It was Liz, her hands white on the wheel, the lines either side of her nose as deeply drawn as Don's. She leaned over and pushed the door open.

Working fast, Clive had turned on her as soon as she spoke in Benjamin's defence. He'd called her a fucking teacher. She couldn't help it, could she? She just couldn't help herself, telling everyone what's what, setting the world to rights. Well, she could fuck off, too. So she did.

Liz was a skilful, studiedly reckless driver. Like her father, she rounded corners at a lick, pushed at speed limits, talked and yawned and shouted as she drove. The Ford bounded across dark, rain-chilled hills towards a necklace of amber lights, a necklace that became a glowing screed, a hot system. They were in flight, the two of them, with the whip of night lashing behind. Liz's mobile rang. It was Don, on speaker. His voice rattled the dashboard: 'What's going to happen to me?' he cried. 'He's gone mad. I'm outside – and he's in there with Mum. It's just her and him now you've gone. And *me*.'

The signal disappeared into a foggy hollow dragging Don with it. As the car surged upwards into the cold clear air, Liz's phone rang again.

This time it was Arnold's neighbour. He'd got back and had a heart attack, or maybe a stroke. They were waiting for the ambulance. Could Liz come? She'd tried Don's number, but he wasn't answering. Where were they now?

Liz and Benjamin got there in twenty minutes but it took the ambulance men another two hours to find Arnold's flat, up the skiddy slope of a 1950s estate. In a chair, and very much like a chair, beaten so as to restore its shape, the old man sought Liz with his eyes as the paramedics docked him into the back of their green and yellow van.

She assured Arnold that he would be all right now, and immediately he transferred his attention to Benjamin.

'You're leaving me,' he whimpered.

'We are not leaving you, Arnold,' said Liz. 'Mum is dying and we can't be everywhere at once. I'm sorry you're not well, but I think you're going to be OK from now on, I do, and we'll check on you in the morning. One of us will get out to see you, I promise.'

'You're leaving me,' he said again.

'Bye-bye, Arnold,' Liz called out as the paramedics shut the back doors. 'You'll be all right. Bye-bye.' The ambulance slid away and Liz said, 'He'll cop it in hospital. That's what happens.'

It was four in the morning when they finally reached

the guest house on Bathwick Hill and let themselves in. Together Liz and Benjamin lay side by side in a double bed in the attic. Far below and outside, the dark canal moved in an iron and stone dream under the bridges and through the town. Liz slept but Benjamin stayed awake, afraid to move in case he woke his sister.

Just after dawn, Don rang, still shouting: 'It's me again, isn't it? The same old thing. Piggy in the middle.'

Liz struggled to reason with him before exasperation got the better of her.

'I cannot help you,' she said, her voice furred with sleep and sleep deprivation. 'I have been up all night with Arnold. I cannot help you, Dad. I am not responsible for Clive. I cannot make it better. I can't, I'm sorry. I am not his father. What can I do?'

'Piggy in the middle.'

'Dad,' she screamed. 'He is *your* son.' Don swore down the phone at that. Then, once more, as if she might din the idea into him or free herself in the process, Liz said: 'He is your son.'

Like men who hang around second-hand bookshops or fringe political meetings striking up conversations, paranoiacs seem to want the stage to themselves. They are chatterers in class. But give them the stage, clear a space for them to speak, and they suffocate. This at least was how Benjamin interpreted matters when he phoned the home after breakfast and heard that Clive had taken himself off at first light, and returned to Hastings. Work needed him. He needed to work.

He had been tearful with remorse, Don said, going on about how he was cursed, a marked villain, the instrument of injustice. It got wildly incoherent, with Clive rolling about the corridors and bumping into walls.

Liz returned to Peasedown, Lotte got straight back on the train and did the same. Benjamin went for a walk on his own, along the Kennet and Avon Canal. Here the boat-houses sprouted pot-plants and stove-pipes while the towpath crackled with cyclists. On Beechen Cliff, hundreds of feet above the city, gulls made lazy figures-of-eight over the highest trees. The branches of the trees were visible, right down to their fingertips, weirdly clarified by mist.

At the bus station, where people talked, the distant quiet of the hillside advised: don't think, don't speak, don't do anything.

Don't upset him. Don't get him going.

It was hard not to hear in the air the sad echo of Emily's rule of thumb for handling Clive. But children know when they are being lied to, long before they are able to justify to themselves how or why it was necessary that they should be deceived. And in deferring to Clive, and to his famous temper, the family had concealed themselves from him – had in effect lied about what they thought and felt. The tactic never worked, because it enraged Clive's deeper sense of fair play, which turned from the fear in their faces and despaired at the only explanation it could find for what it saw there. *Some evil, welling up inside.*

Benjamin walked back along the green canal and down through Sydney Gardens, over the railway and past the tennis courts, around memories of drinks fountains, ice-cream wafers and shoulder-rides, out onto Great Pulteney Street, where the Bath Half-Marathon was about to start. A crowd of numbered runners champed and scuffed the road, some eager to start, others less certain, plumply serious, running for charities maybe. The crowds on either side of the road were three or four thick and Benjamin had to peer for a view.

The first competitor he saw clearly, not five yards away, was a school contemporary, Derrick Someone. Not a close friend, but known to him: shy, diligent, untypical of the sporty crowd in his moderate and orderly approach; Derrick, whose handwriting was small and neat, who played chess and collected stamps and tea cards even in his teens, but who ran fast and was a fine cricketer; who was not mean, who was very good at geography and nothing else; whom other boys didn't mind (or notice) and teachers praised when they remembered to. He lived quite close to the Alldens, on the same estate as Arnold.

Benjamin called out just as the gun fired, 'Derrick!'

The thinning-blond figure looked once, a little crossly, to his left as he jostled for a space in the pack. Benjamin waved at him speeding off, and at the mad idea of hailing anyone like that, forgotten until now, across the street. Derrick Milli – Mini – Minner – what was his name? 'To be perfectly candid,' Benjamin spoke into the noise of the crowd, 'I don't rightly know.'

What detained her, Benjamin wondered? At first he'd thought it was the smothering presence of others, holding on to her. Surely she was a wounded animal who needed to crawl to the back of the cave and die. Now it occurred to him that she wanted encouragement.

She lay, a skeleton with hair. Benjamin found her with his father, who counted long imaginary breaths. Don was holding her hand, very tenderly, eyes half-closed. The girls were in the kitchenette.

Don lifted his wife's Spillikin wrist and said, 'Incredible.' His voice, not even a growl, drifted like smoke from a hole in the ground.

'Dad, I've just come to say goodbye,' Benjamin said. 'I need to get back and wash some clothes. I'll come down again in a day or two.'

'Sure, sure.' Don jerked his head, as though waking. 'Thanks for everything.'

Benjamin went over to his mother and kissed her on the forehead.

'Don't worry about Clive,' he said. He was going to say more, but more seemed inappropriate and impossible. He would say it later. Emily's chest rose a full inch, sinking gradually with a whistle that wasn't breath. Her smell, her decay, had finally silenced Jim in the corner.

'That happens a lot,' Don said, yawning.

On his way out, Benjamin saw that it was hair day at the home. Doris, Peggy, Myrtle and Violet among others were in the day room, their egg-brown faces laid in baskets of white. At one end a joyful girl in her twenties combed and sprayed. She'd wheeled in one of those salon setters, a conical affair, the sort that turns suburban ladies into extraterrestrials.

Vikki approached, coughing and laughing. 'Benjum,' she said, 'Benjumum, my love. What's the matter? Come here, my love. Be strong.' After a short while she checked, 'You strong again? You strong?'

The priest was there, too, by the double doors. He'd loosened his collar, and for a moment Benjamin imagined him coming off shift in the Radstock pit, doubling up jobs as people often did in the country.

Feeling that he had nothing to lose, Benjamin said: 'It was good of you to come yesterday. I'm sorry there was a scene. Perhaps,' he paused pathetically, 'you're used to things being difficult.' He waited for reassurance, and then, wanting the encounter to be over, asked, 'Do you come here often?' That sounded odd. Terry the priest laughed. 'I mean, do many people ask for you at the end?'

'Yes, quite a few. Perhaps more than you'd think.'

The doors clicked to release them. In the forecourt, the priest extended his hand. Benjamin took and shook it.

'You know, I love my job,' Terry said. 'I'm paid to do something I believe in.'

Lotte called Benjamin the next day to say that Emily had died. Benjamin made a few calls himself. The train parted veils of fine rain on its approach to Bath and the sun was out and shining by the time it pulled in. Liz's son Matt, the one who never charged his phone, or complained about anything, had driven down first thing and was at the station to take his uncle to Sunnybrook.

'It's fantastic to see you,' Benjamin couldn't help saying, because it was true. He always wanted to tell Matt how proud he was of him, how at ease and equal he made him feel. And in Matt's freedom and practicality – the fact that he could drive already (he was barely seventeen) and was smart without being clever-clever – he saw through to the truth of Liz's instinctive love.

'Man,' Matt said. 'It's pretty sad stuff.' Almost without a pause he added, 'She looks really nice. They've got her in flowers and – well, you'll see.'

Peggy met them at the entrance, by the lift, her favourite place.

She said politely, 'Are you going up?'

'We are, Peggy.'

'I'm not. I'm going down.'

Matt laughed, and blushed. 'Er, I don't think so.'

'This is the ground, Peggy.' Benjamin tried coaxing her. 'This is your floor. There isn't another beneath this one.'

'Beneath this one, that's right.'

*

When he saw the corpse, Benjamin let out a roar. It had nothing much to do with his better feelings – he could have cheered, he felt so relieved; but grief and death are a body blow, being mortal facts, and nothing can wish them away.

There was something in the idea of death's perfection, however, because Emily's face had set with a sheen to it. Benjamin never would have guessed that the plaster saints and painted martyrs, with their creamy skin and heads leaning to one side, eyelids lowered in ashen ecstasy, owed anything to real bodies, but there it was. They did. The halo of lilies looked vaguely comical.

Back at the house that evening, Liz, Don, Benjamin, Lotte and Matt cooked and ate a peculiar meal in peculiar high spirits. Arnold was still in hospital, better but not well enough to come out. They'd spent the afternoon with him.

But all Don could talk about, to Matt's polite consternation, was Georgie Fame and the time he – Don – had bid too low for a painting by Boudin at the local Bonham's, which wasn't Bonham's then. How Georgie Fame led to reflections on missed opportunities to acquire a masterpiece wasn't altogether clear.

'No one knew it was Boudin, except me,' Don said. 'You wouldn't get that now, with the Internet. Just wouldn't happen.'

They went to bed early, in beds or ancient sleeping bags that Benjamin hadn't seen since their last holiday in France, but Don was up again in a couple of hours with diarrhoea. Benjamin heard much padding about up and downstairs, amid stifled groans and a few forced words of sympathy from Liz.

'I told you to wash your bloody hands. Last *week* I told you.'

She found an old bottle of kaolin and morphine in the mirrored cabinets of the bathroom, shook it vigorously, measured out a tablespoonful and handed it to Don, with a look of not quite fond disbelief.

'Honestly,' Liz said, that word for all seasons and Alldens. 'What a pair.'

From the bathroom window she looked down at the lower lawn and the bushes that separated it from the garden next door. There were fewer than formerly, she estimated, just a hawthorn and some kind of pyracantha. There'd been a cherry-barked tree with white-green leaves, when she was growing up, and a heavy-laden bramble. She had climbed the tree for the pleasure it gave her.

No – there it was. Still there, but smaller. Cut back for the winter.

There You Are

The dampness of the guest-house basement room had an acrid tinge to it, something from the intensity of childhood Benjamin was trying to retrieve. He closed his eyes and followed its trail – and found a boy sitting on a square patch of grass with a magnifying glass, shrinking light, making it smaller and smaller, brighter and brighter until the shred of paper he was holding began to smoke and a tiny black hole appeared, replacing the dot of solar white.

'Benjamin?' A voice was calling from the kitchen. 'If you help me nicely at the laundrette, I thought we could have fish and chips at Evans's.'

After the black hole, nothing much else ever seemed to happen.

'Would you like that?'

The paper never completely caught fire. You could make another sun and another hole, that was all. The prospect of fish and chips was appealing. The more Benjamin thought about it, the more exciting it got, not least because it came after doing something else he enjoyed, which was putting powder on the clothes,

closing the lid and listening to their wet, thumping pun-
ishment.

At the laundrette Benjamin wondered about the heat
from the tumble-dryer. It wasn't as hot as the waft from
the oven and it smelt nicer than the prickly breath of his
grandmother's Hoover, which came when the bag swung
in a certain direction or the machine had to be turned off
and picked clean of hair.

'Has Gran ever Hoovered her teeth by mistake?'

Emily gathered the bags of fresh clothes together and
gave Benjamin a folded towel because he liked to help.

'Don't be silly. Mind, now.'

In a voice which he half-knew couldn't be heard in
the street, Benjamin explained that only this morning,
when he was at No. 4, Granny had removed her teeth
and dropped them on the floor. She ran them under the
tap and put them back in, then got the Hoover out. What
if she'd not replaced her teeth? The Hoover would have
found them. She would have had to send off for more.

Benjamin was almost in tears, later, as they waited
for the bus into town. He didn't want to be silly or in
trouble. As they were walking through Abbey Green he
slipped on a cobble. The mystery of his childishness so
worried him that he barely noticed and got to his feet in
a daze.

'Enjoy your trip?' said his mother, smiling.

Evans's was a palace: it had big fryers behind the
counter and the menu at an angle between ceiling and
wall, sliding-door cabinets with skinny red sausages in

them, a till with jump-up numbers. Tables and chairs, too, with sauce bottles and pear-shaped vinegar bottles, tiles on the wall and pictures of boats. It echoed with activity and chatter and the sound of whistling and cutlery.

There was a moment's anxiety when he asked for his own portion and saw an exchange of glances between his mother and the man serving them. But when it arrived his fish was the same size as his mother's and covered in chips.

After a bit Benjamin admitted that he'd had enough.

'Goodness me,' his mother said, 'you *have* done well.'

Nothing, after that, could dent the little boy's mood, not even the cruel boredom of walking around Woolworth's without being allowed near the pick and mix. 'I just need to get one or two things in here,' Emily said, and he trotted after her, not holding her hand because he didn't have to and because he had the about-to-pop feeling of his lunchtime treat to consider.

'Come on,' she said at the door, 'we're going into Marks and Sparks.'

Emily walked ahead of him in the dark corridor that linked the two stores. It was always dark in Cleveland Passage and Benjamin put on a little burst of speed to catch up with his mum at the back entrance to M&S.

She was holding the door ajar. He was through the door, or almost through, when he realized something was wrong. The door was still being held open. He stopped and looked at the mass of shoppers and women assessing jumpers and skirts, pushing hangers along metal racks, spinning carousels.

'Are you lost?' said the lady holding the door.

'No,' Benjamin said, and ran back to Woolworth's, feeling sick. He didn't like the way the woman spoke or looked. He was confused, with the urge to cry and shout building at the top of his cheeks and behind his eyes.

He stared out of his periscope head at the people in Woolworth's and thought he saw Emily by a counter, in her headscarf. 'Mum,' he called and barged the doors until they gave way. And now he was completely muddled. Had they been in M&S when Mum said, 'Come on,' with that flick of her head which meant 'hurry up'? Or Woolworth's? The woman in the headscarf was not smiling at him and not remotely like his mother.

All he could think of doing was running between the shops. He went back to where the first lady had been, the one holding the door, and stood on the top step, looking out over the noisy expanse at the wrongness which was the truth of being scared. This, the wavering feeling in his legs said, is the end. He heard his pulse. And hooves thundering nearer on a dusty path. He had to think himself away from the sound. It was like wrenching yourself awake.

He walked up to a shop assistant who'd already spotted him.

'Excuse me,' Benjamin said, 'I'm lost. I've lost my—'

The shame of saying it was nothing. The loss was suddenly too real.

'Oh, darling. Don't cry. Don't fret, lovey. It's all right, we'll find her. Your mummy's around here somewhere,

that's for sure. Where did you last see her, can you remember?'

'I was in Woolworth's. She said she needed to get a
few things.'

The initial explosion of grief faded quite rapidly, because Benjamin felt that the assistant understood, but it
was replaced by a growing fear that it was useless in the
end because the person who mattered had gone.

'Can you see her? Let's have a walk and you tell me if
you can spot her.'

There was no one. He saw only legs and trousers and
baskets and old people and tights. They came back to the
counter and after a discussion with a man it was decided
to pop Benjamin on top of the desk so that he could see
and be seen. An important announcement was made
overhead. People turned to look at the skinny boy in the
striped T-shirt, with the pot-belly.

The assistant steadied him with her hand on his ankle,
though in the grip of his uncertainty Benjamin wanted to
shake her off.

'Oh,' said Emily, returning to the counter, 'there you
are.'

She seemed calm, not at all upset or cross. She put
down a bag and reached up with her arms, grinning and
calling to him.

'That was sensible of you,' Emily said as they walked
to the bus station to catch the 207, 'to ask for help like
that. You should always do that, if you're in trouble. If
you're lost.'

It wasn't about anything much, this little traffic in light and shade, but for some reason it was what Benjamin saw when he tried to remember something, and it was true. He wrote the gist of it down on a jotter and went to sleep murmuring 'there you are' against the pillow.

There was to be no formal eulogy. They had half an hour before the next congregation filled the chapel and it was agreed that as many of the Alldens would speak as wanted to. Arnold had prepared a speech and Clive wished to say a few words. The girls would step in if required. Only Don was clear that he wanted to say nothing. 'Dear God,' he'd said in the pizzeria the night before, 'I just want it *over*. All this stuff about the past. I was the one who bloody well lived with her all those years. What does anyone else know?'

He had a point, Benjamin felt, as he watched the chapel of rest fill up the next morning. Deference to ritual does strange things to people's grasp of priorities, and funerals are hardly ever without an element of morbid one-upmanship. It was all a little odd. Neighbours, friends, local characters who'd moved in and out of Emily's daily life seemed relegated to the rear half of the room while, nearer the front, irrelevant cousins and their eager-looking spouses, none of whom had been near No. 2 in years, whispered and nudged. The actual family were squashed together two or three rows back, and when Benjamin finished playing the introit, they had to budge up even more.

Among the mourners at the back it was good to see

Vikki and Tricia from Sunnybrook, their faces placid yet not quite expressionless, set apart by experience from the artifice of their surroundings. It was to Vikki that Benjamin looked when the priest – not Terry, sadly – told the dearly beloved that there was no dementia in Heaven. Encouraged by the horrified silence, he said it again – 'It's true, there's no dementia in Heaven' – and Vikki lowered her eyes.

After the priest, it was Arnold's turn. Liz and Ben wheeled him centre-stage, so that he could address both sides of the crematorium. Again, Benjamin caught the acrid hint of smoke, and shuddered to think of its origin before realizing that it came from his uncle, who wore a mothballed woollen coat.

Arnold faced his audience and gaped. The stroke made speaking difficult; or perhaps it was the urge to be heard that in some way overrode the ability to think in words and phrases.

'I am Emily's brother,' he stuttered, before embarking on a long exposition of the circumstances surrounding her birth, their mother, the drawer that did duty for a cot, Emily's mop of hair, their father's death – 'and she would have been his darling daughter.' On and on it went until the priest eyed the clock and Liz hauled her uncle off, saying, 'That was *very* nice, Arnold. Very good. We haven't got much time, though, and Clive wants to speak.'

Arnold's wet mouth pleaded silently and Benjamin through his tears found himself wanting to shut it forcibly.

An unfeeling he couldn't name, which blotted out the faces around him, made his brow hot and sent seahorse motes swimming across his field of vision. It hid the world and revealed it again. And in the middle of the revelation was Clive, softly audible.

'My mother wrote many letters in a fine style,' he said, 'and this isn't the best of them, but it gives some flavour of the woman – of her stoicism, I suppose. It's the letter she wrote to me after her diagnosis.'

'*Dear Clive,*' Emily had written, '*I do not want you to be scared or worried for me, although I know that you will be, you perhaps most of all . . .*'

Clive soon sat down and the priest signalled to the chapel organist.

Liz said, 'Have we time for one more?'

'I'm very sorry,' said the priest. 'We have to stick to thirty minutes. I have to be fair, for the sake of the others.'

The annoying thing, Benjamin discovered afterwards, was that Emily's was the last funeral of the morning, possibly of the day. There were no others in waiting, no ladies in black gathered at the front doors, no hearses. He saw the organist walking up the cemetery hill, past the silos of cypresses, waving at the last minute to some invisible triggerman or gatekeeper.

He was stranded between worlds at the funeral tea. The garden was moist and green but Benjamin again heard hooves on a foreign path. It wasn't just that the afternoon dragged, as another of Don's pals cornered him to say, 'Which one are you?', it was the way he fell back into the role of the youngest child, without years or significant experience of his own.

'Of course,' said a man in a woollen tie, with cakecrumbs on his lower lip, 'this was long before you came on the scene, back when I shared a flat with Don in Wesley Row. And we were mates with John Hammick.' He paused. 'I don't suppose you know who I mean, do you?'

'The batsman.'

The little man held up a finger. 'Not just any batsman . . .'

'Oh no,' Benjamin agreed. 'The *batsman's* batsman.'

'That's right!' The man was delighted. 'The very same. Now he *was* a super chap. Hell of a drinker, mind – *oof*, we had some big nights, I can tell you – but a super chap. And he and I were, shall I say, just a bit miffed about your dad and Em getting together, because back then, Clive, Emily, *your mum* – she was an absolute stunner. Stunning she was. Cor! It's true. What the two of us wouldn't have given to – to, you know, take her dancing. John especially.'

'You and John?'

'Hammick,' agreed the red-faced man, who for an instant looked angry. And, going a deeper red, coughed dramatically. 'But it wasn't to be, was it?'

At which point he walked off and Benjamin felt the

day relax into chaos, a sort of frenzied reminiscence in which well-wishers avoided talking about Emily for fear of seeming indelicate and talked about themselves instead. Almost any subject would do: an air of hectic improvisation prevailed, which part of Benjamin wanted to capture and preserve, or pin to a cork tile.

His father sat on the great plan chest in the studio, revisiting scenes from his childhood at the prompting of cousins and friends. Clive, next to him, listened with his head bowed, and a tense near-smile on his face.

At Benjamin's approach he looked up, his emotion burnt off, reduced, somehow resolved into a single wobbly expression of compassionate disbelief. Behind them both, against the wall, the two long sides of a substantial timber frame stretched up to touch the plaster-moulded ceiling. Thus enclosed Clive and Don made an intimate if unlikely double portrait, one holding forth for the hell of it, the other quiet, still reckoning.

'Basher Barnes we called him,' Don was saying, recalling the headmaster of his hated public school, Bembridge, on the Isle of Wight. 'It was like something out of *If* . . . – remember that film? Malcolm McDowell? Terrible. Only worse, because the beatings were in front of the whole school, every week. You had to assemble, come in and sit down and watch. Yeah. Awful. And then you – if you were the one being caned, which I was, once – then you had to walk back down the hall, between the rows of boys, and try not to blub or at least not scream, which you *felt* like doing. Of course you did.'

'Totally barbaric,' said Eleanor, Don's sister, who'd flown in from New York. 'Imagine doing that to a child. Ugh. What was Mother thinking of, sending you there? Don? Didn't you say anything?'

Eleanor was a throat specialist, the family brains. She was a rare presence in England, but prized whenever she came over for her patience and truthfulness. She'd emigrated to America at nineteen ('because I didn't want to be cold any more') and married a Broadway composer, met Steve McQueen, hung out with Harry Belafonte. Harry used to ring her on her birthday.

'Oh yeah, sure,' Don said, cowed by his sister's clarity. 'Well, no. No – I didn't want her to know I'd been in trouble, did I?'

'Right,' said Eleanor, disbelievingly.

'But I did tell her about the cabinet minister's son.'

'Ugh,' said Eleanor again. 'I remember that, too.'

Don's marble gaze settled on Benjamin as he explained. The bald man next to Benjamin mumbled the word 'sadist', to which Don responded:

'Oh, completely, completely. Got a huge kick out of it, I'm sure.' He paused. 'And not only was he homosexual, but he also interfered with the younger boys, you know, hands down the trousers, that sort of stuff. We all knew about it. I don't know – I don't think there was any actual buggery.'

At 'not only' Clive turned his head towards his brother.

'I mentioned it in a letter to Mother. I can't remember

how I put it. I mean, I probably thought it was par for the course. I knew it wasn't normal, but . . .'

Benjamin asked: 'Did it happen to you?'

'Me? No.' Don sniffed. 'I wasn't his type, too old. But I knew someone who'd had the . . . treatment, as it was called.' He laughed, horrified. 'I told Mum, probably quite guilelessly, just because I thought it was a piece of news. I wasn't even that interested. Christ, I had to fill up a couple of sides every week, which was a tall order for me. Anyway, she knew the boy's father, who was in the cabinet, the new – Attlee's government. And she wrote to him. And that was the end of Barnes. Woomph. Out on his ear.'

'Was he arrested?'

'Oh, no.' Don seemed surprised by the suggestion. 'Nothing like that, he was just, you know, removed. Threatened with exposure, I imagine.'

The bald man gave a snort and swirled the ice in his glass. Eleanor seemed to want to say something consoling to Benjamin, but for the moment he didn't want to hear any more expressions of sympathy and went upstairs to his sisters' room for a lie down. There he lay for an hour, inhaling the never exactly clean, never unclean fragrance of the spare bed and the spare duvet. Wary of self-pity, he wondered about grief, which seemed blanker, odder by the minute.

He'd been with Jason for a year and still missed him every day. The smell of the bed summoned the homelier smell of Jason's bed, which nestled between boxes of thematically arranged CDs, bought mostly in second-hand shops.

'Shhh, shhh,' his boyfriend said, one night, when Emily was on the slide and Benjamin could only apologize, 'if this isn't making love, I don't know what is.' In the small hours he'd listened to Jason's contented snoring and not known what to do. In the full morning, while Benjamin was in the narrow kitchen, filling the kettle, Jason had stumbled towards him, yawning, stretching, rubbing his belly – and they had gone at it on the skiddy tiles, quietly at first, then with comic abandon, grappling for a hold, braced between oven and sink.

Afterwards they watched a cartoon together – *Monsters, Inc.* – and Benjamin, his head on Jason's chest, really did think it was brilliant.

No great emotion attached itself to these reflections now, as Benjamin lay in Liz's old bed and people trudged past the door on the way to the bathroom. The lingering sense of humiliation was just wounded pride. The silliness of it, the fleetingness, made him smile. Only the smell – a coincidence of similar detergents and would-be restfulness – was far from silly.

Laughter broke out downstairs, one man's in particular, his gaiety seconded by others. Someone was coming up the stairs, saying, 'Oh, Jesus,' sounding stunned. Benjamin got up and went out onto the landing to greet Clive.

Behind him, a few stairs down and doubled-up, was the bald joker, Jeremy Naish, the man with ice in his glass. Jeremy's moustache had survived the years with limpet disregard for the loss of hair elsewhere. Clive, meanwhile, was struggling to understand what had happened, trying to make light of something, his hand unsteady as it shadowed his mouth and face.

'Ben,' spluttered Jeremy, 'it's a classic, really it is. We've been having such *fun*. I'll let Clive tell you. Oh – I know I shouldn't laugh . . .'

Don't, then, thought Benjamin, turning to his brother.

'He said he was Ken Livingstone,' said Clive, in a delayed panic. 'I didn't recognize him when he came up to me and said hello, and – after he said, "You don't recognize me, do you?" . . .' – Clive quivered – 'he told me he was Ken. Said he'd had enough of being Mayor of London: he'd sorted out the traffic there, and now he was going to sort it out here.'

'Did he tell you?' Jeremy asked when Benjamin came back downstairs, and Benjamin nodded, strangely emboldened by what he perceived to be the other man's deeper guilt and confusion.

'I suppose there is a resemblance,' Benjamin said, lightly. 'A faint one. I've always liked Ken.'

Jeremy hesitated before replying. He twisted his glass in his hand, crunching the last of the ice. He wore an instantly familiar blazer with frayed cuffs, from which one of the gold buttons now hung by a thread.

'Clive's a funny lad,' he said at last. 'Always has been. Is he all right?'

'Not really,' said Benjamin.

Jeremy appeared to ignore him, distracted by the elderly woman with big spectacles and round, expectant eyes, who hovered nearby. Both men waited so that she might introduce herself. Jeremy made a small gesture from which the woman shrank, her round eyes growing rounder with alarm.

'I couldn't help noticing his teeth,' the dentist confided. 'I realize that may seem, ah, impertinent, but I expect you know – it's one of the signs. Ah. Has he – got anyone?' It wasn't an enquiry that hoped for a reply.

Benjamin, however, explained that he'd tried once before to coax Clive into making an appointment. It had been a covert operation: an attempt to get his brother on the books of the mental-health services in Hastings by recommending a sympathetic dentist who treated people with problems. Jeremy nodded.

'You can't force it,' he said. 'And that's an important point. Unless they're a danger to themselves or to others . . . Millie? Come back over here, darling, You remember Benjamin, don't you? Emily's youngest?'

The owl-eyed lady with short hair drifted back. Jeremy touched her shoulder comfortingly and Benjamin struggled to see in her the battleaxe who'd watched her first husband drive off thirty years ago or more. Where was the wig? The hatred? She could barely speak, managing just a tremulous 'hello' and some highly self-conscious murmurs of assent, rather than thanks, when Benjamin offered his belated congratulations.

'Good God,' he said to his father, some moments later. 'Jeremy and Millie.'

'Yeah,' Don said. 'Been ages now. Rather him than me.'

'Is she all right?'

'Who, Millie?'

'She seems very withdrawn.'

'Oh, that. She's always been miserable. An absolute drag, I'm sorry to say.'

'But she's got an illness, Dad. She's ill.'

'Yeah, always.' Don, still framed by the two bits of timber, sucked his breath in and straightened up. 'I wasn't surprised when they got hitched. Everyone else in the street was, but not me.' He brooded and Benjamin wondered if he should leave him alone. Then his father said, 'It does seem to be a pattern.' He chuckled drily. 'First the accident, with Peter – never forget that, awful – then Julie, and now Millie. Underneath that smoothie-chops exterior, there's something going on. He must be what Lotte would call a *natural carer*, shall we say?'

'Aren't most people, in the end?'

Don took another deep breath. 'Maybe. Yeah, try to be. Try to be.'

In the room they'd once shared, Benjamin found Clive pointing at a wall of stacked paintings where the piano had been.

'Surely it was yours,' Clive said. 'Weren't you upset?'

He thought about it for a moment. 'Was it his to sell? I'm surprised Mum didn't put up a fight.'

'She may have done, I don't know. I don't live here, do I? It's not my home.'

'Is that what you think?' Clive said, quickly. 'I'm afraid it's still *my* home. I can't think of it in any other way.'

Together they considered the paraphernalia of framing that had moved in from the studio next door, the mitre vices and foot-operated Danish guillotine – the Morvø – the lengths of moulding in the alcove where Clive's copies of *The Ring* magazine used to sit next to Clausewitz, Herodotus, *The Gallic Wars*. On the one remaining shelf, a few older books still hid between newer volumes, staring back at the brothers, daring them to take notice.

'You were good at the piano, weren't you?'

Benjamin hesitated. He was in the mood to admit something and aware of the moment's power over him.

'No, I wasn't,' he said. 'I'm not sure how that rumour got started. I suspect I may have spread it about a bit myself.'

Clive frowned. It seemed to him that his brother lacked subtlety: there was no shame in being an adept, and no virtue either. He wasn't appealing to Benjamin's self-estimation. He wanted to establish the truth, nothing else.

'I play the same things,' Benjamin went on, 'and I don't mind that I play them badly because I'm not playing them for anyone else. I'm dogged, that's all.'

Clive listened, intently.

'Perhaps,' he allowed.

'You're a better writer than me. More talented.'

Clive went to the bookshelf and traced a few spines with his grubby fingers. They paused at *War and Peace* before settling for *Grave Humour*, a collection of waspish epitaphs for the unlamented.

'The thing I really remember about Jeremy Naish,' Clive broke out, 'the thing I always hated, was his chumminess.'

Benjamin found himself surfacing in the middle of the conversation.

'He was always so bloody nice to me,' Clive continued, 'even though I knew he didn't like me. Or maybe wasn't interested – that might be nearer the truth. At least you know where you are with Dad.' He sniffed. 'If Dad isn't interested, he yawns at you – it's that simple. But when I went round to Julie for my maths lessons, Mr Naish – or Jeremy as everyone seems to be calling him – used to clap me on the shoulder and shake my hand and . . . go through this charade of being pleased to see me, which I never could stand. Still can't. What's it for?'

Clive's eyes glittered. He had a magician's way with recasting humiliation so that it became a moral breastplate, a sign of introverted grace.

'He might as well be Ken Livingstone, mightn't he? It's just all *wrong*.' He flicked through a few pages. 'And by the way, Benjamin, I'm pretty sure I didn't encourage him by being nice myself, because I had no respect for the man.'

As usual, faced with Clive, Benjamin was at a loss. It was impossible to comfort him. It was impossible to disagree.

'What I mean is – *I couldn't be bothered.*' Clive widened his stare. 'And it was the same thing with the maths. All I used to do was turn up, talk to Julie, drink tea and eat cake. Every week. I'd already decided that since I couldn't be very good at it, I wasn't going to try at all. And that's the nub of the issue, really, Benjamin. This business of being dogged, as you put it, the method or the pace – behind all that is a *decision*. Whether or not one is objectively able to do something isn't the point. If you decide you can't, that's it.'

Whatever Clive said, you ended up believing. However brutal, however shorn of compassion, or maddened by strange, secret fears, whatever he said blazed with truth. It resolved to a point of incendiary simplicity, like the dot of sun on a child's scrap of paper.

'What's this?' Clive murmured, replacing *Grave Humour* and taking the next book along on the shelf. It was a Penguin Classic in the old black livery. '*Poems of the Late T'ang.* I don't recall buying any poetry.' He glanced at his brother. 'One of yours? Since when were you interested in the late T'ang? *Were* you?'

'No,' Benjamin confessed. He took the slim volume and turned it over. 'Three and six, you see, which was 17.5p, so I could afford a book that looked like yours and get five chews with the 2.5p left over from my pocket money.'

Clive raked his hair. 'If you say so,' he said, tiredly. 'Doesn't sound quite natural to me. But if that's what you did, that's what you did. I'd have spent the lot on sweets.' He smiled. 'Or women.'

The note of dismissiveness was not meant. Benjamin picked up his bag and started to leave. As he did so, tears flushed unexpectedly from Clive's eyes. He apologized and turned a tight circle in front of the alcove.

'You're not going, are you? I thought you were staying the night.'

'I want my own bed,' Benjamin said. 'I've got work in the morning. What about you – when do you have to be at the factory?'

'It's not a factory, it's a – a warehouse.'

'The warehouse, then.'

'Not until next week.' Clive spoke into his hands. 'Some time.'

'Why don't you go back early? That's the other thing about work. It sees you through. You don't have to do it very well. You just have to keep going.'

Clive looked at Benjamin out of the corner of his eye, his head on one side, and for a vanishing instant he was fourteen again, considering the discipline of heroes and the eye of the camera, waiting for the blinding flash.

People were leaving. The studio was empty. From its bay, Benjamin looked down on the remaining guests, enjoying the warmth of the afternoon. Apart from Liz and Lotte – and Arnold, grappling with some pie – they were mostly strangers. Then he spotted a figure he did know, on the arm of a young woman, the two of them picking their way down the steep path at the back. The man's face was hidden; there was nothing much to go on – apart from the companion, chic as her mother in a black dress and grey sweater, her hair messily gathered up. Instinct identified the family doctor Neil Pattison – and his daughter, whom Benjamin had only ever touched through the skin of her mother's belly, in France (and then only because he knew Mrs Pattison, being French, would not mind).

He considered running after them to say hello. He saw a ghost in shorts act on the thought, skidding down the grass and being caught before he hit the garage wall. Benjamin preferred the happening vision to the prospect of an encounter made awkward by the doctor's desire to be on his way.

Above the departing Pattisons rose Bellevue Crescent, where Millie used to lean forward as she sat on her up-stairs loo. And above that row, the rest of the city waited in stony tiers, the faces of nearby houses personal and complete with curtains and window boxes, the far side of the valley always lusher than one remembered it and more available, somehow, to the imagination.

In the middle of the hill opposite, directly above Sydney Gardens, the railway and the canal, lay Sham Castle – a Victorian folly nibbled by blackberry bushes in Benjamin's youth, and now lost to view behind bigger trees. But it was still there, he felt sure. The Romantic masons had cut crosses into the facade. They were bitemarks, Dad said – the traces of savage tyrannosaurs from the hell of prehistory – and bitemarks they remained.

'I *am* gullible,' Benjamin said out loud. As the light dimmed in the garden below there seemed the possibility that this was not a matter of shame, merely the truth of his character. He had always believed what he was told. Others were more likely to be right. He would always be found out.

Don liked putting stones on the ledge of the sash window. Benjamin picked up one of these stones and saw that it was a fossil, probably from a field near Devizes, where the ploughs unearthed a new crop every year.

He recognized it as a brachiopod – an ancient shellfish, that is; not, as he had long preferred to think (until an incredulous Jason put him right), a piece of petrified brachiosaurus shit.

He knew enough to know that he knew nothing. As he waited for his train, it struck him that his brother's fear of mediocrity amounted to the exact opposite. Clive thought he knew something, and discovered that it wasn't enough.

Hastings bus station was closed because of a burst water main, so the coach stopped a fair way back in the new town, almost in St Leonard's, which was a place Clive instinctively avoided. The white-lit square had him cornered. To his annoyance, he found he did not know how to get out of it, or where the roads led. He didn't even know where the seafront was: a gradient could be deceiving. It took him an hour to get home to Church Crescent on the far side of Hastings proper and another ten minutes, in the sludgy murk at the bottom of the steps, to seethe, lose his cool, dance about and then find his keys.

Inside the flat he almost tripped over the jars of fat. The door squealed: Clive remembered how frightened he was of the mice in the cellar.

It was cold. He had no gas, no food – apart from a tin of chunky chicken, somewhere – and anyway the oven was gummed up. He had seen a mouse in there, too, behind the glass, doing circuits. In Irene's old breadbin there were some softened ginger nuts. Clive ate them standing up.

He decided to go for that walk. He located a couple of cigarettes, and cradling the lighter's flame as he walked began to feel that things were not so bad.

He'd been pondering his conversation with Benjamin and growing more convinced of his position, which was that decisions, not abilities, guided one's fate. As he turned left at the bottom of the High and out onto the western end of the front, where the A road curled up the hill and Rock-a-Noy became shingle, Clive realized he'd been making a decision for a long time.

The first part of which had been to let the money run out. Agatha, Don's mother, had left each grand-child in the region of £10,000. It was a lot of money, if you did something sensible with it. The second part was the difficult vow not to sell any more books back to that charlatan antiquarian who'd fleeced him in the first place. The third was to forget about approaching Barry, after Clive had seen him bottle a defaulter in the Tanners' Arms on New Year's Eve. The debtor's soft cheek had split like raw pastry. That was the real Hastings for you, in case you were wondering. And now he was on the beach, the foreshore, waiting for the guy in the sweatshirt, punching the air, to move on. The youngster jogged slowly, stopping to try combinations, his progress slowed by pebbles. Soon he vanished between flaking skiffs and black-louvred boathouses.

Clive was alone at the slopping sea's edge. He found the stretch he wanted, with the rubber underlay of bladderwrack, and lay down in it.

Something came to him, as he entered the water: the sense that he was doing this though his body might object; but also the vivid elation of the far side – not so far now – streaming into view along with his mother in the spectators' gallery, above his retching coughs and the echoes of fraught kids and bored teachers; something about Benjamin wanting to go home, saying in that smug way he had, but affecting a tougher voice, where is *your* home, where do *you* live?

The questions stopped but the put-on voice continued, speaking to others, giving names, a description of where they were on this hot night. *Oh, let it,* Clive thought, warmly. Benjamin, if you could credit it, was wearing a sweatshirt from Westhill Boxing Club. Typical. Since when had his kid brother started wearing sweatshirts? Who did he think he was?

Stop thrashing about, the teacher shouted, you're doing it, you're doing it, yes you are I can see you, that's it, *there you are*.

Whatever Power

'Nearly there, nearly. Ya de da. Christ, it'll have to do.'

Don read it over again, mumbling and tutting, then stuffed the piece of paper in his back pocket and came down the stairs. Liz, already behind the wheel outside her house, with Matt in the back, watched her father's jagged sideways momentum carry him unsafely over the threshold.

'Careful! Take it slowly . . . *slowly* . . . lock the door, that's it.'

'I thought you said we were late.'

Liz smiled at her son in the rear-view mirror.

'We don't have to be there until eleven, so we can *all relax*.' There it was: the sound of her own voice. The thing that made her stiffen when she caught it. 'No one's waiting to turf us out,' she went on, more evenly, as Don got in. 'I spoke to Ygor, and he said he'd leave the hole open. All we have to do is turn up, do our bit and go when we're finished. Now – if the chariot would be kind enough to start, there we are, there – no, once more – thank you, we can be off.' The car bucked and stopped. 'Handbrake. Got it.'

'Oh, man.'

'Matt. Calm down. *Everything* is under control.'

They pulled out into the South London traffic, and after the usual hiatus – that moment of kin limbo that comes when families embark on a much-anticipated voyage – Liz asked if Don was happy, or at least satisfied.

'Hell, I've no idea. Words, um, not my thing. Probably a load of crap.'

Moments later, into reflective silence, Don said, 'Your spare room is a really nice room, Liz. To work in – well, to be in, stay in. Very restful. If I were a writer, I could just see myself at that desk, looking out . . .'

Liz thanked him. If she hadn't been driving, she might have been more effusive. He was such an easy guest, coming with wine and odds and ends of food, and a list of people and exhibitions he wanted to see. The remark about the house was personal: a coded compliment. It was his way of saying he was proud. He said it the way he could. And yet it was tinged with sadness, for her, because she yearned not to speak in code, and the wariness of his affection implied that she was somehow intimidating.

They made it to St Pancras and Islington Cemetery in good time, only to be barred from using the parking bays by an official who waved his arms behind tinted glass. The sign by the raised barrier read: 'Drop Off Only'.

Liz wound down the window to demand an explanation from Clive, who'd made his own way from Hastings by train and was now considering the problem of the bays with his customary sideways glance.

'They're for the use of patrons,' Clive said. 'Obviously you can't have the whole world knocking on the door. There's no room. Look at the place.' He indicated the huge acreage of graves and sepulchres behind him. 'And these are just the people waiting to *park*. God knows where the bodies are.'

One bay was nevertheless in use, filled by a black cab from which Lotte and Benjamin were in the process of removing Arnold, whose orthopaedic boot had become involved with the fold-away wheelchair. Struggling to maintain his dignity, Arnold, as ever, persisted in thanking the driver for his patience.

'You've been so kind.'

The driver took a cup of coffee from a holder bracketed to his dashboard and sipped it twice ('oh, my *foot*') before punching a new postcode into his GPS.

Liz left the car on Finchley Road and doubled back. At last they were assembled, with Clive and Arnold at the head of the procession as it moved out into the maze of lilac-grey lanes and pathways.

Most plots were open to the elements, in bright sunlight or grazing rain – but not Emily's. Hers belonged to an older part of the terrain, in a close-knit, ivied and eroded grouping so overhung by field maple and oak and yew that a visitor might pass it by and not know anyone was there. The faded names on the other stones made room for her, offering the bleak reassurance of ultimate anonymity. She was to be interred with her parents, Irene and Arnold, at the far end of the cluster, away from the road.

There was a standpipe by the entrance to this imperfect glade, and a torn plastic tub – the bottom half of a petrol-carrier. Clive filled it with water and brought it back to the graveside, where Don did the planting.

They'd all brought something to put in or around the urn: Liz had flowers – the geranium Don was firming into the earth – and a bead necklace she'd made about the time of her first trip to France, Benjamin some sprigs of oak he'd grown and a page from his old blue notebook. Lotte and Clive came with flowers, too, though their main contribution was the headstone, with three names simply inscribed above a line from a poem written by Emily herself, which Lotte had discovered in a drawer.

Benjamin asked Don if he minded the fact that there would be no room for him next to Emily when his turn came, and he seemed surprised. 'No, no. It's not that I don't care, but – well, I don't. Not particularly. I'll be gone, won't I?'

The urn contained a surprising quantity of ash.

'Let's put a bit of her around the pot – around the roots,' Liz suggested. 'Get her into the soil a bit more.'

'Good idea,' said Don. Then of course the others wanted to sprinkle their mother into the earth and a sort of routine developed, even if Arnold couldn't throw his sister very far and had to be tipped forward at the grave's edge.

'Not sure what I've got here,' Clive said. 'Feels like a leg. Who's got the other one, that's what I want to know. Liz? Benjamin?'

Clive stood by Lotte, who took his arm. Don was usefully employed, mixing ash and soil, watering, pressing down. He finished, got to his feet and was about to speak, it seemed, when Arnold took his place ('I would like to say a few words') with a broadly familiar eulogy. But there was no hurry, after all, and this time round, a year on, the sentimental anecdotes – the mop of hair, the drawer for a cot, the darling daughter – had a less anxious, happier fluency.

Liz thanked her mother for bailing her out when she went to school drunk – 'how did I manage that at nine o'clock in the morning?' – and for 'letting me bring twenty of my friends back from the pub one Christmas Eve and never complaining'. Benjamin remembered fish and chips at Evans's. Like Liz, he posted his words inside the pot, and at last it was Don's turn.

Brief and unsparing, his letter bore the imprint of a life's work. It was written in the clear and truthful register of one who doesn't suspect himself of having much to say, still less of being equipped to say it: 'You cannot know, Emily, how much I miss your patient, good advice.

'Here is the lace butterfly given to us by Miss Voy, our boarding-house landlady, on our honeymoon in Dorset. It was to bring us luck, she said, and we had need of that even then, when the car I'd hired turned out to have no brakes.'

The children, having never before seen or heard of this delicate enclosure, had their one chance to inspect it before Don folded the wings together and placed it inside the urn. Neither Clive nor Lotte wished to add more, and as they left their mother the Alldens each in turn, caught up in the universe of their improvised ceremony, nodded to the young gravedigger in the Arsenal shirt, who stood leaning on his space at the glade's entrance, waiting for them.

'It felt like a family,' was Clive's verdict, as he said good-bye to Benjamin at London Bridge. 'And Dad's letter was – well, I was impressed.' He scanned the departures board. Clive, so unlike Don in other ways, was similarly amazed that people did and thought of things he hadn't himself anticipated.

'He *kept* the butterfly. Or no, I suppose Mum kept it. Let's not get carried away.' They both smiled. 'The point is, he knew what to do with it, which by the way confirms something I've always felt about Dad.' Clive stopped and shifted, as though kicking off a pair of formal shoes. 'Which is that if you can let go of the fact that he's not ever going to be very sympathetic – and why the hell should he be? – you've still got someone who's utterly dependable. He doesn't deliberate. He does things unquestioningly.'

They were standing near a baguette franchise. A radio babbled behind the sandwiches, intermittently audible in the mid-range of hard soles and phone calls, pierced by gate alarms. The noise ebbed briefly and an enthusiastic woman could be heard saying, 'Jill, in Manchester, with *her* boredom, has rewound all her wool into very neat balls. Here's a song for you, Jill.'

'On which note,' Clive said.

But Benjamin could sense his brother's disappointment. Clive cared about the manner in which he said goodbye. Leavetakings left an impression.

'When do you go walking?'

Clive had wanted to go walking in the Lake District for his birthday, and Lotte had said she'd go with him. Clive was greatly looking forward to his holiday: he'd bought maps. Lotte had booked the pub hotel.

The moment I wake up, before I put on my –

Gesturing towards the music, as if it must be relevant in some way, Clive said, 'Two weeks' time. Yes, it should be good. I'd better get in training for the Wast Water Round.' He patted his stomach. 'I've been telling Lotte to do some preparatory walks, too, but she's not taking any notice.'

'She'll be fine.'

'Will she? It's not just any old walk. It's pretty punishing with a load. Fifteen miles at least – and the path isn't always clear. You need to have your wits about you.' Clive summoned the wilderness, and with it the spectre of Don scoping the Welsh hilltops for knackered Paras. 'I won't be hanging around if she twists an ankle or falls into a tarn. Mountain Rescue will turn up and there'll be nothing left but a few eagle feathers and a bloodstained copy of *OK!*.'

Clive was now pointing at Benjamin and jabbing occasionally. He caught himself, perhaps saw the joke distorted in the glances of people running for their trains, and lowered his arm. He could still rant, evidently. The old ability flapped around a chamber in Clive's mind, but its claws were blunted, its fire relaid in a swept-clean hearth – and how or when this change had occurred none could say. Don, with a practical emphasis, spoke approvingly of Lotte's pursuit of the social services, of Liz's help with the flat; Benjamin, too, had taken Clive to see the doctor and written letters. Above and beyond that, the transformation, or was it retrieval, had been self-willed. Bereavement shows us who we are and demands a response. And Clive had responded: after years of lying about a non-existent job, he now weeded the grounds of a local hospice. It was a start. Other ghosts were laid: he had been to the dentist. He could even hear his father say, 'Hey, nice *teeth*!' and comfortably resist the urge to clobber him.

At the ticket gates, Clive's haversack got trapped and Benjamin saw his brother's face pale at the mad, one-note alarm. An attendant rescued him and sent him lumbering away down the platform, feeling for the straps as he ran.

Benjamin heard voices in his head – Clive's, principally, saying, 'No one ever changes: it is our fate to become more and more like ourselves,' but also his own thin plaint, 'What if we don't know ourselves very well? What if the person, and the story, we recall could be here now, to say: Oh no, you've got it wrong. *I am who I was, but you – you are always a different person.*'

Clive stepped into the carriage just as the whistle went. At the Underground entrance, Benjamin saw a startled middle-aged man close in and then turn turtle in a crowded sheet of glass. It was an unsettling encounter: the reflected face a perfect blank. God forbid, he thought, that we should find we were neither as confident and clever nor as shy and troubled as we've been making out.

In the predawn of his childhood there had been a period of some weeks when Benjamin got up every day at six in the morning, while the others were asleep and the painted colours of the front doors in his street were still emerging, and wrote in his blue notebook. The poems he produced were the spontaneous effects of waking, about trees, cats, shadows, volcanoes, time and God, whatever he could bring to mind. He'd lost the book but the experience of writing it laid down a circuit that came alive forty years later, in his flat, before dawn.

He'd been dreaming about the Formica table at which he used to sit, the little books he made from cheap lined paper and the gas fire on miser rate.

He searched the dream for a meaning, which faded as he searched and saw, through his blinds, that the curtains in the house opposite, like the doors of child-hood, were not yet day-coloured.

For some reason, it occurred to him to say: 'What made you wake me so early?' and the circuit leapt: an-other dream in place of the first.

His shoulders were being shaken by his mother.

'Wake up,' she was saying. 'It's a beautiful day. Let's go to the seaside. Never mind about school!' She grinned at her mischief. 'It's just one day.' So they went to the seaside, to Weymouth, the two of them.

So Benjamin went once more to the seaside, to Wey-mouth, though not directly. (The delaying tactic was itself dreamlike.) First he caught the train to Dorchester and then the bus to Abbotsbury, near to the Portland cove where Liz and Lotte went camping with the chil-dren every year. He found them on the beach, just out of the water and drying off in their tents, in various states of exposure.

'It's, like, so cold it's not even funny,' said Ade, shiv-ering with laughter. 'Liz doesn't care. She's a seal. She's already waterproof.'

'I'm all right,' said Lotte. 'I've got a fleece.'

'My fleece,' Ade pointed out.

'That's right, and you're not getting it back.'

They made a fire on the beach and took pictures of Liz and Benjamin buried under a mound of pebbles and shale. 'Now stay there,' said Ade.

'I'm so pleased you came!' Liz said, walking her brother back to Abbotsbury. 'What made you think of

it? Such a nice surprise. We've been coming for years.
I've often thought of asking you but I didn't . . . I know
you're busy.'

They kissed each other goodbye, and Liz was moved,
a little tearful.

It was the beginning of September, the end of the
school holidays. Benjamin stepped off the bus onto
Weymouth promenade where the warm wind was full of
brackish ozone and beer and fish and chips, cut by wet
sand.

He followed his nose and poked around the back-
streets, which were surely unchanged. The assortment of
pubs and toyshops with flimsy orange nets in doorways
and cartoon-stencilled plastic rings, and real fishing
shops with real rods and tackle – all felt familiar. There
were the seaside bookshops, too, with their sun-bleached
displays of guides to the Jurassic coastline, novels by
Winston Graham and large-format railway-maritime
histories; postcards in shoe boxes, some in plastic wal-
lets; horror paperbacks and green Margery Allinghams.
Further back, where the High Street stores reasserted
themselves, there were also charity shops, reminders
of Saturday afternoons with Jason lost amid the odd
glasses, odder shoes and pictures of frosty riversides.
Benjamin returned to the beachfront. He walked past the
beach cafes, with their red, white and blue awnings, and
the trampolines. A vacancy had replaced – something.

The woman in the Lifeboat shop expressed her aston-
ishment.

'You can't find the donkeys?'

She gave a pregnant lady on a stool a large mug, almost a jug, of tea, stirring it for her and keeping hold of the spoon.

'Our donkeys are famous, my love. Mind, I spec they've finished now the little buggers've gone back. That's what it is.'

She took a tea towel from a cardboard box, shook it open and sighed at the words 'Cromer Lifeboats' emblazoned across the top.

'They win a prize every year, the donkeys at Weymuff.'

The lady on the stool made cooing noises, as if to say 'Yes, they do, and deservedly, though no one else knows about it or cares'.

'They're the best-kept donkeys in the whole country,' the shopkeeper went on. 'And I'll tell you something else – they've more rights better than what we have. They have a lunch break, a coffee break, you name it. It's the life of Riley, that's what I reckon.' She gave the box of tea towels a pat. 'If you're a donkey.'

After a pause, the pregnant lady blinked at Benjamin and returned to an earlier topic of conversation in tones of unmissable confidentiality. (She'd asked why she was so large, and the doctor said, the doctor said . . .)

A part of the town Benjamin did not recognize was the park – Nothe Gardens – overlooking the harbour and, on their far side, a not quite convincing Victorian fort. The Gardens circled the headland in tiers, with seats and flower beds lower down and a wilder, thicker band of trees and linking paths higher up.

The trees were relatively young, with golden bark the colour and sheen of hazel, growing in clumps around what looked like much older remnants: English elms, a notice said. Benjamin had not seen a native elm before, and was surprised to find the leaves covered in fine hairs which irritated slightly, like mild nettles. He looked around for seeds and became aware that he was being watched by a groundsman sitting in the cab of his van with the door open. Embarrassed, Benjamin explained what he was doing. The man scratched his arm.

'Don't have seeds, do they.'

'Oh.'

'They sucker – all round.' With his finger the man traced the perimeter of the Gardens and the road which followed it. 'They're suckers.'

'I probably shouldn't ask, but can I take one, a heel?'

The ground beneath the elms was covered in succulent woody shoots, the suckers of suckers. The man mouthed 'no' and shook his head.

'It's habitat for the *hairstreaks*,' he said, with factual disdain. 'Protected.'

Leaving the path and, later, Weymouth, Benjamin felt disappointed, and because the feeling was one he'd slyly sought out, foolish into the bargain. He'd tried to make a pattern out of unrelated things: the moment of inspiration on waking, the family holiday, the charity shops, the groundsman and the elms, the absent donkeys. He could see the potential for a few postcards, maybe, but no more than that. And the lesson was that you shouldn't go looking for significance: it wasn't ahead or behind. If it was anywhere, it was by your side, an invisible companion.

He stayed the night at a guest house in Winterbourne Abbas, halfway between Abbotsbury and Dorchester, and decided to pay the extra for an evening meal.

The only other guests were a pair of elderly women, one friskily alert and poker-thin, the other meekly contorted, with a windswept spine. Impossible to tell the nature of their relationship, though when the tall thin lady barked over melon and ginger that she was really a DRIVING INSTRUCTOR, Benjamin glanced again at her crushed friend and found himself wondering.

To mask his curiosity, he told them quickly about Emily and Don, on their honeymoon in Dorset, in the car with no brakes. The thin lady roared.

'That sounds DANGEROUS,' she said, before lapsing into a digestive silence. Then, as if in response to an unspoken question from a hidden guest, she added, 'Oh, yes, we've been coming here for years.'

Benjamin signed the visitors' book in the morning. In the comments column he echoed the sentiments of the other guests. Wonderful. Relaxing. Very peaceful. 'Demented,' Clive whispered in his ear. 'Thronging with lesbians.'

He took the train to Bath.

'Hey! Ben!' Don grabbed him by the shoulders and bundled him inside the house. 'I want to show you this. I've just finished it. *What. Do. You. Think?*'

It was Emily's black-and-white quilt, or a large part of it, with a complex polygonal star shape in the centre. Benjamin recognized the frame from the day of the funeral. It had been in two halves then, on top of the plan chest. But now that they were mitred together and the surface treated, distressed, as if ornament had been applied and stripped away, the effect was weirdly disturbing.

Splendid, of course – Benjamin said – but maybe too grand for a chamber piece? For something that had not wanted to be made into art.

'Not that,' Don said, steering his son away from the wall. 'Jesus, no. I got that completely wrong. Got to do it again, much plainer. No, *this*, over here. I found it by accident, in one of his old folders. With the battle scenes.'

The intricate drawing showed a winged figure, a man, the wings not fully open, propelled outwards from a pair of closing gates. Above the gates, and lining the ramparts of an immense fortification or garrison with towers like organ pipes, soldiers and dogs observed the expulsion, which bore no single sense: some of the men waved, others jeered and threw stones.

Out into empurpled darkness the winged figure strayed, towards a billowing mass that formed a face, whose cheeks were stellar clouds the colour of the gas fire before dawn, whose nose became a bridge and steps and, finally, a throne.

In a scrolled box, such as you might find in the bottom corners of an old map, Clive had written in red and black italics:

> *. . . thither he plies*
> *Undaunted to meet there whatever power*
> *Or spirit of the nethermost abyss*
> *Might in that noise reside, of whom to ask*
> *Which way the nearest coast of darkness lies*
> *Bordering on light . . .*

The whole extraordinary envisioning was done on a piece of exercise-book paper with drawn margins. An elaborate doodle. Don had floated it in a deep aperture, given it a large mount so that the tiny figures had room to breathe in their ivory-white surroundings. The moulding itself was plain oak.

'Pretty pleased with that,' Don said, picking it up. He took it to the window and held it at arm's length. At a certain angle, the glass became the reflected sky of the real world and the Devil disappeared into the light.

It was Don's birthday present to Clive, along with a sketchbook and a case of pencils. He would be fifty. Benjamin stared at the fiend, at the fresh creases in his wings. He felt the blast of heat singeing his eyebrows, hurting his face. A question arose from the abyss: 'What is a hairstreak?'

'It's a butterfly,' the landlady replied. 'And I want you to have it.'

Emily protested. The work was crochet, but done with a very fine crochet hook. Even Irene would have taken a long time to do something as intricate. The lady who had might well have been a Dorset lace-maker.

'I don't want any arguments. I want you to have it and keep it. For luck.'

Emily knew the value of such a gesture. She felt its kindness and said so. And now that it came to it, she could hardly bear to say, 'How much do we owe you?' because you couldn't put a price on some things.

'We've had such a wonderful three days.'

Don was in the drawing room, signing, waiting for inspiration. His pen circled the page. He could hear the two of them talking in the hallway, Em laughing, the pause as she got out their new chequebook.

'It's a joint account,' she said, and Don smiled because he could picture the landlady's smile in her silence. 'The first cheque, too. *You're* lucky now.'

'Mrs Henrietta Voy. V-O-Y,' she said helpfully.

'Voy,' Emily repeated. 'But my mother's upstairs neighbour was a Miss Voy. Matilda. She used to read tea-leaves.'

'That's right,' said the landlady quite calmly.

'Mum was always going up to Miss Voy before we were evacuated. She said she just wanted to know we would be safe.'

'And you were!'

Emily laughed to recover herself – she could not quite banish the image of Miss Voy shaking in terror on the lip of a bomb crater, the relish with which Irene had described the calamity – and Don once again found himself distracted by the women's exclamations. He would be called as a witness at any moment, though he'd still not found the right words to express his own gratitude or his happiness. He mistrusted them – the words, not the feelings.

'Tilda was a good soul. She made everything up, of course. She used to say, "I do it to give people hope. And people trust tea, so where's the harm?" '

'Your sister. Oh, *Don*!'

His pen stopped circling.

'I can't believe it,' Emily was saying.

But Don could. He finished writing, reflecting as he did so that no one reads a visitors' book, or returns to it after they have made their mark, unless it be to find, one rainy afternoon years hence, that very mark a shade smaller in retrospect.

Emily would not now sign it herself. She'd found a story to absorb her in other ways and he was grateful. He would be sorry to have his tenderness held up to inspection and to see her read the distance between his thoughtless manner and his careful heart. Or not sorry. What did it matter? Sometimes you have to say what you have it in you to say, however you can say it, and leave it at that.